Music
Is
Murder

Music
Is
Murder

A Musical Murder Mystery

B.J. Bowen

**CAMEL
PRESS**

Kenmore, WA

CAMEL PRESS

A Camel Press book published by Epicenter Press

Epicenter Press
6524 NE 181st St.
Suite 2
Kenmore, WA 98028

For more information go to:
www.Camelpress.com
www.Coffeetownpress.com
www.Epicenterpress.com
www.barbarabowenauthor.com

This is a work of fiction. Names, characters, places, brands, media, and incidents are either the product of the author's imagination or are used fictitiously.

Cover design by Scott Book
Design by Melissa Vail Coffman

Music is Murder
Copyright © 2021 by Barbara J. Bowen

ISBN: 978-1-94207-816-6 (Trade Paper)
ISBN: 978-1-94207-817-3 (eBook)

Printed in the United States of America

In loving memory of Mamacita,
Emma Frances Bowen Barnett,
who awakened my love of music
and always supported my writing.
I wish you had seen the book.

ACKNOWLEDGMENTS

Many people inspired this manuscript and helped turn it into a book. I would like to acknowledge a few here. In no particular order they are:

My agent, Dawn Dowdle, who had confidence in me and in this book, and provided support when I was most discouraged.

Jennifer McCord, my editor and publisher, who took the risk of publishing me, an unknown author, and expressed and shared her love of music with me.

La Dolce Vita Writers Group, which started me on this project.

Clark Wilson, the bassoonist whose description of the instrument's boot joint gave me the idea to use it as a murder weapon. He acted as consultant on all things bassoon. If I have made any mistakes, the responsibility is mine.

Nancy Andrew, who patiently answered my questions about the flute, flute music, and flute playing. I am to blame for any errors.

Jim Cara, who provided technological expertise, humorously getting past my technophobia and reexplaining many times. Any inaccuracies are my own.

Lena Gregory, who gave unstintingly of her time and knowledge to help me find my way through the unfamiliar world of electronic promotion.

My daughter, Amy, who didn't mind when I forgot to make

dinner as long as I was writing, and who read the first chapter approximately 1,387,942 times.

The Writers of the Roundtable—Marylin Warner, Ann Kohl, Leisel Hufford, Mary Zalmanek, and Eve Guy—who read the first chapter *another* seventeen times, as well as the rest of the book, gave me excellent advice, provided encouragement, got me to the finish line and, most of all, were my friends throughout.

ONE

OLIVE'S VOICE ON THE LAND LINE made me cringe. If I'd known it would be our last conversation, I'd have been more patient.

"Emily, I'm in such pain!"

Oh no. Not again.

Olive suffered pain—southern-tinged, emotional pain—on a regular basis. This time Gardiner James, her section leader, the symphony's principal bassoonist and her unrequited love, refused to talk to her. No surprise. "He hung up on me. It's fate that we're in the same place, playing in the same symphony in Colorado. We were meant to meet and fall in love. He just won't admit it."

Please. Not me. Not in the middle of a crucial practice session. I wanted to be there for my friends, especially someone who'd given me as much time and sympathy as Olive, but this was a repetition of a conversation we'd had a million times. I didn't want to hurt her feelings though so, bowing to reality and knowing I wouldn't get back to practicing for a long time, I put my flute on the counter and boiled water for tea as we talked.

Olive continued to whine. If my nephew had whimpered that way as a toddler, I would have put him in time-out. But I summoned my patience—again. "Gardiner asked you to leave him alone. You can't have a relationship by yourself." I used the most persuasive tone I could muster.

Olive dismissed me. "Why can't he understand we're meant to be together? It's kismet, Emily."

I held back a sigh and tried to think of a new tack.

The conversation went on like this for way too long; it felt like hours. In reality, no more than fifteen minutes went by, Olive moaning it'd be a great relationship if Gardiner only let it. I paced the floor with the phone and my tea, reminding her that a relationship took two, while casting longing glances at my reluctantly abandoned flute.

"Emily, help me. I can't think straight." An understatement for the record books. She explained that she had to play a 4:00 quartet rehearsal and desperately needed to talk to Gardiner first.

I wanted to help, but I became more and more exasperated. How many ways could you say "He's not interested. Forget him"? I hoped she'd listen when I said, "He's not worth it, Olive. I don't know what else to tell you." I shook my head. I'd said it to her so many different times and ways.

She almost cried. "But he's gotta talk to me!" She pronounced it "tawk." Her accent always got more pronounced when she grew emotional, and now threatened to render her unintelligible. "If he does, he'll come 'round."

She wasn't listening to me. Hardly news. "Olive, I wish I knew how to help, but I don't see any way forward for you and Gardiner. You don't want to be accused of stalking him, do you? My advice is to get on with your life."

She cried, "I can't!"

With a headache building above my eyes, I finally said, "Olive. Go play your rehearsal. I have to practice."

She started to say more but, without any other important words of wisdom, I said, "Gotta go," and hung up.

I retrieved my flute and returned to my aborted practice session. My job as second flute in the Monroe Symphony depended on practicing, particularly in this concert, and my responsibilities demanded my attention.

Ravel's second *Daphnis and Chloe* suite started with an important flute passage, and I wanted to be ready for the first rehearsal.

Besides that, I anticipated the side effects of practicing: calm, focus, and a sense of accomplishment. I'd discovered over the years that without words in the way, I could express my feelings and center myself in music.

I sat down and ran through the opening passage but couldn't concentrate. I'd said all I had to say in this and many previous conversations, and Olive hadn't listened to me. She worried me. I wanted to take a stand for sanity, hers and, more importantly, mine. I'd done that, but did I have to say goodbye so hurriedly? She'd been close to tears. Different approaches chased themselves around in my head, but I couldn't think of a right way to help Olive. I didn't know what words would help her let go of dreaming of a romance with Gardiner.

I'd almost regained my focus when Clara James called. Gardiner's ex-wife played violin in the symphony, so we were all members of the great big dysfunctional family of the orchestra. Gardiner and Clara had been divorced about a year, and I knew from previous conversations she wasn't taking it well. Watching while Gardiner flaunted his desires, flirting with every female in the symphony, strained her good nature. And his obvious lust for Leanne Johnson, the violinist who happened to be Clara's stand partner, hurt her deeply. She pasted on a smile and tried to ignore the seductive games they played under her nose, though. I had divorced around the same time and felt a certain camaraderie with her. In my book, Clara deserved sainthood. It must have been obvious because she called me a lot.

Clara exploded, "I don't believe it. Olive just phoned me . . . again."

I settled down in the big easy chair, flute across my lap. "Why?"

"She calls all the time. It's infuriating. I try to be polite. But she always wants 'insight' into Gardiner. This time she wanted me to tell her how to make him talk to her. As if I know how to make Gardiner communicate!"

Clara and Gardiner had stopped talking long before their marriage ended, and nothing had changed with their divorce. Weird for Olive to consult Clara about Gardiner in my opinion but, in Olive's world, I had to assume it made sense.

"Why does she insist on phoning me?"

Clara didn't stop long enough for me to answer.

"With Olive excavating the past, dredging up my feelings all the time, I can't move on. It's excruciating." I could hear the irritation and pain in Clara's voice. "Well, I've had it. I'm not taking her calls anymore. I'm blocking her number."

"I don't blame you a bit."

Clara vented a bit more, with me affirming her decision, before we said our goodbyes.

The phone calls, first Olive and then Clara, had upset me. Why put me in the middle of this squabble? I tried to resume my practice session, but my mind circled back again to Olive and my frustration with her.

Time for a break. Here in Monroe, Colorado, the weather in February can range from brutally cold to sunny and mild. Today, with the sun shining in a cloudless sky, Mother Nature seemed to be offering me a temporary reprieve from my frustration. Olive had mentioned a 4:00 rehearsal. I figured if I stayed away from the landline and turned off my cell phone until then, I'd avoid her phone calls.

I put away my flute, turned my cell off, and bundled up to walk my retriever, Golden.

Just before we left, the landline rang. The phone ID-ed Olive as the caller. I didn't answer this time, and as I left, I heard, "Emily, phone as soon as you can. Gardiner still isn't answering and I gotta talk to him."

Golden and I took refuge in the greenbelt, one of our favorite walks. I let her off the lead, so she could run free. She always stayed in sight or checked in, and the path led away from traffic, so I didn't have to worry about her. I really came here, though, because the greenbelt's peace soothed my soul and restored my perspective and sense of well-being.

I stayed 'til the beauty of the spot worked its magic, then called Golden. She came right away, smelling terrible, with brown goo all over her fur, looking extremely satisfied. I smiled, glad she had enjoyed herself and resigned to cleanup. I had become used to seeing her, and smelling her, like this after a romp outside. All part of having a canine friend.

When we arrived at home, we went in through the garage. There I kept a large aluminum tub especially for bathing Golden. I filled it with warm water from the garage tap and lifted her in, first forelegs, then hind end.

Noticing her betrayed and miserable looks, I said, "I'm sorry, Lovedog, but you brought it on yourself. I'm just making you socially acceptable again. It'll be okay."

She didn't look any happier.

I washed her thoroughly before I let her go. While she shook off, soaking everything, I emptied the tub, then dried her as best I could with old towels I had for the purpose. I gave her one last inspection and opened the kitchen door.

Once inside the house, I turned on the cell phone and checked for messages. I found a missed call and a text.

The call came from Leanne Johnson, Gardiner's latest fling, and the message she'd left seethed with anger. "Emily, you have to do something about your friend. Olive phoned while I visited Gardiner. He saw her name on the caller ID and, of course, didn't answer. But then she had the nerve to call my house and talk to my kids, hoping to find Gardiner. The kids were home alone. I'd left Steven in charge—he's thirteen now, you know—and he knew I should be at Gardiner's. But Olive told him no one had answered the phone there. She scared him. He called me on my cell, and I calmed him down, but I shouldn't have had to. Olive's your friend. Talk some sense into her." The recorded phone banged down noisily.

I was taken aback. Why was I somehow supposed to take care of this situation? Surely Gardiner's mistresses could settle things without me. Although, scaring kids was crossing the line. I vowed once again to try to reason with Olive.

The text was from her, time stamped 3:28 p.m. "In trouble. WRU? CMB!"

What kind of trouble could Olive be in? Probably more about Gardiner. I only had so much energy for Olive in one day. Besides, she would be in rehearsal now, which gave me a good reason to delay phoning her. I had already heard about the calls she'd been making. I would call later when her perceived crisis had passed.

After a quick dinner, I paid some bills and reveled in an evening with no commitments, free for practice. The phone left me in peace, and I did some good, solid work. At last, prepared for rehearsal, I realized I hadn't yet returned Olive's call or text. I glanced at my watch. 11:30. Time had passed unnoticed, a frequent occurrence when I immersed myself in music. If I wanted Olive to respect my time, I had to respect hers. I wouldn't call this late. I'd wait until morning and hope she had finally let go of her fantasies about a relationship with Gardiner. She deserved better.

TWO

ALICE SMITHSON, CELLIST IN THE MONROE SYMPHONY and my main connection to the grapevine, phoned and interrupted my morning routine. I don't know how she learned the things she did, but her news was faster and more reliable than MSNBC. Usually when she called, she had some bit of gossip, unimportant. With the phone propped between my shoulder and ear, I only half listened while I opened the drapes to my stunning view of the Colorado mountains, the main reason I'd bought the house. Carrying my mug of tea with one hand, I shook open the newspaper with the other, and sank into the recliner in front of the window. A lively house finch ate from the bird feeder.

"Isn't it chilling?" Alice also had a flair for the dramatic.

"What's that?"

"Olive. It's on the front page of the paper."

"Why would there be anything about Olive? I'm looking at the front page, and I don't see anything about her."

"Look below the fold, at the bottom. The lower left corner."

UNIDENTIFIED HOMICIDE

An unidentified body was found yesterday evening at 225 Maple. The death is being investigated as a homicide . . .

Olive's address. I scanned the article. Pretty sketchy. It didn't mention her name.

"It can't be her."

"Killed with her own bassoon boot. Beaten to a pulp, Alesia O'Malley says. David, that's her husband, discovered the body."

I knew the O'Malleys. Olive lived in a duplex. They were her downstairs neighbors.

I absorbed Alice's information. Olive's bassoon boot? The bassoon, largest of the woodwind instruments, pulled apart into five different sections. The "boot" was the bottom section, a heavy chunk of wood with metal caps and keys. I pictured Olive dead beside it. To put as much love and time into playing as Olive did and then be killed with her own instrument. Ironic. Sad. And more than a bit bizarre.

I felt sick. Golden knew something was wrong. She sat in front of me and put her head in my lap.

Impossible. I'd just talked to Olive yesterday. I remembered how impatient I'd been with her, and my throat tightened as Alice babbled on.

"Who would . . .?"

"It's just awful. I put it on Facebook, but I know you don't use Facebook much, and I had to be sure you'd seen it, since you and Olive were friends. I have to let my Twitter followers know, too. Lots to do. We'll talk later."

Olive. Dead. What had happened, and why? I'd miss her. Even her accent. My first impression of her had been her Texas twang. Now I'd never hear it again. Or listen to her honest, unvarnished opinions—opinions that often made me laugh, sometimes in spite of myself, for her views were always truthful, but frequently unkind. Olive, gone. The lump in my throat grew.

The memories kept flashing through my mind.

Olive had joined the orchestra at the beginning of the season, six months ago. Her outspoken opinions had attracted attention from the very first rehearsal. At one point, the conductor, Felix Underhayes, told her to match pitches with the first flute, Sandy Baines. "But if I do that, we'll be flatter than my momma's pancakes." Not a wise response for Olive to make, particularly in front of the entire symphony. But, unlike me and just about everybody else in the orchestra, Olive didn't worry that first flute was royalty, while second bassoon was lower middle-class merchant. Nor did she worry she might be wrong.

She fascinated me. What made anyone that confident?

During the first half of rehearsal, I noticed Olive kept a paperback on her stand and read while Felix ground through long string passages. I loved books and wanted to know, was she fascinated by the book or bored by the rehearsal? I asked her at break.

It turned out to be both. She had read all but the final pages of the book, and eagerly looked forward to the solution. But Olive always had a book. Anytime she felt bored or had an opportunity to read she pulled it out, so she never stressed, no matter what happened, or didn't. We discovered we were both interested in whodunits and thrillers and we'd read a lot of the same ones.

At the end of rehearsal, Olive gave me the novel. "You take it. I'm done."

Our meeting at that first rehearsal bloomed into a friendship. Books gave us excitement we shared, and something to discuss besides our daily routine and often boring lives. We explored Monroe's bakeries, too. For me, our meetings provided an excuse for the occasional doughnut. And Olive kept me laughing with her perspective on the orchestra, men, mutual friends, and life.

As I came to know Olive better, my respect for her grew. She generously contributed to animal shelters and literacy causes, and often gave me gifts for no reason. Things that were perfect: a book, a golden retriever welcome mat, or a dog training CD . . . wait, was that a hint? But no, Olive didn't hint. If she thought Golden ought to have better manners she would have said so, straight out.

She always spoke honestly, at least from her perspective. When she described her family, I gathered her father controlled his family with an unyielding hand, even though Olive adored him. Her mother found comfort in the bottom of a vodka bottle. She didn't talk much about her sister. Not always knowing what to say, I just listened.

Olive listened, too, when I talked . . . and talked . . . and talked about my divorce. She sympathized with the gradual deadening of feeling I had gone through, and the ensuing years of numbness as my ex insisted time after time that he loved me and would never hit me again—and then hit me again. When I told Olive that in the end he took a lover and ended the marriage, she comforted me by telling me I was better off without him, and made me laugh about it when she nicknamed my ex-husband's twenty-one-year-old ballerina girlfriend "Bimbo the Ballerina" and said, "The thoughts in her head are probably as light as her body." Somehow, it helped restore my sense of perspective, and release anger and sorrow.

Olive had been a good friend . . . until Gardiner.

THE DOORBELL RANG, INTERRUPTING MY THOUGHTS. I wasn't dressed for company. I wore sweats and hadn't showered, and my dark brown hair was uncombed. Besides that, I was grieving for a friend.

I cautiously looked out the peephole. A man, a stranger. What could he want? My curiosity got the better of me and I opened the door. "Yes?"

"Emily Wilson?" Well-proportioned, lean, muscular, and extremely tall, with a strong, deep voice, Olive would have called him a hunk and dragged him inside.

I nodded.

He pulled out a badge. "Lieutenant Gordon, Monroe Homicide. I'm here about Olive Patterson's death. May I come in?"

I backed away to clear the entrance.

He stepped onto the sun porch and Golden gave her usual bouncing welcome to a visitor. Lt. Gordon pushed her away.

I grabbed Golden's collar, pulled her aside, and held on firmly. "Down, Golden," I said. She had to content herself with continuing to wag her whole body.

"Olive's death is such a shock." My voice wavered. "I just heard about it a few minutes ago. I can't believe it."

He cleared his throat. No other response.

"But I'm being rude. Please, come in."

He wiped his shoes on the welcome mat, then crossed my sun porch and followed me down the hall to the living room. I held

Golden. Despite my cries of "Heel! Heel!" she tried desperately to reach the lieutenant all the way. I had to drag her to keep her beside me.

In the living room, I pulled Golden out of the way and told her to sit. She sat, but wriggled on the floor, her whole body wagging with delight, trying to inch her way toward Lt. Gordon. Holding on to her collar, just in case, I perched beside her. The lieutenant sat kitty-corner from us in one of my armless straight-backed chairs.

Olive murdered. Surreal. But no matter how discombobulated I felt, my mother's training took over. "Can I get you something? Coffee, tea, water?"

"No. I'm fine, but if you'd like to take a minute . . ."

I took a deep breath. "No, I'm okay. I want to help however I can."

He unzipped his quilted parka and shook his hands out of the sleeves. Then he pulled a notepad and pen from his jacket pocket. "You knew Olive Patterson?" He asked the question quietly, without expression.

"Yes."

He didn't mince words. "I'm here because she was murdered."

"She's really dead?"

"'Fraid so." He paused only a moment. "We're starting our investigation by interviewing symphony members. How well did you know Miz Patterson?" He lifted his gaze to mine, and his eyes shone with an intensity that told me he expected the truth.

"We were colleagues. You probably already know I play second flute in the orchestra."

He nodded. "Mhmm."

How to sum up our relationship? "We were friends, too. Close friends once."

He arched an eyebrow. "Once? What happened?"

"It's kind of a long story."

"That's all right. Take your time."

If he wanted the whole story, I would tell it. It would actually be a relief. I couldn't think about anything else, anyway.

Sensing the lieutenant would be too busy to listen to trivia, I confined my description to, "We met in orchestra and connected right away over books and bakeries." That covered the facts, and the statement satisfied him.

"What happened? Why'd the friendship go south?" the lieutenant asked.

I started tentatively, without getting to the point. "Well, her slant on the music world started to bother me."

"How so?"

Even though Olive was dead, I was reluctant to criticize her, so I commented as carefully as possible. "It didn't seem important at the time. Later, her views on music and being a musician started to upset me, though." I delayed, taking time to scratch my nose. The lieutenant didn't rush me, but waited patiently.

When the silence stretched out and became too long, I continued. "She acted like a world-class bassoonist, but she wasn't. Not in my opinion, anyway." I took a tissue from the box on the coffee table and devoted my attention to refolding it neatly along the crease lines. "She'd put someone else down and try to build herself up. It made me uncomfortable and created tension with other musicians."

I avoided the lieutenant's gaze.

"And as much as I appreciated her intelligence and sense of humor, her descriptions of fellow musicians didn't show understanding for anyone's feelings. She poked fun at people. It started to rub me the wrong way and made me even more uneasy."

"How did they react?"

"I don't know. I never heard Olive laugh with anyone, only *at* them, behind their backs. If she laughed at me, too, I wouldn't be surprised."

"Did that make you angry?" He leaned forward.

"Not angry. I didn't think about it at first. But later, when the friendship sounded sour notes . . . I guess I felt cautious about sharing anything with her."

"Sour notes? Something else must've happened."

I answered, "Not something, someone. Gardiner. Olive was my friend. If it hadn't been for Gardiner, we might have worked things out."

"Who's Gardiner?"

"Gardiner James, our principal bassoon."

He made a note. "They were dating?"

"Well . . . not exactly. Olive wanted to date him in the worst sort of way."

"He didn't like her?"

"Who knows? I couldn't tell you. He bedded lots of women."

The lieutenant raised his eyebrows quizzically.

"Gardiner's usual 'type' was a willing and sexy musician. Even though she was willing and a musician, Olive wasn't any cover girl. But she began to change after she fell for Gardiner. She tried to seduce him by fixing herself up, wearing makeup and showing off her full-blown curves in tight clothes. I don't know if they ever dated, but Gardiner wasn't above going to bed with her."

"How do you know that?"

"She told me, of course. She told me every detail, whether I wanted to know or not."

He pursed his lips and frowned. "Sounds like she trusted you, but you were annoyed."

I didn't respond right away. "I wasn't annoyed, but frustrated, yes. Her friendship with Gardiner . . . relationship . . . whatever . . . went on and on and became more and more twisted. Olive didn't like my advice to stop seeing him. I repeated it whenever I had her ear."

"Did you ever tell her why you felt that way?"

"Of course. The way he treated her was horrible."

The lieutenant's look was a question.

"Gardiner and Olive shared an interest in the bassoon. Maybe that appealed to him?" But I also had to be honest. "He dated other women whenever he wanted, though."

"Did his dates know he slept with Miz Patterson?"

"Everybody did. I was embarrassed for her." I didn't add that a gentleman wouldn't repeat details the way Gardiner did. Lt. Gordon would meet him and come to his own conclusion.

"She had a reputation as a tramp?"

"I would *never* say that about her." I took a deep breath and a few seconds to calm down. "It's only she'd do anything for Gardiner."

He jotted a quick note. "Sounds like he got around. You date him?"

"Me? No, no." I paused while I argued with myself, but reluctantly decided to be completely truthful and added, "But we did have one meeting outside of orchestra."

He didn't have to ask his question out loud.

I figured a policeman was like the doctor. If you lied or hid anything, it could hurt you and keep him from doing his job. I'd handled hard things in the past. I'd learned to set aside my shyness and play big solos, even though everybody in the audience stared at me, hadn't I? I used the same methods, took a big breath, and ignored my embarrassment. "We only got together once. Before Olive," I answered. "It's awkward to tell you about it."

"It's okay. I hear all kinds of things."

I marshalled my courage and continued. "About a year ago Gardiner and I were both newly divorced. I'd had enough of men for the time being, but I didn't think twice when Gardiner said he wanted to organize a quintet. Sandy Baines, the first flute, had turned him down because the rehearsals conflicted with family commitments, and it sounded like fun and a good opportunity to expand my professional contacts."

The lieutenant stayed quiet, but his look was both skeptical and inquiring.

"Gardiner suggested meeting after rehearsal to talk about it. It turned out he expected . . . he expected . . . well . . ." My face heated. "Let's just say it didn't end well. We never played quintets, and I never told Olive."

"So, she talked honestly with you, but you didn't come clean with her?"

"Of course I did."

"But you never told her about your unfortunate meeting with Mr. James."

"It was a . . . mistake . . .on both our parts."

The lieutenant scribbled in his book.

"Are you writing that down?"

"Just making a note. In case Mr. James turns up dead."

His straight face never faltered, and it took a moment for me to realize he had actually made a joke.

My smile was fleeting, but I felt encouraged. "I guess I wasn't pre-disposed to a good opinion of Gardiner, but the way he treated Olive ... well..." I searched for a word and failed to come up with one. "... I wouldn't have put up with it. I know Olive admired his musicianship. It was enormously important to her. But she overlooked a lot. Too much, I thought."

"What do you mean 'overlooked'?"

"I thought Gardiner was awful to her." I struggled to find a word strong enough. "Cruel."

"Cruel?"

"When Olive didn't leave him alone, Gardiner ignored her. Then he started making snide remarks, and, by the end, he humiliated her on a regular basis."

"Humiliated?"

"He flirted with other women right in front of her, never took her out, and then expected her to be available for his booty calls when he wasn't busy with someone else. If that isn't cruel and offensive, what is?" My stomach churned angrily at the memory.

Lt. Gordon ignored my rhetorical question and scribbled a note. "How did Miz Patterson react?"

"In her eyes, Gardiner was her soul mate. The universe wanted them together. No other possibilities existed, as far as she could see. The 'relationship,'" I made air quotes, "should have ended. I hoped she'd find someone else, but she wouldn't let the idea of a relationship with Gardiner go."

"How so?"

"She tried to keep other women away from him." I shifted gears. "She did crazy things. I wanted to help. So, on one of our bakery visits, I convinced her to see a psychotherapist."

He wrote rapidly. "How did that work out?"

She had talked to me in confidence. It didn't feel right to reveal her secrets. But now that she'd been murdered, if it would help, I'd tell the lieutenant what I knew.

"Not the way she wanted. She saw both an expensive psychiatrist and a not-so-expensive psychologist. Olive told me the psychiatrist wrote her a prescription for an anti-anxiety medication. Neither doctor encouraged her interest in Gardiner. The psychologist wanted to know why Olive chased him so frantically."

"Isn't that the important point?"

A reasonable response. "You know it and I know it, but Olive wanted someone to tell her how to win Gardiner. She gave up on psychotherapy and told me that if she just tried harder, he'd realize the two of them belonged together."

"Do you know the names of her therapists?" His question interrupted my train of thought.

"I recommended a couple psychologists, but I didn't know the psychiatrist. Do you want the names and contact information of the ones I told her about?"

"After we're done."

It took me a couple seconds to regroup. "Olive's behavior grew crazier and crazier, and eventually, I started to suspect she was one note short of a full scale."

"Crazy? What'd she do?"

"Went on spy missions. Questioned Gardiner's friends, peeked at his mail, and quizzed his dates to find out what he liked. She even broke into his house and snooped when he left."

"How do you know about that?"

"She . . . mentioned it." I'd folded the tissue too small to crease again, so instead I inspected my nails. Veeeery carefully.

"You knew about it but didn't report it?"

"No. No, I didn't. I had no proof except what she told me. I wasn't sure I trusted her state of mind. And she was a friend. I couldn't report her. If you're asking if I approved, or even approved by my silence, no, I didn't. I reminded her she violated Gardiner's privacy every time she pried and strongly suggested that she stop."

"Did Mr. James ever call the police?"

"I don't know. It would have been a rational thing to do. But nothing about their so-called relationship made rational sense. Gardiner didn't do anything about her behavior as far as I know."

I paused, then continued. "I didn't understand it. I thought

Olive should move on. Find someone who appreciated her good points. Life's too short. She shouldn't have settled for anything less than respect and kindness. But no. She committed herself to making it work with Gardiner, whether he cooperated or not."

Reliving my puzzlement and distress, I hesitated. "I'd seen Olive at her best—funny and giving, interested in everything. She had so much to offer. I wanted my bakery buddy back—my friend—not this Gardiner groupie she'd become. I missed what she had been before her obsession with Gardiner."

I gave the lieutenant time to scratch in his notepad, while I continued to try to recover from my shock at Olive's death.

When he finished, he asked, "What did you do?"

"Olive made me laugh and patched up my . . . well, my psyche . . . after my divorce. I didn't want to give up on her. I tried to distract her with every subject I thought of—the conductor's quirks, her family, her career path—but Olive always led the conversation back to Gardiner. I didn't know what else to do." Thinking about it now, I balled the tiny, soggy tissue between my palms. When I looked up, the lieutenant stared at me.

He made a note in his book.

Whatever. I took a deep breath and shrugged. "Bagels and books didn't interest her anymore. She didn't listen to me about Gardiner."

Lt. Gordon asked, "That ended the friendship?"

"As it had been. I didn't enjoy seeing Olive anymore. Dealing with her felt like dealing with my ex-in-laws. I don't like conflict, and I tried to avoid her, but if I didn't answer her phone calls and texts, she showed up at my door. If I made the mistake of letting her in, I couldn't make her leave." I rubbed my eyes. "Based on my own experience I had no respect for Gardiner, and he treated Olive so poorly. I didn't understand what she saw in him. I couldn't support her chasing him at the expense of her self-esteem. Unless and until she forgot about Gardiner I couldn't be sympathetic." *How sad it all was.* "But even though I didn't understand her taste in men or her behavior, I cared about her. I saw her at rehearsal, and we played in the same orchestra. I tried not to hurt her feelings, but she kept calling. When she did, I was as compassionate as I knew how to be, without encouraging the relationship, or even the fantasy of the relationship, with Gardiner."

"So, if it hadn't been for Mr. James, you'd be close friends today?"

I started to reply with an emphatic "Yes," then thought better of it. "Who knows? It's hard to guess at a future that will never happen." My eyes filled with unshed tears.

The lieutenant spent a couple long minutes scribbling in his notepad then looked up at me. "According to her phone, Miz Patterson called you twice and texted you once yesterday. The text was her final contact."

And I never answered it. My sense of guilt multiplied exponentially.

The lieutenant continued, "Can you tell me about that?"

I cleared my throat. "She wanted to reach Gardiner. She told me all about it in the first call. The second call came as I left to walk Golden. I didn't want to hear any more about Gardiner, so I let the voice mail record her message. The text came while Golden and I were out walking. The message said she was in trouble and asked that I call. She didn't say why. I figured it must be about Gardiner and didn't respond."

He leaned forward. "Let me get this straight. Your friend—and you were at least nominally friends—texts and tells you she's in trouble, asks that you call, but you don't bother to answer?"

At first, I avoided his eyes. "No, I didn't. I meant to. In the morning." Then I raised my gaze and met his. "Sometimes Olive could be highly emotional, usually about Gardiner, and I'd already talked with her many times about the two of them. I'd even taken a call earlier in the afternoon about the relationship, or lack of it, between them. She often called about everyday matters and asked for my help, claiming she was in trouble. Why would I suspect the text was any different? She'd cried 'wolf' so many times. If I'd responded maybe she wouldn't be dead now, but I didn't know she needed anything special or different." I looked quickly away.

He jotted a note. Again, he didn't waste a word. "You erased the message?"

"Yes."

"Does your answering machine have a tape or cartridge, or do you use the telephone company service?"

"The phone company."

"What about the text?"

"It's still on my cell."

"May I see it?"

I pulled my phone from my pocket and showed him.

"Okay." He made a note. "What happened then?"

"Just dinner, bill paying, and practice, for several hours." Sadly, I realized that Olive had been dead or dying while I practiced. How ironic. "I didn't suspect a serious crisis. I accomplished what I wanted to around eleven-thirty and went to bed intending to call her in the morning."

He took a long time to jot down all that information and then switched topics, "Who saw or talked to you yesterday afternoon and evening?"

"You're asking if I have an alibi?"

"Yes." He glanced up from his notebook and raised his eyebrows. "At this point, we're checking out everybody's story." He put the notebook and pen in his lap, rubbed his eyes, and leaned forward, knees spread. "Answer the question, please. I've been working all night on this."

He did sound tired. And he looked like he'd slept in his clothes.

I backtracked, took a deep breath, and tried to treat him with respect. "Sorry." I hoped for a friendlier tone but made no effort to avoid a touch of sarcasm. "One of my friends has been murdered. I may be a bit grumpy."

"A friend whose calls for help you ignored yesterday," he said in a matter of fact tone.

Heat rose in my cheeks. He was right. I didn't know if I could forgive myself.

He changed the subject. "Who'll replace Miz Patterson in the orchestra?"

At least this question didn't pack any emotional bombs for me. "I don't know. You'd have to ask the personnel manager or Gardiner."

He made a note and changed the focus back to me. "Okay. Describe any interactions you had yesterday afternoon."

"There weren't any."

"Anyone join you for dinner?"

"No. I ate a few quick bites, paid some bills, and then practiced all evening."

He summed up. "No one can verify your whereabouts after your first call with Miz Patterson?"

"Clara James phoned me. We hung up around three fifteen."

He jotted that down. "And then? Call anyone else? Text? See anybody?"

"Just Golden."

At the sound of her name, Golden cocked her head, but she wasn't talking. I scratched her behind the ears.

"For our daily walk."

He frowned at me. "And you didn't watch any TV?" He sounded skeptical.

"No." I paused.

"Unusual. If you could describe the programs, it would help establish your whereabouts." He frowned. "Anything you did do that would corroborate your story? Use your computer? Send any emails? Get on Facebook? Tweet?"

"It was just me, Golden, and Ravel."

"Ravel?"

I felt depressed, guilty, and upset; he'd admitted he was tired. The mood wanted lifting. I'd hoped to cheer him up, to raise my spirits and his, but people often didn't understand my attempts at humor. "The composer. He wrote the music I practiced." Just in case, I clarified further. "He's been dead since nineteen thirty-seven. You don't have to investigate."

He stopped writing and looked at me for a long moment. "Oh." Apparently, I disturbed his concentration.

He returned to business. "You don't have any proof of your activities?"

I gave up and kept my comment factual and short. "I guess not."

He made one last note, stood, and gave me his card. "If I can have the contact information for the therapists, I'll be on my way. Please give me a call if you think of anything else. Thank you for your cooperation. I assume you'll be available for more questions if it's necessary?"

The interview had been painful. "The symphony's in session for the next week. After that, we'll have some time off. I don't know what I'll be doing then."

He gave me a long, silent look, then said, "The department would *appreciate* it if you're available to assist in our investigation."

In other words, I had no choice. Fine. If any further questions were necessary, I hoped they would be easier, or I'd be in a better frame of mind. "As far as I know, I'll be here."

I wrote the names and phone numbers of the psychologists down, handed the information to Lt. Gordon, and closed the door behind him, sagging against it with relief.

THREE

FRIDAY, FEBRUARY 7, 2010, 7:00 PM

I'D BEEN EXCITED ABOUT PLAYING Ravel's *Daphnis* since the symphony first scheduled it and hurried toward rehearsal, the first we'd had since Olive's murder. The shock of her passing five days earlier and the emotions police questioning stirred were settling down. Now, I wondered about the latest developments in the police investigation.

My musical life took place at Fleisher Hall, the city's performing arts auditorium and my second home. A gray concrete structure built in the 1990s, it had been state-of-the-art at the time. Now, dated colors, stains on the carpet, and frayed furniture in the green room began to give away its age. Urban renewal in the form of a new office development dazzled the audience in front of the building, but I parked in back and walked through the neighborhood of pawn shops and junk dealers that surrounded the stage door at the rear of the hall, heading toward *Daphnis* and my friends.

The last I'd heard, the orchestra grapevine (Alice, again) reported that the police had questioned Gardiner at length, first at his house, then at the station, before they released him. He must know, or at least guess, the investigation would be pointed his way. How did he feel about that? Gardiner, besides being an abusive chauvinist, provided the woodwind section with unnecessary drama. Despite moments of charm, his temperamental outbursts were insulting and often made colleagues uncomfortable, even if their roles were limited to that of bystander. Should I brace for a scene? An emotional flare-up would distract our colleagues and surely be unpleasant for me, too.

When I arrived, I found Gardiner already on stage, warming up and trying to find the reed with the best sound and response, which could vary with the weather. Tall and thin, he expanded to twice his size when he breathed, reminding me of a toad under attack. I went to my chair, hung my coat on its back, and gave Gardiner a cheery hello.

He scowled at me. Judging by his past actions, he considered social politeness a waste of time, so I didn't take his lack of friendliness personally. Apparently, I was wrong.

"Don't you have anything better to do than discuss my affairs?" he snapped. "How come you set the cops on me?" He flushed, his words clipped.

His hair-trigger anger was his usual response to anything he didn't like.

"You and Olive weren't exactly keeping secrets, you know. I didn't tell the police anything they couldn't have heard from somebody else. I assumed the police would question everyone who knew Olive."

He snorted. "I don't know why you all can't mind your own business."

I decided to ignore Gardiner until he calmed down. Silently, I took out my flute.

Symphonic music fits intricately together. The composer has written every note and rhythm to fit precisely into a whole. Mistakes throw eighty-four other people off, so I tried my best to eliminate errors. Preparation, both mental and physical, helps accuracy and focus, and every musician has his own warm-up routine. Mine involves long tones and scales. Tonight, though, I just moved my fingers and blew softly while I watched Gardiner and listened to his conversations. He told someone he'd been questioned, but as new arrivals began their individual warm-ups, cacophony prevailed, and I couldn't hear in the hubbub.

At 7:30 sharp, the conductor, Felix Underhayes, tapped his baton on the podium to begin rehearsal. After the concertmaster took the A from the oboe and we tuned, Felix officially announced the tragedy, in case anyone had missed it. Taking as little precious and expensive rehearsal time as possible, he let the orchestra know there would be a moment of silence at this series of concerts in memory of Olive. A touching tribute, good showmanship, but probably insincere. Felix didn't get to know his musicians on a personal level and wouldn't be grieving, beyond being annoyed that the second bassoon had to be replaced. He couldn't ignore the case though, since by now Olive had been publicly identified as the victim, and her murder had been splashed all over the local news media. The symphony's PR department had to have come up with this solution. Olive would have loved the attention.

After Felix's brief announcement, we started *Daphnis*. A finger-twister for the flutes, it required my complete concentration. I didn't think about the murder again until break.

As I made my way backstage, various colleagues congratulated me on my part in *Daphnis*. They didn't have to notice or comment, but they did anyway. I smiled and thanked them.

I heard snatches of conversation everywhere about Olive and the case.

"... She called me at three in the morning even though I had to be at work by six ..."

"... Olive didn't worry about money. She told me the dividends were enough to ..."

"... She even offended the custodian and the electrician. They should've hit her with a ladder when she ..."

I heard my name once or twice, and Gardiner's more often. He must have, too, and I made a point of avoiding him.

Lt. Gordon stood backstage in a corner. He'd apparently been busy because, in the five days since Olive's death, he'd set the grapevine buzzing with his interviews. Certain he'd overheard at least some of the comments, I wondered what he made of the gossip.

"Hi," I said.

He nodded in my direction. "Did you think of something else I should know about Miz Patterson?"

"No. I just stopped by to say hello."

He answered, "I can't socialize. I'm trying to work."

I took the hint and left.

Just then, Diane Gelbart, a plump, friendly woman, President of Friends of the Symphony, the Symphony's fundraising arm, approached. "Emily, I know this is terrible timing, what with Olive's murder and her being your friend and all, but the printer wants the program for this month's meeting, including the list of music and musicians."

I'd promised to arrange entertainment for the next Friends luncheon, but Olive's death had totally pushed it from my mind. "Sorry, Diane. I'll get right on it. Can I email the final info to you tomorrow?" Although I'd planned to play Beethoven's Serenade for Flute, Violin, and Viola and could give her that information, I hadn't lined up specific players.

"Sure, honey." She gave me a hug which enveloped me. "Hang in there."

As I continued my intermission activities, the sight of violinist Chuck Holcombe all alone in the green room gave me a heaven-sent opportunity to follow through on my promise to Diane. "Hi, there."

Chuck was one of the nicest guys you'd ever meet, a real teddy bear. You could rely on him if you needed help. I counted on that today. Tall, probably over six feet, toned and muscular, he had a gentle manner, and dimples took up his whole face when he smiled. He could sweet-talk anybody out of anything and played a $450,000 Amati violin he'd convinced a collector to loan him. By playing it, Chuck kept the collector's violin from deteriorating due to lack of use. At the same time, he performed with a magnificent instrument. A win/win situation.

I'd already approached him before I realized he looked like he'd lost his best friend.

"Emily. Hi." Making an effort, Chuck smiled half-heartedly.

"Terrible news about Olive, isn't it?"

"Yeah." Chuck wasn't normally a monosyllabic kind of guy.

I realized, too late, he wanted to be alone. An uncomfortable pause followed. "Chuck, I didn't mean to disturb you, but I'm in charge of musical entertainment for the Friends of the Symphony fundraising luncheon this month. I thought it would be nice to do Beethoven's Serenade for Flute, Violin, and Viola. I'm hoping you'll help me out. All I can pay is a free lunch. Based on past experience, it will be cold by the time you eat it, but the gig might be fun."

"Sure." Despite his response, he didn't look at me or ask any questions.

"I don't want to impose. If you don't want to do it, tell me and I'll find someone else."

"Sorry, Emily. I *am* willing to help you out. What are the dates?" He pulled out his cell.

I told him and included the times.

"Looks okay." He gave me another weak smile. "I guess I'm not too enthusiastic about anything right now."

"Anything I can do?"

"No. Nothing," he said hopelessly. "It's Celia. We're splitting."

He *had* lost his best friend. "I'm sorry." I hadn't expected this. Chuck usually glowed with domestic content. Shock momentarily silenced me. "What happened?" Exactly the wrong thing to say, but my mouth moved before my brain came up with anything better.

Fortunately, Chuck treated the question more politely than it deserved. "I'm not sure. Money's always a problem . . . the kids . . . and her folks have never liked me . . . but I thought Celia . . ." His voice trailed off. Another wan smile. He tried to put a good face on it. "It's okay. We're working on it. We love each other."

To my relief, Phil Gray approached just then. An intense, focused, and energetic violist, he barely came to my shoulder. At my height of five feet six, I felt like a giant when I talked to Phil. Oily dark curls covered his forehead and thick glasses magnified his eyes. His passions centered around playing music, very seriously; fixing his original VW bug, very seriously; and reading true crime magazines, also very seriously. He joined the conversation, apparently unaware of the awkward undercurrents.

"You guys hear about Olive?" This was clearly a rhetorical question. Since Felix had announced it at the beginning of rehearsal we had to have heard.

I nodded.

"Who do ya think did it?"

Chuck just stared dumbly at him. Poor guy. A million miles away, he obviously hurt.

At least I could take the pressure of conversation off him. "The police haven't arrested anybody, but you sound like you have it all figured out."

Phil responded enthusiastically. "Most of it. Did you hear she was murdered with her own bassoon? I just have to figure out someone with motive and opportunity. Motive shouldn't be hard. She pissed people off. But opportunity? I figure it had to be somebody in the orchestra."

"The orchestra!" I wasn't prepared to hear that theory. "Why?"

"Well," Phil ticked points off on his fingers: "A, she hadn't been in town long, and she didn't know many people outside the orchestra. B, statistically, most murders are committed by someone the victim knows. Ergo, C, it must be someone from the orchestra." Phil sounded sure of himself. He must have felt that reading true crime magazines gave him some sort of expertise.

I listened to Phil expand on his theory for a few minutes, but, at the first opportunity, I changed the subject.

"Listen, Phil. I need to find a viola player to do Beethoven's Serenade at the Friends of the Symphony Luncheon the first Saturday next month. It doesn't pay, but you'll earn the admiration of the ladies of Friends, as well as my undying gratitude and a free lunch. Are you available?"

"Sure, Emily. I like playing with wind players. Text me the dates. I'll put them in my calendar."

I excused myself and made my exit. With a one-track mind, Phil enthusiastically returned to his theory about Olive's murder as I left, while poor Chuck stared off into space.

In the restroom the conversation centered around her.

From the stall I heard, "Olive told him his haircut was too short.

Can you believe that? What's the point? What could he do? Glue his hair back on?"

Vintage Olive—funny and accurate, but not considerate, and now bittersweet.

I washed my hands beside Janet Archer, our second clarinet.

"Emily, good job on *Daphnis*. How've you been?" A slim, willowy black woman, Janet walked with a dancer's toe out. She had wanted to be a ballet dancer until she grew too tall. Now she took ballet lessons for exercise.

She joined me, floating along gracefully, and we left the restroom together on our way to the drinking fountain.

"Same old same old. How 'bout you, Janet?"

She began, "I—"

But before she answered, I heard my name in the crowd.

"The cops went to Emily Wilson's, first thing." Thirty years in the symphony had ruined the white-haired trumpeter's hearing. His conversation soared through the chaos of intermission, and I had no trouble hearing it, though Janet and I pretended to ignore him and his friend.

"Emily?" His friend spoke loudly enough to be heard in the next county. "I wonder why. I'd say she's too nice to be involved in a murder."

The trumpeter answered, "Everybody's friend, huh? She used to be Olive's pal, for a while. But the two of them had a falling out. Why do you suppose the police questioned her for so long? And the lieutenant talked to her again just now. I bet Emily killed Olive."

Janet looked horrified. I felt horrified. These people were my colleagues. I thought they were my friends.

"Emily, that's not . . . they're just talking. Oh, please don't pay attention." She hugged me. "Nobody believes that."

Janet's words were comforting, but I wanted to defend myself. On impulse, I turned and walked straight toward the trumpeter and his companion.

They quit talking mid-sentence, and the trumpeter blushed; his friend ducked his head and shuffled his feet.

Under any other circumstances, their guilty looks might've

made me laugh. But instead I fumed. Was the grapevine buzzing? About me?

"Clyde. Steve." They knew I'd heard them. "You shouldn't spread rumors."

They stood there silent, while Janet and I moved on.

Fortunately, the rest of the rehearsal didn't require the concentration of *Daphnis and Chloe*. The conversation I'd overheard circled in my brain. Two people who knew me connected me to a murder. All because my friendship with Olive had soured, and Lt. Gordon had asked me a few questions.

How could anyone believe that I would hurt Olive? She might not have been perfect, but she didn't deserve to die the way she did. Janet, at least, believed in me. Thank goodness. I calmed down a bit. The trumpet player didn't represent the good people of the orchestra, my friends. My guilt at not returning Olive's last call and text didn't leave me though, and my mind continued to churn.

As I drove home, I wondered if I should hire a lawyer. I didn't have money to waste on an attorney if I didn't need one, and real evidence couldn't exist. I didn't kill Olive. But our friendship had withered. Did I look guilty? The grapevine busily churned out rumors about me. That wouldn't help me with the cops. And, with no alibi, the police had no reason to believe in my innocence. Having a lawyer couldn't hurt and it would be a wise idea to talk with one of them, or at least have an idea of who I could contact.

I tossed and turned and had a hard time going to sleep as I wrestled with the problem. Then I remembered Barry Reitman, an attorney a matchmaking friend had fixed me up with a few months ago.

I'd resisted the idea. I wasn't interested in dating and didn't believe we'd have anything in common. But my friend told me Barry's ex-wife ended up with the house and adequate child support, despite Barry's legal connections. I figured that meant he had to be either a nice guy and a good father, or a bad lawyer. Since my friend also painted Barry's success in glowing terms, I decided he must be a nice guy *and* a good lawyer, and that he might make a good friend. We agreed to meet for coffee after a symphony concert.

He came away from our one meeting with amorous intent. He asked me to a gallery opening, then a play. His interest made me realize I didn't want to risk failing at another relationship, and I enjoyed my life as it was. Kicking myself for starting something I didn't want to finish, I'd rejected him. Gently. Both times the symphony schedule provided an excuse that didn't hurt his feelings.

Would he be willing to listen to me? Tell me whether I should hire a lawyer, or point out that my fears were unreasonable? If I did need an attorney, I believed Barry would take the case and maybe even give me the starving musician's discount. He'd told me the symphony—eighty-five people working together in harmony—represented a major miracle to him. He spent ten hours a day mucking about in the nastier sides of life.

The thought of having an attorney in my corner who knew me relaxed me for the first time since rehearsal. Reason returned. I wouldn't bother Barry over gossip. But if at some point in the future I thought a lawyer necessary, I'd talk with him about my case.

I turned over and, finally at peace, went to sleep.

FOUR

NINE DAYS AFTER OLIVE'S MURDER a memorial service commemorated her life at Chapel of the Pines. Since her death I'd focused on our good times and been feeling guilty over my failings as her friend. Last night I spent a sleepless night. I finally fell asleep sometime after 4:00 in the morning. Consequently, I overslept and had to rush to make the memorial service, scheduled for 11:00 at the Chapel. I threw on a black dress—orchestra musicians have lots of black outfits—put on makeup at stoplights, and sped, actually arriving early, to my surprise.

Outside, bright sunlight reflected off snow, and I blinked, momentarily blinded, as I walked into the comparatively dark artificial light of the foyer. As my eyes adjusted, I recognized a few orchestra members. More arrived as I watched, and eventually I realized that if everybody had brought their instruments, we could have held a concert for Olive. She hadn't had that many friends. Did the players come out of a feeling of duty or curiosity? Certainly audience members wanted to show respect and encouragement, too. City bigwigs showed their support for the symphony, and the mayor and several members of the city council were there. Rumor had it that Olive's sister, who had planned the service, would come, but I didn't see anyone I thought might be her yet.

As I waited for the chapel to open, I caught a strong whiff of expensive perfume, and realized I stood next to Leanne Johnson, Gardiner's latest love. As angry as she'd been at Olive that last day, I hadn't expected to see her here. "I didn't think so many people would come."

Leanne shrugged. "I didn't either. I wouldn't have shown up, but Gardiner said we should, for appearances. Do you suppose they're all as glad as I am that Olive will never bother them again?"

Olive couldn't defend herself anymore, and I felt offended enough to stand up for her. "Isn't that a little unkind?"

"C'mon, Emily. Look around." Leanne's gaze took in the crowd and she nudged me with an elbow. "See any tears?"

"Well, no." Even I wasn't crying.

But Leanne apparently hadn't finished. "People Olive ticked off are all around."

"What do you mean?" I looked to see who surrounded us.

She nodded back and to her right. "Hester Crabbe's here."

Another orchestra member, second oboe. What did Olive do to "tick off" Hester?

"Olive stressed her friends. Hester has stories."

So did I. I didn't bother to ask questions.

"Or David O'Malley." Leanne nodded forward and to the right again. "He discovered Olive's body. Ask him about life with her as a neighbor. You'll get an earful." Leanne jerked her head to the left. "There's Clara James, Gardiner's ex."

"Yeah. I know about Clara. No love lost there."

Leanne looked farther to her left. "Craig Neil's over there. Olive picked on him mercilessly, and in front of all his colleagues, when they played the musical together."

Leanne's knowledge of negative gossip about Olive bordered on encyclopedic. I knew Olive had been a thorn in Leanne's side, but did she have to be so negative? And at Olive's funeral?

"And what about the people who aren't here? Sandy Baines'll never forgive Olive for embarrassing her in front of the whole orchestra at the season's first rehearsal. And Janet Archer has to be glad Olive'll never meddle again."

"What about Janet?" She generally kept no secrets from me, but I remembered at rehearsal we'd been interrupted by the gossips and hadn't finished our conversation. Had Janet been about to tell me something? Leanne ignored me and sped on with other gossip.

"You ever hear Olive compliment anybody? Never a kind word. Even for you, Emily." Leanne talked faster and faster.

"But she . . ."

"And then there's Gardiner and me. Olive harassed us unmercifully. She stalked him, tormented me, even hounded my kids. But she had to force herself on someone or be alone. No one wanted her." Leanne tsked. "What a loser."

I was frozen by Leanne's intense hostility and couldn't think of a word to say.

Meanwhile, her voice had been rising, and she'd begun to attract attention. Lt. Gordon had just come in. Had he heard her?

"She didn't leave us a moment's peace. Let me tell you, she'd've been dead long ago if I had my way."

That did it. I gripped her arm. "This is Olive's funeral. No matter what you think, she didn't deserve to die the way she did. Be civil and don't speak ill of the dead."

Leanne looked around and lowered her voice but didn't apologize or soften her words. "I don't know why you're acting like Miss Holier-Than-Thou. Everybody knows you were plenty annoyed with Olive. You should understand. Even dead, she won't leave me alone. Now it's the police. 'When did you last see Miz Patterson?' 'Where were you at the time of the murder, Miz Johnson?'"

Had circumstances been different, I might have laughed at her imitation of Lt. Gordon. But my protective instincts had been aroused by her comments.

Forgetting herself and letting her voice rise again, Leanne continued, "Honestly, Emily. You're pretending to be concerned, but you can't fool me. You might've even killed her." Leanne's antagonism took me by surprise.

I looked around. Lt. Gordon can't have missed her tirade.

My common sense told me a confrontation dishonored Olive.

It wasn't the time or the place. I took a deep calming breath, put my anger aside, and concentrated on de-escalating the situation. After a few moments, I asked calmly, "But you're alright? You have an alibi?"

"Well, of course I do. The day Olive died, I visited Gardiner. You know that. I called you from his place."

I remembered the angry, convoluted message she left on my answering machine.

"Lucky thing, too. Lieutenant Gordon is hot to prove Gardiner did it. If I'd left when Gardiner stomped off to his studio in a snit, he'd be in real trouble. As it is, I can swear he worked at home all afternoon and evening."

Studio . . . something about that jogged my brain. It took me a minute to remember. Gardiner had invited the entire orchestra to his housewarming two years ago. He'd been especially proud of the studio. It had its own door to the outside. "Students won't have to traipse through the living room," I remember he'd said. Now I asked Leanne, "Why didn't you leave?"

"And give him the satisfaction of running me off? I figured he'd calm down so we could discuss our spat. If he didn't, I wanted to set an example. Be available and willing. I settled down in the living room to wait with a book. It turned out to be some boring coffee table thing with no plot, and I dozed off. Three hours later, Gardiner woke me, and we made up."

Three hours? A long nap. Was she lying? On the other hand, I imagined Gardiner quite capable of being in a "snit," as Leanne put it, for three hours. Why didn't these women just leave? More to the point, though, was Gardiner really *in* the studio all that time? Supposedly, Leanne read or slept for three hours. Did Gardiner leave by the studio door and go to Olive's? It didn't sound like the thought had occurred to Leanne. Had it occurred to Lt. Gordon? And what about Leanne? With her and Gardiner out of contact for that long, neither of them could give the other a believable alibi. If Leanne snuck out, did she go to Olive's and murder her? Or maybe Leanne and Gardiner worked together?

Gardiner showed up just then. As the funeral staff opened the chapel doors, he approached Leanne and me, interrupting my speculations. Ignoring me, he took Leanne's elbow, pulled her aside, and talked quietly in her ear. Red-faced and scowling, he bent over her. Abruptly, she pulled her elbow away, straightened, then twitched her shoulders, turned her back on him, and hurried forward. He followed, and I stood watching as they settled into a pew. Leanne removed her coat with no help from Gardiner and shook back her long blonde hair. Gardiner ignored her, a telling space between them. They deserved each other. Gardiner must have overheard our conversation. For that matter, I'd guess lots of people had heard Leanne. I wondered again if Lt. Gordon had been one of them.

As people entered the chapel, organ music played softly. Stained glass windows admitted only dim light, and a damp, newly sanitized smell tickled my nose. Olive's urn sat in the front, elevated on a red velvet stand. Ironic that such a small container held what remained of a human being. What about the real Olive, the ideas and hopes and fears? Where were they?

The ceremony gave the impression of being hastily put together by someone with little knowledge of Olive's wishes. The minister admitted he hadn't known Olive and gave a short biography in which he mispronounced the name of the Julliard School. The service consisted of generic remarks about eternal life. He mourned the brevity of Olive's career and said no more.

Olive would not have approved of the music. She'd been passionate about playing historically accurate performances and a snob about discovering unusual pieces unknown by the masses. Yet now an elderly gentleman with scraggly white hair banged out arguably the best-known classical piece in the Western world, Pachelbel's "Canon in D," on the piano. The piano hadn't even existed when Pachelbel composed the Canon, for heaven sakes. Olive would have known that. The piece should have been played by a string quartet or chamber orchestra. It made me sad that no one, even her own sister if the grapevine could be believed, knew her well enough to put together a funeral she would have liked. I could have planned a more appealing service. I should have volunteered to help. I wished I had thought of it. Another way my friendship had failed Olive.

I waited for the final notes of the postlude. A stranger, a red-haired woman, sat in the front row, in the family section. She had to be Olive's sister. She must have arranged the funeral long-distance. The sister sat by herself. I could speak to her; it was the least I could do.

After the service ended, I left my pew and went down front, introduced myself, and offered my condolences.

"I'm Patricia, Olive's sister," she said in a soft Texas drawl. "You're Emily? If you'll wait 'til I've greeted people, I'll take you to lunch."

Patricia's invitation touched me. I couldn't leave Olive's sister all alone. It didn't look like she would be mobbed by mourners. I took a quick look at my watch and decided to wait. Only two people approached Patricia, and they were gone within a few minutes. There should be plenty of time for lunch with her before my students arrived.

She turned away from the last well-wisher, regret or relief plainly written on her face. "Can you choose a place where we can talk? I don't know the city."

"The Articulate Artichoke's just down the block. It's usually quiet, and the service is good." Monroe, a conservative place in its food preferences as in every other way, under-patronized the Artichoke, in my opinion. Being unusual, its vegetarian menu ensured customers were sparse, and its classical music and dim interior soothed the psyche. It was one of my favorite spots and perfect for this meeting.

After we had seated ourselves and ordered, Patricia made small talk until the main course arrived, and I studied her closely, making automatic replies. She looked to be in her mid-thirties. Stray wisps escaped from the dull red hair she pulled straight back, and everything about her drooped. Her blue eyes looked bloodshot and watery, and her voice quavered now and then. She appeared tired and worn, but her sister had been murdered. I'd look tired and worn too, under those circumstances. Though the coloring differed, I recognized the family resemblance and saw Olive's posture and bearing, as well as her nose and mouth, in Patricia.

She fidgeted with her napkin as she spoke, twisting it this way and that, and I took it as a sign of her distress. "I guess it's unusual to ask a stranger to lunch like this, but I wanted to meet you."

"Why?" I asked.

"Olive didn't mention many friends, but she emailed me about you. You're easy to talk to and forgiving. 'Accepting,' she said."

Accepting? Guilt knotted my stomach. I hadn't "accepted" her awful relationship with Gardiner. And I'd judged her to be lacking in good sense and self-esteem. Patricia hadn't known that, I hoped.

"Were you close?" I asked.

"Not really." She leaned away and her eyes focused above my head. "Our family . . . it's unpleasant. Olive spent her life trying to please Daddy, but nothing she did ever satisfied him. He disapproved of . . . well . . . everything. A perfectionistic, overbearing man. I don't think he *could* be pleased. I just wanted to be sure I didn't end up like Momma, who became an alcoholic. For different reasons, Olive and I both escaped as soon as we could."

That explained a lot. Olive's determination to be seen as the best, her willingness to accept Gardiner's treatment of her, and her efforts to please him, could all be explained by her family background, and particularly by her father's demanding and unsatisfied attitude.

"We kept up on Facebook and she emailed once in a while, but I hadn't heard from her in at least three months."

That explained why Patricia didn't know about the strain between Olive and me. Three months ago, Olive and I were exchanging books, laughing together, and visiting bakeries. The crush on Gardiner had just started, full of hope. It hadn't gone south yet.

"She told me how good you'd been to her." Patricia leaned closer. "She valued your friendship."

I felt embarrassed and guilty. I wished I'd followed Mom's longstanding advice, "Never do anything you'll be ashamed to have me catch you at." Mom would never have approved of being unsupportive of a friend. Patricia continued, "Olive'd want us to know each other."

"True. If only she were here." I said it, and I meant it. "How long will you stay in town?"

"As long as it takes to settle Olive's affairs. The police aren't letting me use Olive's place. Under the circumstances, I don't want to." Her eyes filled and she took a moment before she continued, "I'm staying at the Regis."

"Let me know if I can help."

"Thanks. I may take you up on that. Two heads are always better than one."

"I'm willing to do whatever I can. Thank you for lunch." I gave her my phone number and then left quickly, feeling conscience-stricken.

I'd dismissed Olive when we last talked and ignored her last messages. Now I'd never have a chance to apologize. Her funeral had been drab and friendless—lonely—even though lots of people attended. I knew her brilliant wit and generosity, but not many people had seen that side of her. Now she was dead, and no one would ever see it.

I felt depressed, but I knew that wouldn't do anyone, especially me, any good. My guilt over not returning Olive's communications only grew stronger. I wanted to make it up to her, but she was dead. What if I helped find her killer; figured out what happened?

Leanne and Gardiner interested me. They both had motive and opportunity, and I kept remembering what Olive had told me in our final conversation. She wanted to find Gardiner. I could easily see Gardiner committing murder. And Leanne?

A glance at my watch reminded me of my afternoon students. And I had to make some phone calls first. Unless I hurried, I'd run out of time.

FIVE

I RUSHED HOME TO FIRM UP DETAILS with Chuck and Phil for the Friends of the Symphony luncheon rehearsal. My students would start arriving in half an hour. Trying to ignore the beginnings of a headache, I looked out the windows but saw only drab branches of winter-dead shrubs and trees. That didn't help. I made a cup of tea and sat in my cheery yellow kitchen to sip the hot liquid. Better. I called Chuck and discussed the particulars.

"Okay. We're set for Monday the twenty-fourth at my place. I'm calling Phil anyway. I'll give him the details," Chuck volunteered.

Gratefully, I crossed that phone call off my to-do list. I didn't ask about his situation with Celia and the kids, figuring it might be a painful subject, and hung up instead.

Thanks to Chuck, I had a few minutes to myself. I sipped my tea thoughtfully. I knew only what the grapevine told me about the police investigation of Olive's murder. The gossips suspected me, and it rankled. I would never have hurt Olive. What had really happened? My desire to do one last service for her, irritation at the rumors about me, and my curiosity all prodded me to find more facts. David O'Malley, the neighbor who'd found the body, might have more solid information. Leanne had mentioned something at the funeral. "Ask David about life with Olive as a neighbor. You'll get an earful." Had life in close proximity to her been a strain?

The doorbell rang, signaling the arrival of my first student. Instrumental students are a good way to supplement the symphony salary, and I usually enjoy teaching flute lessons. But today my mind wandered. As Olive's downstairs neighbor, David was the only person I knew in Olive's life who didn't play with the symphony. She had introduced us on one of my visits. I'd seen him several times and knew him casually. What did he know? Eagerly, I waited to talk to him, and the afternoon's teaching drug endlessly on. When the last student left, my curiosity gave me wings. I had just enough time to squeeze in a conversation before dinner and rehearsal. I hurried to David's.

He answered the door. "Emily, what are you doing here?"

Normally an amiable, capable guy, David lived with his wife and two small kids on the lowest floor of a treeless new duplex not far from me. Olive had lived on the upper level.

"Olive's death shocked me. You don't expect your friends to be murdered." I hadn't had a chance to pick his brain at the funeral. "I just wanted to talk to somebody. I figured you'd understand."

David's crew-cut head sagged, and up close, dark circles underlined his eyes. "Maybe not. Depends."

I should have taken the hint. "Can I come in?"

"No." He paused, his gaze not meeting mine. "My wife's napping on the couch with the baby."

I heard sounds of movement and a baby's cooing inside and knew he lied. I felt as welcome as a broken violin string, mid-solo.

Leaving me outside on the porch, David's body blocked my view of the interior of the living room. "What did you want to talk about?"

At least he didn't threaten to slam the door in my face. Relieved, I thought about how to answer his question while he continued.

". . . 'cuz I don't know if I should be talking to you."

Why should David worry about talking to me?

With the air of a man letting secrets out of the bag, as if he'd read my mind, he said, "I saw you that day, you know."

I didn't get it. "What are you talking about?"

"I told Lieutenant Gordon about it." His gaze avoided mine.

"I spotted you less than a block from here, on the greenbelt with Golden."

Now I understood. "Really, David? You think I had something to do with Olive's death? And that I'd take my dog along if I had murder on my mind?"

"I just know what I saw. Somebody killed her. Cops think she knew her killer, or her place would have been torn up a little. They kept asking questions about the afternoon and early evening. I told Lieutenant Gordon I saw you late that afternoon." He sounded increasingly mistrustful. "I know you and Olive used to hang together, but I haven't seen you lately. You must've been pissed at each other. Did you have a reason to kill her?"

I had counted David as a friend, or at least a friendly acquaintance. I defended myself, trying to ignore my hurt feelings. "It's true she annoyed me. You'd have been annoyed, too, if she'd asked for advice as often and listened as little as Olive did to me when I tried to help. But that's not a reason to kill."

He looked at me and folded his arms. "I'm not letting you in with my wife and baby." Silently, he glared at me.

I figured I may as well get to my main question. On the basis of Leanne's hint that there may have been some strife between him and Olive, I bluffed. "What about you? Lieutenant Gordon might like to hear about your *neighborly* relationship with Olive."

"It doesn't matter what you tell Gordon. He's already been told." He sounded angry and bitter.

I continued bluffing. "Does he know it all?"

"Apparently, the neighbors heard the whole thing. Gordon knew all about it."

"So, you started making insinuations about seeing me because the police think you're the killer."

His face contorted and he balled his fist. "If they do, they're wrong. I wouldn't have hurt her."

As the sun went down, I stamped my feet and rubbed my arms to warm myself and ward off the cold. "Tell me."

"I thought you knew all about it."

"I knew her side. Tell me your side," I asked.

David watched me wordlessly.

I met his gaze but remained quiet and held my breath.

He apparently took the silence for pressure. He shook his head and then, to my relief, began talking. "Listen, Olive started it. I asked her not to practice later than eight, okay?" David snapped. "She kept the kids awake." Imitating Olive, he stood up straighter, cocked his head, and said in a high, nasal voice dripping with a fake southern accent, "'I'm preparing for an audition and I do my best practicing at night.'"

"A bad Texas accent didn't get you in hot water with the cops," I insisted.

"It couldn't have, if that's all they knew. But the day before she died, we stood on the sidewalk. She'd come home from wherever, and I quit shoveling snow to talk to her. When I asked her to keep it down in the evenings, she threatened me."

"Threatened you?" I guessed that David stood at least a foot taller than Olive. What could she do? Play louder?

"She said she'd call the landlord." David helped the landlord with yard work in exchange for a break on the rent. The duplex's yard radiated the results of his work, one of the best-kept in the neighborhood. Without the landlord's goodwill, though, the deal could fall apart. I figured Olive's complaints were a serious threat to David's financial well-being.

He continued, "She said the lease didn't prohibit practicing, that she'd checked before she moved in, and that I'd have to take it up with the landlord. Her voice could have been heard anywhere in a five-mile radius. She said the landlord 'paid' me to make sure she had no complaints and that if I kept bothering her about her practicing, she'd report harassment to the landlord, and that violated the law, forget the lease."

I should have guessed at Olive's belligerence when her music was threatened. It represented both her first love and her livelihood. But she'd been aggressive and obnoxious, attacking before she'd made any effort to settle the disagreement amicably. "You just tried to work it out. Peaceably. For your kids."

"That's what I thought. I've dropped my work to help her lots of times, running errands and all. When she walked off mumbling something about 'cheap white trash,' I lost it."

"Lost it?"

"Yeah. You know. Lost patience. Shouted at her."

"Shouted what?"

A long silence followed, and I thought he'd keep the rest of it to himself. After all, I asked nosy questions. He didn't have to answer me. The way he avoided my gaze, telegraphed his shame. I stood on the porch, waiting. The weak winter sun had almost sunk down behind the mountains. A chill breeze blew, and I shivered visibly.

David moved back. To my relief, though, he didn't close the door entirely and talked through a tiny crack. "I guess I might as well tell you. Everybody knows anyhow." He paused again, then continued slowly. "I yelled, 'You inconsiderate bitch! We'll see who's harassing who. You'll be dead before I let you bother my kids!'" David looked at his shoes and the door opened a little wider. "I shouted and the neighbors had to've heard. Then I discover her body not twenty-four hours later."

"That doesn't look good, does it?"

"Not even a little." David shifted his weight to the other foot. "The next day, the afternoon of the murder, she kept playing some loud classical thing over and over and over. I thought she did it to drive me crazy, make a point. She kept it up for a couple hours. Around six o'clock, I finally went upstairs to tell her to knock it off." He stopped and ran his fingers through his hair. "Her door was ajar. God, it was awful. She lay on the floor, still and white. The blood—so much blood. I didn't even go in. The music kept playing, I'll never forget it. I called 911 right away. When the cops arrived, they finally turned the CD player off. They said she'd set it on repeat. I can hear that music pounding in my brain even now."

We looked at each other silently.

Finally, David continued, "I guess the cops decided I wasn't stupid enough to report a murder I'd committed or that I didn't have much of a motive in the first place. I dunno. They might still think I did it. I'm just glad they let me come home."

I had a rush of both sympathy and understanding. The grape-vine had taught me how awful it felt to have groundless suspi-cion leveled at you. He knew he wasn't the murderer, and so he'd accused me. As sick as he'd looked when he described the blood, my intuition told me he wasn't the criminal, either. "We can help each other. I don't believe you killed Olive."

Some of the tension faded from David's face.

I remembered the trumpet player at the orchestra rehearsal and Leanne at the funeral. "I didn't either, even though some people think I did." I shifted my weight to the other foot. "Can you think of anybody else who might have committed the murder? You knew who came and went better than anybody."

"Emily, I've turned my brain inside out trying to figure out who it might have been. I didn't see anybody or hear anything, other than the music. As far as I know, you, Gardiner, Red, and Vince were the only visitors she ever had."

I knew about Gardiner. "Who are Red and Vince?"

"Guys she went out with a few times. Heard them clomp up and down the stairs." He shrugged. "I think she said she met Red at your place."

"My place? You mean my adult student? Red Calloway?"

"Yeah. That's the name."

I remembered how they'd met. Red, an enthusiastic and faithful adult student, relaxed from his high-pressure job by playing the flute. He had scheduled an extra lesson because he'd volunteered to provide the background music for the can-dle lighting at a cousin's wedding and wanted to go over the music. I'd squeezed him in before a shopping trip with Olive. She'd arrived early, before my session with Red ended. I intro-duced them. Neither Olive nor Red divulged they'd ever dated. I thought Olive told me everything. I guess not. "How often did Red and Olive go out?"

"You're asking me? I wasn't her social secretary." He bristled at me again. This time I took the hint.

"Well, thanks for talking to me."

He had the good grace to blush.

"We can chat more some other time. You're under a lot of pressure. I'll just get out of your hair now."

David painted a grim picture. He'd noticed Olive and I weren't the close friends we once were and he'd told the lieutenant about it. He'd placed me near the scene of the murder and hinted I had a reason to kill Olive. The police would take note. But he'd also made it clear he'd had his ups and downs with Olive.

He might even have killed her. Apparently, the police were thinking along those lines already. I didn't believe that theory, though. I decided to forget about David for the moment. What about Red? And who was Vince?

I had lots of questions and no answers. One thing had become clear, though. I probably was on the list of suspects and moving toward the top. Time to call a lawyer, the only one I knew. Barry Reitman.

SIX

WEDNESDAY, FEBRUARY 12, 2010, 9:00 AM

I PHONED BARRY FIRST THING NEXT MORNING. He worked for a big firm, and I had to get through a business-like assistant before I talked to him. It had been a while since I'd seen him, and, surprisingly, the joy in his voice warmed my heart.

"Emily, it's great to hear from you. How have you been?"

I responded to his social chitchat until he wound down.

Clearly puzzled, if happy to hear from me, he finally asked, "To what do I owe the pleasure?"

"It might be nothing, but I'm worried, and I'd appreciate your professional advice. Do you have time to see me?" I wanted to be vague but clear that the meeting would be strictly business.

I could hear confusion in his silence. "Professional advice? You know I don't do wills, right? I'm in criminal law."

"I know." I didn't say more. Somehow, the phone didn't seem like the place to tell an admirer the gossip-mongers' theory that I'd bumped off a friend.

Barry rallied admirably. "Well, sure, Emily. I'll be delighted to see you. Let's see . . . hmm . . . I can move my two o'clock. Will that work?"

I'd have to cancel two students, but I'd make it work. "Two o'clock is perfect. Thanks, Barry."

That afternoon, as I entered his office, he greeted me warmly, wrapping me in a friendly bear hug. "Emily, you're a sight for sore eyes." Barry's salt-and-pepper hair framed a big, warm smile.

"Thanks." I chewed a fingernail. How could I keep his good opinion yet confess that some people, who knew how many, thought me capable of murder?

"It's great to see you." His enthusiasm sounded real.

"I'm glad you're here, Barry. I might be in trouble."

"I can't imagine it." He escorted me to a comfortable padded armchair in front of an enormous, unnaturally tidy glass-topped desk. "Sit down. Can I get you coffee?"

"No coffee, but if you have tea . . ."

"Sure thing." Barry turned, his hand on the doorknob. "Sugar?"

"Plain is fine. Thanks."

While he fetched the tea, I settled my purse on the floor. This was my first visit to his office, and I looked around. A large leather chair sat behind his desk, which held several framed pictures. No woman could be seen, but there were photos of the same boy and girl at various ages, and I thought again that Barry must be a proud and caring father. The Native American rugs and arts decorating the walls reminded me that he spent a month every summer living on a Hopi Indian reservation, working *pro bono*. A blank yellow legal pad and pen on the desk clued me in that Barry would be taking notes, and a computer on the L-shaped extension bounced a quote against all four sides of the screen from that distinguished philosopher, Anonymous. "Every great achievement was once considered impossible." An encouraging sentiment for your lawyer to be familiar with. Manila file folders formed a neat pile on the floor beside the desk.

I soothed my nervousness with butterscotch candies from a dish on the desk. At our first and only meeting a month or so ago, we had talked about everything from Incan ruins to my Aunt Patty's quilts. The thought of employing his intelligence to my benefit comforted me, and I settled back in the chair.

When Barry returned, he brought tea for me and coffee for himself. He was now, though, coolly professional.

He gave me the tea, put his coffee on the desk, and parked himself in the chair, leaning forward. "What brings you here?"

In answer to his question, I told him the whole story—Olive's murder, her last text, my lack of an alibi, Lt. Gordon's visit, the orchestra gossip, David's placing me near the scene of the crime—and watched Barry's expression become more and more serious.

"Em, this isn't good news."

The affectionate diminutive surprised me, but Barry used the nickname good-naturedly. I concentrated on the rest of his message, which wasn't reassuring. "Ya think?"

"But you don't have to be too concerned, either." His voice, low and comforting, soothed me.

"No?"

Barry hesitated a moment, then leaned back and laced his hands over the modest paunch that assured me he was neither a fitness nut nor a comfort-food junky. "The cops need more than coincidence and a non-existent alibi to arrest you." Barry sounded confident and assured. "They've gotta show probable cause. Something that points in your direction. Motive. Something."

I felt like a load had been lifted from my shoulders. A little uneasiness remained because the grapevine didn't see me as innocent. But I'd told Barry about that. I consciously relaxed.

"At this point, it's unlikely the police will arrest you." Unfortunately, Barry didn't stop there. "Having an attorney's a good idea, though. And if they do arrest you, don't say anything except 'I want my lawyer.'"

"But—"

"Don't give me any 'buts.' I know you think you haven't done anything wrong and that telling the truth can only help you." He sounded as if he'd given this speech many times. "That's what everybody thinks." A slight pause followed. "The trouble is that anything you say can be twisted or misunderstood, taken out of context, and used against you."

I nodded. "Okay."

"And for you, I'm available any time. Call me right away if there are any problems."

"Oh, I will. I'm not afraid to ask for help when I need it."

He pulled a business card out of a holder on the desk and

scribbled on it, then handed it to me. "Here's my cell number. Keep it with you, and don't be afraid to use it. You'll be alright." He smiled. "Don't worry, Em."

"Thanks." My stomach relaxed, knowing someone had my back. "What do I owe you?"

"Oh, anything's fine. Just something as a retainer if you want me to represent you."

Thinking of my checking account, I opened my purse and gave him my last five dollars. "Is that okay?"

"Sure."

"It's not much."

Barry chuckled as he stood. "You haven't gotten the final bill yet."

I rose, and we moved across his office to stand next to the door.

He positioned himself close enough that his aftershave enveloped me.

He looked into my eyes. "Look, Em, my schedule is full this afternoon, but I'm done at six. Why don't we go to dinner? I'd love to talk with you some more. You can bring me up to speed on the symphony."

"I'd like to, but we rehearse tonight. No rest for the weary." I paused. He seemed like a nice guy. I didn't want to hurt him, but I didn't hold high hopes for any relationship right now. "Besides, it sounds like a bad idea to be dating my attorney."

"Then it's simple. I'll refuse to take your case."

I must have looked as panicked as I felt, because Barry immediately grabbed my hands. "Sorry, Em. A joke. A bad one."

He squeezed my hands.

I pulled back my hands, turned quickly away, and hurried out the door without looking back.

On the way home, I annoyed myself by remembering, in magnificent detail, Barry's welcoming hug, the scent of his aftershave, and his kind words. It would be nice if . . . but I knew better than to get a case of the warm fuzzies. Men had a knack for turning tender hugs into cold prison bars, metaphorically speaking. My ex had done it, and the relationship had not turned out well.

I shuddered and decided to call my mother before the afternoon's students arrived. Mom has been on her own for forty-odd years, emphasis on the odd. She is . . . well . . . uniquely colorful. She lives in Denver, where she's close enough in an emergency, but too far away for everyday visits. She was divorced soon after I was born and as far as I knew, she hadn't looked at a man since. I counted on her to have a clear perspective on relationships.

"I don't know, Emily. Don't be so quick to kick a gift horse in the teeth."

"You mean look it in the mouth," I corrected out of habit.

"Whatever. The point is it might be a good thing. Barry might be one of the good ones. You know what they say. There's always the rule that proves the exception."

"You mean the exception that proves the rule," I said.

"Whatever."

"How can you possibly know, for heaven's sake? You haven't even met him." I hoped my frustration didn't show.

"How bad can he be? For one thing, he's a lawyer. At least you know he's not a felon." A pause. "And there's something in your voice when you talk about him. Who knows, maybe the two of you can even have some fun."

Good grief. This wasn't what I expected to hear from Mom. "I can have plenty of fun on my own. And lots of lawyers are felons. What's with you? I don't see you rushing out to find a man."

"Well, they're harder to find when everything sags around your knees. You're a young woman. You have needs, passion. It's no picnic to spend your life alone, you know."

I marveled at the turn this conversation had taken. You think you know someone. "You never complained before."

"You never asked before. Besides, I haven't been exactly alone."

"Mom!"

"Well, I did my best to set a good example."

"So, you admit that a good example doesn't include a man."

"Stop twisting my words and start thinking for yourself."

She sounded angry, and I felt like an oboist with a bad reed. I hadn't a chance. "Well, thanks, Mom. It's been wonderful talking to you."

"Sweetheart, you're a beautiful and interesting woman who's been hurt by the world's worst snake of a husband." The change in her tone astonished me. "But not all men are like him. Think of your friend Amy's husband. Or your brother-in-law. He worshipped your sister while he lived. Let your luck change. Welcome it. Greet it with open arms."

Astounded by her unexpected praise and shocked into a broader perspective, I recognized the truth that I knew a number of nice men, all married to someone else. But Mom was still Mom.

"And if the lawyer turns out to be a snake, let me know. I'm a fearless snake-hunter, and I won't let my baby be hurt again."

As soon as I put the receiver down, the phone rang again. "Hello?"

"Em?"

"Barry." Heat rose in my face, as I thought of Mom's advice.

"I'm glad I didn't miss you. Listen, I wanted you to know, I've done some checking. I talked to a friend down at MPD. We go way back. I knew he'd let me know for sure where you stand."

"Barry. Thanks. What'd he tell you?"

"Well . . ." A long pause followed, as if he considered his words carefully. "Not what I expected." He hesitated again.

From the time I'd first met him, I'd sensed a deep integrity in Barry. I felt comfortable asking questions. "You're awfully hesitant, Barry. What's up?"

"I'm just trying to decide how much you want to hear."

Torn between believing what I didn't know couldn't hurt me and that, on the other hand, I could only fight what I know, I hesitated only a moment. "I need to understand. You're honest, and I trust you. Please tell me."

Another short pause. "Well, like I said, Tom and I go way back. I told him I wanted all the info he could give me."

His caution made me nervous.

Barry continued. "He told me the cops are real interested in you."

Police interest? In me? "But why?"

After a short pause Barry said, "Apparently, of all the people who hated this lady—"

"But I didn't—"

Barry continued as if he didn't hear me. "—so far you and the neighbor are the only ones they can place near the murder scene."

"What are you saying?" The silence that followed made me extremely uneasy. Finally, he continued in a calming voice. "I'm saying you're not off the hook. They're checking on you."

"Do I have to worry about jail?"

"It's unlikely."

I didn't like the sound of that "unlikely." Nasty things happened to people in prison and I would have liked Barry's terminology to be absolute. Besides, I wasn't Olive's killer. If the police jailed me, somebody got away with . . . well . . . murder.

"Can you keep me out of jail or not?" I didn't like the fact that he didn't answer right away.

"They don't have anything that'd constitute probable cause. They'll need more to obtain a warrant."

"Well, then, there's no reason to worry. Right? After all, I didn't kill Olive. What can they find?" Was I trying to convince myself or Barry?

"Likely nothing."

Again, the small doubt reflected in his words stimulated my fears.

"Let's not worry unless we have to." He paused, and his voice softened. "Now, to more important subjects. That invitation for dinner's open. I'm available for food, encouragement, and general comfort."

I suspected he wanted to assure me he believed in my innocence, since I'd already refused his offer of dinner. Despite Mom's "advice," I turned him down again. "Thanks, Barry, but I have a rehearsal tonight. If I don't play, I don't get paid, and I have to be able to pay my lawyer."

Barry chuckled. "As long as you're refusing for a good reason."

We were laughing when we said goodbye, but as other people's suspicions mounted—the gossips, the neighbor, and now, according to Barry, even the police—I felt my sense of humor slipping away.

SEVEN

WEDNESDAY, FEBRUARY 12, 2010, 7:10 PM

I DIDN'T WANT TO BE A SUSPECT in Lt. Gordon's investigation. Anxious to find answers, I arrived at rehearsal eager to talk to Gardiner again. It also occurred to me that, even though it was hard for me to imagine Clara would ever kill anybody, her anger and frustration had been intense when she'd called me on the afternoon of Olive's death. Should I talk to her, too?

As I stepped from my car and began the dark, crisp walk to the stage door, I remembered Leanne's comment at the funeral about our second clarinet, Janet Archer. Why would Janet be glad Olive couldn't "meddle" anymore? What did that mean? One of my better friends, Janet sat right behind me in the orchestra and talked to me about everything. I would know if she and Olive were at odds. Wouldn't I? Had she been about to tell me something when we'd been interrupted at the last rehearsal?

As it turned out, I had to forget my questions for the moment. I arrived later than usual, and Gardiner was already testing reeds, while Janet practiced selected passages. It would look odd if I interrupted. Clara, like most of the string players, hadn't arrived yet. I began my own warmup. I have to admit I gave more thought to planning conversations than to preparing for rehearsal. Meanwhile, the stage filled, and the usual pre-rehearsal warmups built to a din. When Felix started rehearsal, my mind hadn't focused yet, and I concocted and discarded various conversational gambits instead of concentrating on my part.

"Second flute. You should have a part at letter C."

"Oh, sorry," I apologized. Stalling rehearsal was the short road to professional suicide, I knew. The wake-up call jarred me back to reality. I put my questions away, and concentrated on my part, not thinking about the murder until intermission.

When break came, Gardiner left the stage faster than a sixty-fourth note. Clearly, he must be avoiding me. Clara and a string player I didn't know were deep in conversation.

That left Janet. I turned around.

"Yo, Emily." She put her clarinet on its stand and joined me. "I thought Felix was gonna kill you. Us second chair players can't attract that kind of attention."

I laughed, but we both knew it was no joke. "Yeah. No excuses." There never were. "How've you been?" I hadn't talked to Janet since our last rehearsal.

"Well, sister, there's news."

Her tone announced its importance. Maybe she was about to finish our interrupted conversation? Because we had only so much time at break, we walked in the direction of the restroom as she spoke.

She took a deep breath. "Alan split."

It didn't surprise me. Janet's marriage had taken its cue from the Capulets and the Montagues ever since I'd known her. According to Janet, the couple's problems had started when Alan lost his job. Janet got work with the Monroe symphony, first as an extra, then as a regular when our aging second clarinet retired.

For a year and a half after that, Alan took care of the house and kids. By the time he found a new job, their bills looked like the national debt. Inconceivably, Alan wanted Janet to quit the symphony because he "didn't want his wife working." Janet felt pressured to pay off the loans. Besides, she enjoyed her symphony job and felt she'd worked too hard to quit.

By then, their marriage had survived fourteen years. They had two children. The kids had two dogs, a cat, a guinea pig, and a succession of goldfish which, thanks to the kids' neglect, frequently floated to the top of the tank.

Alan and Janet declared war over the work issue, with Janet working nights and Alan working days. Their spare time went to the kids. Creditors hounded them and tensions made them snap at each other. I'd never heard either one of them say anything kind or loving about the other.

"What happened?" A stupid question. As if she could answer in twenty-five words or less. But what was I supposed to say? Somebody should publish an etiquette book for these occasions.

"Olive happened."

"Olive?" My confusion showed. Olive? Mixed up in the breakup of Janet's marriage? I wanted an explanation.

"She convinced that useless jerk I used to call a husband that I had an affair with Gardiner." Anger vibrated in Janet's words.

It occurred to me that we needed more privacy for this conversation. I stepped into an isolated alcove between the curtain and the stage door and lowered my voice. "You've been friends with Gardiner for years. How did Olive, or Alan, make an affair out of that?"

"Last Wednesday, Gardiner and I downed a few at the Blue Dragon."

I nodded, unenlightened. Everybody hung out there for rehearsal post-mortems over a snack or a beer.

"We talked for a long time. Mostly Gardiner groused about Olive. I'm trying not to speak ill of the dead, but putting it tactfully, she put the loons to shame. She followed him around, called in the middle of the night, and showed up with no warning. She even had his answering machine code because, according to him, she stole some of his messages."

I nodded. I knew Olive's crazy side.

"Gardiner kept trying to dump her." Janet's voice rose as she expressed her anger. "He wanted Leanne to move in, but Leanne didn't want to talk about it 'til Olive was history."

I wondered if Lt. Gordon knew that. But we weren't talking about the police investigation. "What about the affair?" Janet had lost the thread of her story.

"Gardiner was wound tight and ticking. Besides his troubles with Olive, he'd stunk up the rehearsal. We closed down the Blue Dragon, and I didn't get home 'til three in the morning."

She paused and took a breath. "Alan was snoring in dreamland when I got there. He knows better than to wait up for me."

"So? Where's the problem?"

"When Gardiner went home, Olive was waiting outside his place in her car. She pounced on him with questions." Janet imitated a whiny nag, cocking her head from side to side. "'Where were you? What were you doing? Who were you with?' He should've just clammed up but, Lord knows why, he talked to her." Janet's eyes narrowed.

I kept quiet.

"Gardiner told Olive he'd been with me. She smelled beer on his breath, put two and two together, and came up with eight."

Janet had begun pounding one fist against her thigh, her agitation signaling the climax of the story. "He tired of the inquisition real quick and he said, 'Yeah, Olive, I've been screwing Janet the whole time. Now get off my property so I can get some sleep.'"

Nice guy. But in her nuttiest mode, reason didn't work with Olive.

I heaved a tired sigh. "And she believed him." It wasn't a question. I had no doubt I knew the answer.

"Worse. She called our house, in the middle of the night no less, and woke Alan, who answered the phone. She told him Gardiner'd admitted we were screwing and demanded that Alan do something."

"Alan listened?" This surprised me. I credited him with more intelligence than that.

"He didn't see Gardiner lying about it."

I guessed Olive had embarrassed Alan. He had years of marital battles in his life with Janet. Then Olive pressured him. He had to do something to save face.

I wanted Janet to feel better. "It's temporary insanity. Once he has a chance to think it out, Alan'll come home."

She looked straight at me, and again, I felt her anger. "He'll have to do some heavy courting if he wants me back. I'm better off without him. After fourteen years, to believe a story like that." She tsked and shook her head.

I understood she hurt.

But Janet went on, her wounds hidden by antagonism. "The evil bitch deserved to die!"

So much for not speaking ill of the dead. "Careful." Our alcove wasn't that private. At her volume, Janet could probably be heard in the suburbs. "You can't talk that way."

Janet blew up at me, at top volume. "I'll talk any way I like! I'm not gonna make her Saint Olive just because she's dead. I'd've killed her myself if somebody else hadn't done it for me."

Janet's rage had me rattled. And it might not just be talk. After all, as David O'Malley had said, someone killed Olive. But my friend Janet?

Apparently, she hadn't had her say yet. "The woman was a nasty slut. She hurt everybody she touched. She trashed my marriage, tried to break up Gardiner and Leanne, and lied about Joe's—"

I pricked up my ears. "Joe? Joe who?"

"Oh, damn! Forget I said that, Emily. I'm pissed. I've got to calm down before the second half."

I couldn't very well pump her for information when she'd just told me to forget it. I gave her a hug, made my excuses, and headed for the drinking fountain.

In line, I ran into Peter Hall, our concertmaster. A nervous man, tall and thin, with glasses, a beard, and dark curly hair, he accepted the responsibility of leading the string section as a continuing burden.

"How are you, Peter?"

"Fine. I've been meaning to talk to you."

Proving that life went on despite death and divorce, Peter asked me to play second flute in the new opera orchestra. "I'm the opera contractor. I'll be hiring the best musicians, I hope."

I allowed his comments to count as flattery. He must consider me among the best, or at least the best available.

Peter went on. "The job'll pay the orchestra well. Should increase the symphony salary by about a third, by the time all the rehearsals and performances for the year are done. Everybody's asking about the extra work. Sometimes it puts me in an awkward position. Chuck Holcombe asked me straight out if I'd hire him for the violin section. He wouldn't take 'no' for an answer." Peter's voice grew louder and more aggrieved. "We knew each other in college and our wives are friends. I like him. I know he wants the money, but business is business. He's having personal problems and hasn't been practicing much. Olive told me he . . . well . . . never mind."

But my imagination connected the dots. I'd heard Olive's critiques of fellow musicians. Kind, she wasn't.

Peter continued, "Plenty of people want the work. I'm paid a lot of money to put a good orchestra together. My head's on the block if the orchestra's not good enough. I had to tell Chuck I couldn't hire him. I felt like the big, bad wolf."

He *was* the big, bad wolf in my opinion. I thought of kind, gentle Chuck, hurting from his problems with Celia. Well-prepared, supportive, and pleasant, he'd always done a good job. If he had personal problems, shouldn't a friend like Peter understand? But there were no second chances in music. Once the word made the rounds . . .

Alice Smithson stood in line just behind me.

I didn't want to say anything I'd regret to Peter. Instead, I turned to Alice. "What's new?" A dangerous question, because nothing existed that she didn't know or have an opinion about, and you never knew how long you'd be tied up, listening to every little thing. In this case, though, the question provided an excuse not to talk to Peter any longer.

"You know the murder investigation? Olive? Well, I just found out from Alesia O'Malley . . ."

Alice talked freely, with no trace of hostile feelings. Maybe not all the gossip convicted me.

". . . that the police finally cleared David, her husband. She sounded pretty peeved that the whole thing took so long. She'd told them he'd been home all day, but they didn't believe her. David discovered the body, and he lives just downstairs from Olive. He had all kinds of opportunity to kill her, and they thought Alesia might be lying to protect him, but I guess a friend had taken a picture of the whole family on David's phone. The living room furniture confirmed the location, and the cops found a timestamp in the photo's data. The friend confirmed that he'd been there most of the afternoon. That and David's browser history finally convinced them."

You couldn't stop Alice once she started passing on the news.

"And have you heard that Leanne Johnson . . ."

Just then, the personnel manager interrupted Alice by calling the end of break. I skipped the drinking fountain but hadn't used the restroom. Fortunately for me, the stalls were empty. I arrived back on stage after the tuning note, just as Felix started to conduct Beethoven's Fifth, the main piece on the program.

"Nice of you to join us, Miz Wilson." He let me and the rest of the world know my sins had been noticed.

Thank goodness for the union's review committee or I'd find a pink slip in my next paycheck. "Sorry, Felix."

He scowled and turned to the first violins, venting his frustrations. Better them than me.

As information rattled around in my brain, I played the Beethoven on automatic. Did Janet decide to have it out with Olive? Kill her in a sudden rage? But I couldn't believe it. Not my friend, Janet. We shopped 'til we dropped. She'd helped me landscape my backyard. If Olive ended Janet's marriage, though . . . and her husband, Alan, might have hated Olive, too . . .

Janet had mentioned a "Joe." Who was he? Another victim of Olive's lies, she'd said. He could, of course, be a Joe I didn't know. But if I knew him, there were only two possibilities. Either he was Joe Burke, the local music contractor, who hired musicians and handled music for non-symphony jobs such as musicals, or he was Joe Rhinehart, orchestra librarian. Joe Rhinehart was here tonight. I'd try to talk to him before I left.

And I wanted to talk to Gardiner. I wouldn't be sorry if he was put away, out of my daily life.

AFTER REHEARSAL ENDED, I PACKED UP as fast as possible, but missed connecting with both Gardiner and Joe Rhinehart. I'd have to catch them at rehearsal tomorrow.

I dragged myself home, disappointed that it would be another day before I made any progress on finding out about Janet's "Joe." My lack of mental attention upset me, too. I'd built professional respect over the years but, remembering Peter's attitude toward Chuck, I feared I could blow it in a matter of days. Fortunately, I'd practiced hard enough that my fingers knew what to do without my brain . . . so far.

As I walked in my front door, I heard my landline ringing. Who could be calling this late? I ran past Golden, who tried to greet me. The caller ID said it was Barry. Breathless, I snatched up the receiver. "Hello?"

"Em? Are you alright?" Barry again. "You sound out of breath."

The late phone calls were getting to be a habit. I scratched Golden's belly with my foot.

"I just walked in the door and ran for the phone. What's up?" He wouldn't be calling at this hour unless it was important.

"I talked to a connection I have at the DA."

"And?"

"When he heard I called about you, he tried to bail out of the conversation."

More good news. "You couldn't find out anything?"

"I didn't say that. He stuck to the official line. 'The police must complete their investigation.' He did promise to let me know if he heard anything about plans to bring charges." He paused. "That's something."

"Great." Somehow, I couldn't summon any enthusiasm.

"I thought you'd be a little more interested."

"I'm sorry. I guess I'm not a very good conversationalist right now. I had a horrible rehearsal. But I did find out some interesting stuff about Olive from Janet Archer."

"Oh? What?"

"Apparently Olive broke up Janet's marriage. Or at least Janet thinks so. If that's the case, both she and her estranged husband would have a motive. I doubt she killed Olive, but her soon-to-be ex might have snapped. And I have a feeling about Gardiner. Is any of that helpful?"

"Sure. Write it all down with names and as many details as you can, and I'll pass it along to the cops."

A short silence followed.

"Em? Are you sure you're okay? Sounds like you need a little cheering up."

I felt tired, discouraged, and I wished for things to go back to the way they were. "All I want is a hot bath, bed, and sleep."

The phone buzzed with silence.

Realizing I'd been short with him I said, "Barry, I'm sorry. A lot happened today. I'll wake up in a better mood tomorrow."

"I understand, Emily. I'll let you know if I hear any more. Take care."

EIGHT

WEDNESDAY, FEBRUARY 12, 2010, 11:00 PM

I CRAWLED INTO BED AND DRIFTED, drowsily falling, falling, falling . . . when the doorbell jerked me back to consciousness. Golden barked fiercely to hold the intruder at bay as I pulled on a robe and tied the belt. I padded downstairs and peered through the peephole. Lt. Gordon? At this time of night? I quieted Golden and cracked the door open.

"Ms. Wilson, I'm here to take you in for questioning regarding the murder of Olive Patterson."

Barry's instructions not to say anything without a lawyer present rang in my ears. "Then I'd better phone my attorney."

He didn't say anything.

I opened the door, and, for the second time in a little over a week, Lt. Gordon entered my home. He followed me down the hall, through the living room, and to the kitchen.

As I picked up the phone he said, "Tell your lawyer we'll meet him at the station."

My stomach and my head changed places. "The station? Can't we just . . ."

"The station," Lt. Gordon repeated firmly.

I made the call.

Even though we'd talked not ten minutes before, Barry didn't answer. Hoping he was in the shower and not out on the town or sleeping so soundly that he couldn't be roused, I left a message and hung up. "He's not answering. I don't want to be questioned without him."

Lt. Gordon tsked. "You can try again from the station." He waited while I went upstairs and dressed. Back downstairs, when I reached for my cell phone, which I'd left on the entry table, he grabbed my hand, "Might as well leave that."

"But you said I could call Barry from the station."

"We have phones."

I supposed he didn't want me making any secret texts or calls.

He took my elbow and propelled me toward the squad car.

The swirling red and blue lights of the police car must have wakened Mrs. Jensen, my neighbor. I saw her watching from her upstairs window and gave a little wave. Her curtain fell shut. By morning, the grapevine would be buzzing. I imagined the talk now. Either I had been "arrested," or, knowing the grapevine, possibly I had a police lover, with whom I had a late-night date.

On the ride to the station, Lt. Gordon didn't say a word.

Not that I minded. My thoughts churned. Dead tired and running on adrenaline, I wondered, how long would this take? How could I keep everybody at the orchestra from finding out where I'd been? Why did we have to go to the station? What if I couldn't reach Barry? At a stoplight, the man in the next car stared. What if I saw someone I knew?

Our arrival at the station gave me other things to think about.

The Monroe police station is downtown in an old marble-columned building much too elegant for its purpose. Lt. Gordon helped me out of the squad car, took my elbow, and led me into the station.

We entered through a back door. He nodded in the direction of a wall phone and ordered, "Try your lawyer again. We have to start."

Praying for Barry to answer, I called.

To my relief, he picked up on the first ring, said he'd received my message, and would head for the police station as soon as possible. Ten minutes, I figured. Next, I had to deal with an overdose of nerves. Feeling embarrassed and desperate, I asked, "Is there a restroom I can use?"

Instead of answering, Lt. Gordon turned to a heavyset, graying officer whose desk nameplate read, "Sgt. Diaz." "Hey, John, where's Millie? I need her to escort Ms. Wilson, here," jerking his head in my direction, "to the bathroom."

"I can get there by myself," I informed him, my dignity suffering and in tatters.

"Sorry. You have to have an escort."

John broke in with, "You may not have much luck with that. Millie and Jackie both called in sick. Nobody's available."

I tried to hurry things along. "Well, it's not going to wait much longer,"

Lt. Gordon muttered to himself, then said, "Okay, I'll escort you."

We walked down a long, dark hallway that smelled like urine and vomit. He opened the door for me, but, to my relief, said, "I'll wait here. I don't suppose you can get into too much trouble in the restroom by yourself. There are no windows, for your information. Make it quick, please."

No cleaner than the hall outside, the restroom had four stalls. I strained to see in the dim lighting, and a moldy smell rose in the air. Relieved to be momentarily free of the lieutenant, I entered a cubicle.

I heard the door to the hall open and close and, when I came out, I had company. A tall, classically elegant beauty splashed her face with water. Her auburn curls were piled atop her head and secured with a sparkly diamond comb. Just a few tendrils escaped artistically. She looked ready for a society fundraiser, except that, as she turned toward me, I saw a purple, swollen cheek. She sniffled softly.

I didn't want to intrude, but I couldn't very well pretend not to notice. "Is anything wrong?" Recognizing a stupid question as soon as I asked it, I didn't give her time to answer. "Can I help?"

Looking in the mirror, she abruptly stopped sniffling, pulled a tissue from her purse and checked her mascara. She dabbed gently at her eyes. "No. But I should be a little pickier about the men I date."

At a loss for words, I thought about my ex-husband. Trying to be encouraging and remembering that she had used the word "date" I said, "At least you discovered his temper before you married him."

She took her gaze from the mirror and studied me then. "You look awfully familiar." Her smile revealed a perfect set of dimples. Cheekbones a mile high and dimples too.

"Have we met?" Her six-inch heels and little black dress were appropriate for a cocktail party.

I felt a surreal sense of disorientation. "Not that I know of. Do you go to the symphony?"

"That must be it." A puzzled pause. "I know. You're Emily Wilson, the flutist."

Amazing. How could I imagine the headquarters for my fan club was the women's restroom at the Monroe police station? "That's right. How did you guess?"

"I'm a flutist, too. KC Giroux." She held out her hand. "But I haven't played in years." She smiled excitedly. "My dates take me to the symphony all the time. Who did you study with?"

I shook KC's hand. I'd run into fellow musicians everywhere I went, but this definitely proved we lived in a small world. "Carol Wincenc."

"Julliard?"

"Yeah." What next? Could we discuss the relative merits of different flute brands?

"I'm so excited to meet you."

A movie star I'm not, but it's nice to know I am well-known in some circles. "Well, it's always nice to meet a fellow flute player, but this would be the last place I'd expect to find one. What are you doing here?" I had a million questions, and they all came out at once. "Why are you dressed to the hilt, looking gorgeous? And what happened to your cheek?"

"Oh, this." The wave of her hand took in her cheek, her ensemble, and the building. "I'm waiting for Madeline."

That answer didn't give me any information. I was considering how to rephrase my questions, but fortunately she didn't stop there. "My 'date' turned out to be a real jerk. I thought we were going to the opening of the Howard collection at the Creative Commonwealth Gallery. It turned out he had other ideas. When I screamed, the neighbors heard and called nine-one-one. Luckily, the cops came when they did, you know?"

"You didn't know your date?"

"No, he phoned the service."

I'm a little naive, but I slowly put the information together. "So, you work for . . ."

". . . an escort service." She finished my sentence, grinning.

I must have looked stunned. I felt stunned. Trying to hide my astonishment, I returned to our mutual interest. "How does a nice flute player like you end up in a place like this?" I waved my hand to include the jail surroundings, purposely paraphrasing all the old films I'd ever seen, and thinking KC a bizarre combination of innocence and worldliness.

Mischief lit her smile. A face as stunningly beautiful as hers should have been in the movies. "How does a nice flute player like *you* end up in a place like this?"

It took a minute to figure out her meaning. I'd momentarily forgotten my predicament. When the light dawned, I laughed at myself. "We are up a creek, aren't we?"

She joined in my laughter. Our amusement didn't have much to do with how funny our situation was or wasn't.

Laughing harder I said, "They think I killed somebody."

Now we guffawed, and I clutched the counter for support.

"Hey! What's going on in there?" A fist thumped on the door. Lt. Gordon.

"That's *my* date." If it was possible to laugh harder, I did. KC snorted.

With weak tummy muscles, barely able to speak, I wiped tears from my eyes and raised my voice. "I'll be out in a minute." I tried to recover, hiccupping with the effort. Then I said to KC, "But seriously . . ." and we were off again. The giggles finally died out more because we were tired than because the situation had changed. I gasped and wiped my eyes. I dispensed with modesty. "You must be smart, if you play the flute, so I'm assuming you have a good reason for doing what you do."

"Oh, well," she sounded serious now, "it's a kind of control, isn't it?"

"Control?" This didn't make sense to me.

"Men will do anything for a woman when they're properly encouraged."

Maybe for her. Encouraging men wasn't my talent.

"And that's revenge."

Revenge? For what? Her comment was outside my experience, but I didn't want to pry any more than I already had. I conceded, "If you say so."

"Besides, most of them treat me nice. They take me to the symphony, art galleries, plays, on vacations . . ."

"What about the ones who don't 'treat you nice'?"

She didn't answer right away. When she did, she defended her chosen profession. "Only one guy's hit me, you know?"

Thinking again of my ex-husband, it sounded like one too many to me. Not okay, but I didn't press. "You like your job, then?"

"Yeah, I guess. It'd be nicer if the flute playing had worked out, though. At least I'd be able to tell my sister what I do."

"You considered it seriously?"

"Oh, yeah. But who can afford Juilliard, or any other school? That's how I started with the escort service. It pays well."

Well, I guess I shouldn't be surprised. Musicians always scrounged for money. I wanted to encourage her, give her a hug, but since I didn't feel I knew her well enough, and we were standing in a restroom, I said, "If you're interested, I'd like to give you lessons."

"Oh, I haven't played for years. I'd be awfully rusty." She glanced down, first shaking her hands then stretching her fingers.

I encouraged her. "Hey, that's what teachers are for."

She looked up again. "I haven't thought about lessons. How much do you charge?"

Feeling like I owed her something on music's behalf, and because our encounter had been such a stress reliever, I hurried to offer. "No, no. It's on the house. No charge."

"Oh, Emily! I can't take advantage of you. I'd want to pay you." She sounded distressed.

"No. I won't take your money. What would I have done if you hadn't been here?" Sincerely I said, "I'd be crying instead of laughing right now. Let me give you a couple lessons as a 'thank you.' In appreciation for your company."

She displayed her dimples again. "Well, I guess if I can take money for my company, I can take flute—"

Lt. Gordon pounded on the door again. "Do I have to come in there?"

"Just a minute." I turned to KC. "Don't forget, now. Give me a call about those lessons."

"Okay. Sure thing."

Hurrying, I pulled a pen from my purse, found a scrap of paper, and scrawled my phone number on it. So far, KC had been the light of my day. Sending her a mental hug, I opened the door to rejoin Lt. Gordon.

NINE

THE LIGHT MOOD I HAD SHARED with KC evaporated with one look at Lt. Gordon. His hands were fisted at his side and he scowled at me. "I told you to hurry, not have a party."

I suppose I should have apologized as a matter of good form, but one of my principles, new since my husband left, was that I never said "sorry" unless I actually *was* sorry. Silently, I turned back up the hall.

I didn't get far before I realized I didn't know where to go. I had no choice but to stop, wait for Lt. Gordon, and follow him meekly.

We proceeded to the patrol room. John still sat at his station. By now it must be midnight. Didn't any of these folks ever go home?

Lt. Gordon jerked his head in the direction of another long, dark hall and asked the sergeant, "Got a minute?"

John looked up from his paperwork and joined us in our trek to a starkly bare room, furnished only with a long beige Formica table and four chairs.

The lieutenant waved me into one of the chairs. "If you'll excuse me a moment, I'll be back with someone to take notes. The sergeant'll stay with you. Would you like something to drink? Coffee? Cola?"

At the risk of annoying him further, but wanting comfort, I replied, "Tea, if you have it."

Lt. Gordon tsked. "I'll try," he said, and left.

John and I looked at each other.

Silence in the presence of another person made me uncomfortable.

John sat in silence.

I was uncomfortable.

I tried a tentative smile. John didn't respond. I interpreted that to mean he didn't want to engage in social chitchat, either. I felt a migraine coming on and reached for my purse.

John beat me to it and didn't let me touch it again until he'd performed a search. He examined my aspirin with a scowl, saw that it was clearly marked and in its original bottle, and eventually let me take one, though he kept the bottle, and examined and removed the penknife on my key ring before he returned it and the rest of the purse.

I swallowed the aspirin dry.

Barry arrived, finally, after twenty very long minutes. At last, I had some company besides John's silent, unsmiling presence.

While the sergeant called Lt. Gordon on his radio, I said, "Barry! Am I glad to see you."

He rewarded me with a huge hug of greeting. "Glad to hear you say so, Em, even if I'd hoped for different circumstances." John continued to speak into the radio. Barry huddled with me in the corner and asked softly, "Have you said anything?"

"Not me. When I pay for advice, I follow it," I responded, also sotto voce. "Lieutenant Gordon makes it easy to stay silent."

"Well, don't say anything, no matter what he says. Let me handle it."

Relieved, and trusting Barry's competence, my eyes filled, and I felt I had to say, "I didn't do anything wrong. I swear."

Barry captured one of my hands with his and gave it a squeeze. "I know, Em. I know. Quit worrying."

Thinking that was easier said than done, I forced a smile.

John glanced up from the radio. "Sorry. Gordon's busy. He'll be here as soon as he can."

We waited. And waited. I paced. By my watch, it took twenty-two minutes before Lt. Gordon appeared. A young Latino man, about my height, with a pock-marked face and carrying a steno pad, accompanied him. No tea, though.

"Sorry to be slow. Eric here was tied up."

As a measure of my exhaustion, his words conjured pictures of a struggling Eric, bound and gagged, rescued by a gallant Lt. Gordon. I almost giggled.

Managing to keep a straight face, I listened to Barry respond. "No problem, but let's get busy so Miz Wilson can go home."

My instincts said the look on Lt. Gordon's face meant that wasn't likely to motivate him, but Barry didn't flinch.

We all sat at the table.

Lt. Gordon reached under it and I heard a click. "I'll be recording this."

Barry pulled a small recorder out of his briefcase. "Sure. I'll record it too, if you don't mind."

Lt. Gordon responded, "Fine. Eric will take notes to make sure we don't miss anything if *both* machines malfunction." He then explained that he wanted to ask some questions in connection with the murder of Olive Patterson.

In response to Barry's inquiries, he replied that, no, they weren't charging me with anything at this time.

I took a quick glance at my watch. One a.m.

Lt. Gordon asked the questions I expected. Where was I between 3:15 and 6:00 p.m. Sunday the second? When did I answer Olive's phone calls and text? Where did I go on my walk? What did I have for dinner? What had I practiced? How long?

Barry nodded, so I gave the lieutenant the same information I'd given him in our initial interview.

The questions took an unexpected turn when Lt. Gordon started asking about my financial situation. How much did I make? Did I have debts? Did I have savings and investments?

Barry stepped in. "My client isn't answering on the advice of counsel."

Finally, Lt. Gordon tsked. "You know we'll get a court order and find the info."

"Fine," Barry responded. "Get it."

Lt. Gordon shrugged and moved on to questions about Olive's will. Was I acquainted with her attorney? What did I know about the provisions of the will?

Barry continued to respond, "My client refuses to answer on the advice of counsel."

My head throbbed, and I wished for another dose of aspirin. How would I know about Olive's will? But I handled it pretty well, I thought, managing to confine my "comments" to surprised sounds.

Finally, Barry had had enough. "It's extremely late, Lieutenant Gordon, and I'll have to insist you either charge my client or let her go."

This whole process hadn't improved the lieutenant's temper, and the look he gave Barry made me feel my lawyer had earned whatever he billed me.

"Fine. Have it your way. This is getting us nowhere," the lieutenant snapped.

"Wait here, Em, just a minute, while the lieutenant and I have a little talk. I'll be right back." Barry winked at me.

Lt. Gordon scowled and followed Barry from the room.

Fifteen minutes later I trotted gratefully alongside Barry out the front doors and onto the sidewalk.

In answer to all my questions Barry mysteriously replied, "I just made sure he'll be a little more careful about disturbing you in the future. You're supposed to stay in town, though."

"Shouldn't I cooperate a little more? After all, I didn't kill Olive."

"He already suspects you're guilty. We're just giving him some motivation to earn his salary."

"But . . ."

"Trust me on this, Em. I know what I'm doing."

I shut up. I didn't enjoy the feeling of trusting someone else to protect me, but I had confidence that Barry knew his business. Obviously, Lt. Gordon respected him, even though Barry worked for me.

We didn't arrive at my house until three in the morning. Golden gave us a wild welcome—bouncing, jumping, and barking—and finally settled down for an affectionate tummy scratch. Though I didn't show it in quite the same way, I was just as happy to see her and soaked in her unconditional welcome.

"Are you sure you don't want me to stay and cook? I make a mean omelet."

"Thanks, Barry, but I just want to crash."

"Well, don't worry about a thing. I'll call my friend in the police department, find out what brought that little session on, and then be in touch."

"It's a relief to have your help. I don't feel so alone."

"Okay." His confidence faltered and he sounded awkward. "Well, have a good sleep."

Relieved I didn't have to struggle to convince him to leave, I realized that one of Barry's positive qualities was that he was a gentleman.

Alone at last, I waited while Golden did her business in the backyard, then stumbled into my PJs. In bed I snuggled with her warm bulk and fell into a dreamless sleep.

TEN

THURSDAY, FEBRUARY 13, 2010, 9:00 AM

IN THE MORNING, SHORT OF SLEEP after the interrogation at the police station, I treated myself gently. A steaming cup of peppermint tea helped. The warmth of the cup in my hands and the comfort of the familiar aroma soothed my psyche. I drew a hot, lavender-scented bubble bath and prepared to let the luxury of its fragrance continue my self-administered therapy. My tea in hand, I immersed my body in the steaming water with a sigh of pure pleasure . . .

Only to have every anxiety I ever had reactivated by the doorbell's strident "bing bong." Golden barked ferociously while I shot out of the tub, threw on my robe, and prepared to discover who dared disturb my peace.

I looked out the peephole as Golden continued barking. KC, the dazzling flute-playing escort from the police station, stood outside my door. A maroon BMW SUV occupied my driveway.

"Golden. It's alright." I cracked open the door, chain on. "KC?"

She leaned toward the door. "Emily? You dropped your wallet. I found it and thought you might want it today." She held it up. "I hope you don't mind. I found your address from your driver's license."

"I didn't even know I'd dropped it." I closed the door, took off the chain, and accepted the wallet. "Where did you find it?"

"It fell along the wall between two of the wash basins."

"It must have tumbled out while I rummaged in my purse. I'm glad you're the one who found it. I would have been stranded somewhere and not had cash or credit cards. You're a lifesaver. Thank you. Can I give you some money?" I opened the wallet. Ten dollars. It wasn't much, but all my money was there.

She blushed. "Oh no, Emily. You've already been so kind. Offering me flute lessons and all."

I didn't know anything about this woman other than she performed a service which encouraged exceedingly questionable business contacts. And she played flute, of course, although that didn't necessarily indicate trustworthiness. But she had returned my wallet. I glanced at Golden. Her tail wagged, signaling her approval. My dog was friendly, overly friendly some said, true, but there had been enough exceptions that I knew Golden would have told me via a growl if she had any reservations.

The memory of our recent shared experience fresh in my mind, I didn't hesitate any longer. "Come on in." I took the chain off, opened the door all the way, and pulled my robe tighter.

Golden's whole body wriggled.

"Thanks, Emily."

"Are you okay?" The swelling on KC's cheek had gone down, but it had turned fiery red.

"I'm fine." She touched her cheek lightly. "It'll start to show some color soon."

KC knelt and held out her hand, palm up, speaking soft endearments, while Golden sniffed her all over. She scratched Golden's ears. "You're a good girl, aren't you? I always wanted a golden."

Golden nudged her head under KC's arm, forcing a pat. KC had apparently passed a thorough inspection.

"Is that your BMW in the driveway?"

"Yeah." She stood. "It's how I pamper myself, you know?"

I briefly wished I had the means to pamper myself that way but changed my mind when I considered how I loved my job, even if it didn't pay very well. "Can I get you some tea?"

She looked up at me and said softly, "If it's not too much trouble, I'd love that."

I led her down the hall to the kitchen and nodded in the direction of the table, wordlessly inviting her to sit, then moved to the stove.

Golden approached KC, tail wagging, giving her a doggy welcome.

While the two of them were getting acquainted, I filled the teakettle and turned it on to boil. "Did you have to stay at the police station much longer?"

"Yeah. I haven't gone to bed yet. It took forever."

"You came here before you slept? That was very kind of you."

"I wanted you to have the wallet, you know? I just took time to change my clothes. Before I can sleep, I have to find somewhere to stay anyway. Madeline wouldn't let me go back to my apartment."

"Who's Madeline?"

"She's my boss. She sets up my dates."

She didn't say the word "madam," but I thought it. Loudly.

"Anyway, I'm sort of *persona non grata* right now since I pressed charges against a customer. Madeline said I 'compromised confidentiality.'" KC made air quotes. "She picked me up at the police station and took me to my car, then told me to find a place to stay and gave me some clothes she had on hand." KC pulled at the thighs of her jeans, which were almost twice too big for her. "They don't fit very well." She hesitated and gazed at me, as if asking that I believe her, but afraid of my reaction. "I'm not in trouble with the law. Really. It's just that Madeleine didn't want me available to answer questions, you know?"

"In other words, you're out of a job."

"Yeah. I guess." She grinned.

I smiled back.

"Actually, I'm kind of relieved. Talking to you . . . you remind me of my mother, or the mother I wish I had, anyway,"

Sounded like high praise, but it made me wonder about her relationship with her real mother.

"I'm getting too old for this," she went on. "It's time to do something with a future. Something I can be doing when I'm thirty."

In about a century. But she gave the impression of being forward looking and practical. Not to mention sensible. "I've saved a little money and, all things considered, now's a good time, right?"

From her history, I figured she might be as old as twenty-three. Makeup made her look all of twenty-eight. But now, scrubbed clean and in jeans and a T-shirt, with auburn curls around her shoulders, she looked eighteen. I had friends with daughters this age. She might have been *my* daughter if I had one. And if she were, I'd hope somebody would help her out.

I was briefly silent while I thought. "Can you cook?"

Her face lit up. "Oh, I *love* to cook. It's relaxing. Such fun. And then I eat what I create." She smiled. "It was my favorite part of Home Ec. in high school."

"Can you cook anything that's kind to the waistline?" I thought as fast as I could.

"The waistline likes slicing and dicing, not cooking." She beamed at me.

I smiled back. I couldn't help it. Irresistible. I thought again that she ought to be in pictures. An auburn-haired Audrey Hepburn. "Well, until you find another place, you're welcome to stay here and slice and dice to your heart's content. If you'll cook, and do laundry and light housekeeping, I'll throw in flute lessons, too." I hesitated. "But no customers." This last condition was non-negotiable.

"Are you sure, Emily? I don't want to intrude. There's a lot on your plate."

I hesitated. "In fairness, I have to warn you. This might not be the best place for you if you're trying to be inconspicuous. There's been a lot of police interest in me lately."

She laughed. "I'm not worried about the cops. They won't even know I'm here." She moved her chair closer to the table. "So, it's a deal? I can stay?"

I chuckled. "It's a deal."

She bounced up and ran to hug me. "You won't be sorry. I won't stay long. Just 'til I find a place. And I'll slice and dice and cook and clean. You'll wonder what you ever did without me. And no customers. Promise." Seeming younger than ever, she crossed her heart with her index finger. "I'm thankful. This is so unexpected. I didn't feel safe alone in my car, and I knew I'd have to stay there at least a little while. And my friends and family are all in Washington state. I didn't know anybody to turn to for help." She hugged me again.

I hugged her back. Like magic her joy and, believe it or not, her innocence had bypassed my staid and carefully built barriers. As she settled in her chair again, I sipped my tea. "Do you have a flute?"

"Oh, sure. Even if I'm rusty, I wouldn't think of selling it. It's in my bag."

"Well, let me know when you're ready for a lesson."

She hesitated a moment. "What about you, Emily? Is there anything I can do to help?"

"You will be helping. I hate housekeeping."

"Oh, that," she waved it away. "I'd be doing that anyway." She paused. "I meant with . . ." Another pause. "The person you killed . . . I mean . . . the person they *think* you killed, you know?"

She looked sheepish, and I started laughing, but she didn't join me. Just sat there holding her teacup, looking serious and worried and sincere.

So, I told her all about it. She had the right, after all, to know she wasn't living with a murderess.

"Now that I know what happened," she said when I'd finished, "tell me the important stuff."

"Important stuff?"

"Yeah. The non-facts. Who was she? What was she like?"

Good question. "Well, for me, at her best, Olive was a hoot. But she could be plenty annoying. And I'm finding out that's the side of her almost everybody else saw." I thought about it a bit. "I liked her. We had fun. She made me laugh, until I tired of laughing at other people." I paused again.

"But . . . ?" KC prompted.

"But she didn't have much sense about relationships." I thought of Gardiner. "She tried to force herself on people sometimes." I realized the rest of her relationships weren't great either. "She could be pretty tactless and self-centered. That's what irritated everybody."

KC opened her eyes wide then shut them for a few seconds. Her voice sounded hurt when she spoke again. "What's tactless and self-centered to you might be painful and cruel if you have a different perspective, you know?" Her eyes filled with tears.

She'd known her share of sorrows, it seemed.

I thought how Olive had ended Janet's shaky marriage with her jealous accusations, the anger and hurt she'd aggravated by poking around in Clara's post-divorce wounds, even the chaos she'd created in Gardiner's life. "Good point. I have to think about it some more."

"Em?"

Was this my new nickname? First Barry, now KC. "Hmmm?"

"I want to be more help."

"If you have any ideas, let me know. I have to think of something before Lieutenant Gordon finds evidence that I started World War III."

She'd finished her tea during the recitation of my troubles. Now she leaned back. "Well . . . I didn't think about it before . . ."

She hesitated.

I encouraged her. "What?"

She looked down at her fingers. "I keep what I do confidential. You have to promise not to tell anyone."

"I'll promise anything to find useful information."

She finally continued. "Curtis Strange? The Symphony Board member?"

I didn't have much to do with the Board, but I knew Curtis as a wealthy land developer in his forties. Single. Not very knowledgeable about music but enthusiastic. I would have guessed he'd be a Rossini fan, going for fast and frothy, but he'd come backstage raving about our performance of Mahler's Fourth, a manic/depressive work if I'd ever heard one. I'd never considered whether that revealed his personality. "Yeah. What about him?"

"Well . . ." Her gaze was penetrating as she looked at me, "You have to promise not to tell anybody I told you this."

"I promise."

"He called the service. He wanted a date for the symphony picnic last fall."

I saw her with different eyes, and realized KC looked familiar. "Don't tell me he was a client."

"Yes, but not the way you're thinking. Madeleine gave me the assignment since I know a little about music. Curtis picked me up in his car and, on the way to the picnic, I made conversation, and asked him if he liked being a developer." She hesitated again and pushed her hair behind her ears. "I don't know why he talked to me the way he did. I think because I wasn't a threat."

"Or because he wanted to impress you."

"Maybe." She shrugged and shifted her gaze. "Anyway, he told me that developing communities is interesting, but the main thing is the power."

"Did you ask him about that?"

"Of course. He said, and I've never forgotten it, 'I love to snap my fingers to hire people I want and fire people who annoy me.'"

"Whoa! And Olive didn't make a secret of her contempt for the Board." I felt like someone had switched on a light bulb. "She'd tell anyone who'd listen that she didn't make enough money and that Monroe needed a stronger musician's union."

We looked at each other in silence.

KC glanced at her hands. "It's a long shot. It might not mean anything."

"Don't downplay your ideas. This might be important. But I don't know anyone on the Board well enough to talk to." I thought a minute. "Can you follow up with Curtis? Phone him and meet with him?"

KC didn't answer immediately. "I thought we agreed. You said no customers."

True. "Okay." I thought, searching for a rationalization, I'm afraid to admit. She'd given me my best lead so far, besides Gardiner. "He won't be a customer because *you'll* be approaching *him*." Oh, ouch. That didn't sit well. "And it won't be more than once or twice, maybe for tea in a public place, or a casual date. And I'm certainly not asking you to do anything unsafe or unpleasant." I hesitated. "Would that work without compromising you?"

She smiled, her dimples dancing. "Sure thing. I'm glad to help."

She didn't speak for a moment. "Do you have his phone number, though? Madeleine keeps all that information."

"No problem. He'll be listed in the symphony directory." I found the book and gave her the number.

"He'll think it's a little . . ." She chuckled. ". . . strange."

It took me a few seconds to realize the chuckle was because his name was Strange, Curtis Strange.

"Usually customers contact me, not vice versa, and it's been a while. But if I call him and act like I'm smitten . . . not too many people are annoyed by being liked. The worst he can do is say no." She thought for a bit. "Okay. I'll take care of it." She stood and took our tea things to the sink. "But like I said before, it's a long shot. I'll bet when it gets right down to it, you'll find sex is behind the murder somehow. It usually is. Or at least it's important."

I thought again of Olive's overabundant curves and decided KC had a warped worldview. On the other hand, lately the world had been seriously skewed. Second thoughts convinced me to consider the idea.

Gardiner had been Olive's only love interest, as far as I knew, and he was deeply annoyed with her. For months, he'd tried to oust her from his life. She'd spied on him and messed up his romances. With a smile, I thought of the time Olive told me she'd gone to Gardiner's, discovered Leanne was there, and managed to yell through the window, "Did he tell you about me?" before Gardiner slammed the window shut. You can only imagine the scene inside. I'd been amused. Gardiner presumably wasn't. Leanne, understandably, wanted Olive completely out of Gardiner's life before she moved in. Killing Olive would have been a sure way to solve the problem for Gardiner . . . or Leanne. Was that reason enough to kill?

"You might be right, KC. If you think of anything else, let me know."

Confidence brightened my day. Her ideas echoed what I'd already been thinking. Our talk had helped me organize my thoughts. The new information about Curtis Strange excited me. That angle looked promising. In the meantime, I reminded myself I'd planned to talk to Joe Rhinehart at rehearsal.

I looked at my watch. Not much time before my first student. "You can stay in the guestroom. It's upstairs on the right." I led the way. "I'll give you a house key, and there's a spare spot in the garage you can use. You may have to move a few things if they're in your way."

Going to the kitchen junk drawer, after some effort, I found the spare key and took it to KC. "I'll give you some towels, and then I'll have to run. My students start coming soon, and I have to dress." Silently groaning, I remembered that I had to clean up my interrupted bath, too.

"Awesome. Thanks, Emily."

I finished straightening the bathroom as the doorbell rang, and I greeted the first of the day's flute students panting and out of breath.

ELEVEN

THURSDAY, FEBRUARY 13, 2010, 7:30 PM

Besides Saturday, Thursday is my biggest teaching day. I taught until the last minute, then accepted a BLT KC shoved into my hand as I ran out the door and wolfed it down while I drove. I barely had time to sit in my chair and put my flute together before the downbeat. I couldn't warm up, talk to Joe, or find my focus.

I felt scattered, but the familiar surroundings and activity soon grounded me, and I felt myself relax as I centered myself in the music.

I didn't connect with Joe Rhinehart, music librarian and section bass player, until the break.

Tall and gangly, he gave me a big smile when I approached him. "Emily! My favorite flutist."

I felt a little silly entertaining suspicions of him. Could such a jovial character commit murder? And he'd had little contact with Olive, as far as I knew. What could Olive lie about, and why would it matter? The worst I imagined her doing to Joe was putting too many pencil marks in the music.

I smiled at him. "I bet you say that to all the flutists."

He grinned. "Guilty as charged. But it's true when I say it to you."

"Liar."

He grinned again, and we made small talk for a few minutes.

Joe's wife finished her master's in June; his daughter was a junior in high school and beginning to hunt for colleges seriously.

Finally, I jumped in. "Did you notice they've replaced Olive already?"

One of the local freelancers had appeared in Olive's place, glad to have the work, even though he'd be under pressure with a big part, only one rehearsal, and the possibility of losing future work if he did a poor job.

Joe's smile disappeared. "Too bad they didn't call a substitute sooner. Maybe she'd still be alive if they had."

Did he know something? "What do you mean?"

"The longer she played, the more enemies she made."

My momentary excitement died. I already knew that. But he might know details I didn't. "Somebody had a reason to kill her?"

"Wouldn't surprise me."

"I know she wasn't tactful, but you think anybody took her that seriously?"

"One man's tactlessness is another man's torture."

I startled and gave Joe closer attention. KC had said the same thing with different words. His matter-of-fact attitude sent a chill down my spine.

"Everybody I know is well-balanced enough to take her thoughtlessness with a grain of salt, or at least to stay calm enough to avoid homicide."

Joe snorted. "Guess we'll only know that for sure when the cops decide who did it."

"You're serious. Who could've been that angry?"

"Who knows? She played six months with the symphony, free-lanced two musicals, and managed to be a nightmare for everybody who had to work with her." Joe's mouth curled down, his jovial sociability completely gone.

"A nightmare?" Wasn't there a kind word for Olive anywhere?

"She had this I'm-better-than-you-could-ever-think-of-being attitude."

That was just her way of bluffing. She wasn't better than anybody else, and she knew it. But she worked hard at the appearance of superiority. Olive yearned to be above criticism. I encouraged him to go on. "True . . ."

"She showed her worst side in the musicals. You didn't play *Cats* or *Phantom of the Opera*, did you?"

Surprised and pleased to have my absence noticed, I answered, "No. I had a conflict with the rehearsal dates both times."

"Well, first Olive sat there and made snide remarks about the conductor. She shouldn't've hurt the guy's feelings." Joe liked everybody happy. "We all tried to ignore her. Like it or not, the conductor's the boss." Joe paused. "But she didn't stop with the conductor. She even picked on Craig Neil. I felt sorry for him."

Craig played oboe, sax, and flute and covered any combination of all three parts, if necessary. When money was limited, he was first choice for freelance gigs, which meant he worked constantly. I had nothing but respect for the solid job he did with three instruments. Craig also liked everybody. Easy to get along with. I'd heard his name recently. It took me a minute to remember. Leanne had mentioned something at the funeral. I was trying to remember exactly what, when Joe tsked.

"Olive just kept raggin' on him. A running critique of his playing, full of bitchy cracks, and him sitting right in front of her. Craig stayed calm, ignored her, and didn't tell her off. Too nice, I guess. She pissed me off, but it was none of my business. Craig endured it the whole run."

"He's a good player." I'd played with him often enough to know he wasn't disruptive, either musically or personally. "Why did she complain?"

"I don't know. He did fine. He'll never make the New York Phil, but he had nothing to be ashamed of. She only wanted to show her superiority and tried to raise herself by putting him down."

Joe took a deep breath, scratched his nose, and then continued more calmly. "He's also a popular guy. By the end of the run, I'd have been surprised if two people in the whole orchestra were speaking to Olive. People shut her out, and I know at least four players, including me, begged Joe Burke not to hire her again. That's why it amazed me when he put us all through it a second time."

I was surprised, too, if Joe's description was accurate. Why not just hire Gardiner? He'd played the musicals for years before Olive came to town. His experience and playing skills put hers to shame. Did he refuse the work? He must have. Otherwise, why bother with Olive?

"And you know all the people around here she ticked off."

I suspected I had no idea, but the personnel manager announced the end of break. I returned to my chair with my questions unanswered.

After we tuned, Felix, the conductor, began the second half of rehearsal. "People, don't forget. Tomorrow there'll be a moment of silence in Olive's memory before we start. I'll make an announcement first. Try to stay completely quiet. No page turning or rustling, please."

I looked around as he spoke. Gardiner's stand partially concealed him, and I didn't want to stare too directly, but he focused intently on something in his lap. Mostly people shuffled music. The second bassoon sub looked uncomfortable, and the brass chuckled at some comment the first horn had made.

Felix ran Beethoven's Fifth without stopping, then went over a few spots, finishing exactly at ten. Since it was dress rehearsal and there wouldn't be another chance to work out problems, several people stayed in groups of two or three, working out last minute glitches. Sandy Baines, the first flute, and I polished the opening of *Daphnis*.

When we finished, I hurried home, looking forward to falling into bed. It had been a long couple of days with police questioning, lost sleep, KC's arrival, lost sleep, students, and two stressful rehearsals. And did I mention lost sleep?

Golden gave me an enthusiastic welcome, tail thumping, and I stayed awake long enough to let her out and check on KC, who slept quietly in the guest room. A fold-away music stand stood in the corner, holding several sheets of music. It touched me to see evidence KC had already begun practicing. I left her quietly sleeping, let Golden in, and, without brushing my teeth, hurried to bed, where I slept a dreamless sleep

TWELVE

FRIDAY, FEBRUARY 14, 2010, 8:00 AM

OTHER THAN THE SYMPHONY, teaching, and walking my dog, I have almost no life, so Golden's bark alerting me to an 8:00 a.m. visitor took me completely by surprise. Rolling out of bed and throwing on a robe, I peeked out the front door, then opened it and accepted a long, white box delivered by a young man from Stan's Flowers, who obviously expected a tip. I checked my purse and then the sofa cushions. All I found was three quarters and a nickel. It would have to do.

I guessed he'd seen better when he said, "Thanks, lady. I'll be sure not to spend it all in one place."

I closed the door, embarrassed.

"Now who . . ." I ripped open the card. From Barry. I opened the flower box. Two dozen long-stemmed yellow roses. Friendship. Well, at least they weren't red. Red—romance—would have scared me. I walked to the kitchen, wondering how to keep them from dying. I'd used my big vase as a door stop in the house I shared with my ex-husband. Where had I put it when I moved? The most logical place was in the pantry. But no.

The phone rang. Barry's name showed on the caller ID.

I lifted the receiver. "Hi, Barry. The flowers are beautiful. Thank you. They just arrived." I kept looking for my vase as I talked, phone receiver between my shoulder and my ear.

"Hi." The voice was deep, and I smiled to hear it. "There's more." He sounded ambivalent.

"Yes?" I continued looking for the vase. Maybe I'd put the vase in the china closet? No. "So tell me."

Eureka! I found it in a box in the storage closet. I pulled it out, took it to the kitchen, rinsed it, and filled it with water and flowers, listening with the phone between my ear and shoulder as Barry talked.

"There's good news and bad news. I talked to my friend at MPD. The good news is you might be rich, if I can keep you out of jail. The bad news is the police are thinking of you as a suspect because they think they've found a motive."

"What? There must be a mistake." I put the vase down on the counter with a thump.

"They hauled you in on a fishing expedition, sure they'd be able to nail you. Olive's neighbor saw you near the murder scene. You knew that. They're putting the murder between three thirty and six because of the timing of her last text to you, and the time the neighbor discovered the body."

"So? There are lots of people who were out and about in that area between three-thirty and six."

"That's true. But you're the only one Olive's will names as a beneficiary."

Barry couldn't have surprised me more. "You're kidding me. She never mentioned having a will. What do I have to do? Pay her bills?"

"Far from it. It turns out Olive was one of the Dallas Pattersons."

"Who are 'the Dallas Pattersons'?"

"They're old Dallas money—or as old as Dallas money gets. The grandfather made his money in oil. The daughter, Sylvia, was a sharp businesswoman who divested the investments in oil just in time and multiplied daddy's money in the import/export business. When Sylvia died, she took good care of the whole family, including her niece, Olive."

"Olive talked about an 'Aunt Sylvie.' She had a fluffy little white dog, apparently."

"She had a lot more than the dog. What she left Olive is now worth about forty million."

Forty million! Who knew?

"Olive's will left most of her money to her sister."

"Patricia?"

"Yeah, that's the name."

"Barry, you said the will named me as a beneficiary."

"Yeah. Well, you inherit ten percent of whatever the estate's worth."

I did some quick mental math and sank into the nearest chair. "But that's four million."

"That's the good news, but it's also the bad news. Now the cops are sure you have a motive for the murder."

I remembered Lt. Gordon's unfriendliness. "They think that's enough to kill for?"

"Yeah. After all, it takes approximately two hundred years to earn that much from your symphony salary."

I didn't know how I felt. I imagined no more broken-down old cars, no more making do with thrift store bargains, no more skipping vacations. But guilt and sadness instantly killed any possibility of joy. The money belonged to Olive. I never thought she cared about me, other than to shop the bookstores and bakeries together and gripe about men. At the end, I wasn't very supportive. I'd even hung up on her in our last conversation, the last before she was killed.

I guess I stayed silent too long.

Barry said, "Em? You there? You okay?"

My eyes filled with tears, and my voice broke. "I'm tired, Barry. I don't want her money. Not this way, anyway. I want Olive to be alive, annoying me, and chasing Gardiner." I sounded tearful. And I was.

Golden padded over, whined, and put her head in my lap.

"What now?"

Barry didn't hesitate. "Just sit tight. The police'll figure out that you didn't kill Olive. It'll be all right. Stay in touch and don't lose my number. You may have to call." After a longish pause Barry continued. "Em, I'm sorry. I'd like to comfort you."

An unnerving thought for me.

Shaking off my mixed emotions, I told myself I didn't have to think about it right now. I *wouldn't* think about it right now. Instead, I took comfort from stroking Golden's fur.

Barry continued, "If I was there, I'd make it right. Let me take you to dinner. We'll go dancing, to a movie, whatever you like. You need to relax."

I wasn't likely to be good company, but I knew Barry would make me laugh. That sounded good. I didn't have time, though. "You've forgotten, Barry. I'm a working girl. Tonight's opening night for *Daphnis*, and I've scheduled a full afternoon of students before that."

"No rest for the weary, I guess." He sounded frustrated. "When *can* I tend your wounds?"

I was scared. This man posed the biggest threat to my independence since I'd participated in the Cancer Society's Jail-n-Bail last year. I put up the first wall I thought of. "You're my lawyer, remember?"

"Yeah. I remember. Can't you forget?"

"Not now. Not with everything going on."

"That's what I feared." He paused. When he spoke again, he'd returned to business. "Well, let me know if you change your mind. I'll tell you if I hear anything more."

Relief rushed through me. As we hung up, I considered the new evidence. It gave me all the more reason to find Olive's killer. Soon.

THIRTEEN

KC HAD SLEPT THROUGH THE FLOWER DELIVERY and Barry's phone call.

I gave Golden a hug, then put the roses on the dining room table and tried to push the idea of money out of my mind.

On my own for breakfast, I had an orange, then thought about the day. I was stunned and upset by Barry's news about Olive's will, but I had a free morning. I wouldn't think anymore about the motivation the police imagined Olive's bequest gave me, or their investigation. I'd return to the immediate problem. Who was "Joe"? Wishing Janet hadn't clammed up the way she did, I wondered what she meant when she said Olive "lied about Joe."

Joe Rhinehardt hadn't impressed me as much of an Olive fan. On the other hand, I didn't know of any direct reason he'd hate her enough to kill her. She hadn't done anything to him personally. I thought briefly and then realized I had the perfect excuse to talk to Joe Burke, the music contractor. He'd hired me to play *Les Misérables* in two weeks. Now was the perfect moment to pick up the part.

Speaking quietly so as not to wake KC, I called Joe and arranged to meet him at ten. Then we chatted about the show and who had picked up the music.

"I wish Olive hadn't been so quick to take hers," he said. "I guess I'll have to replace it. I was about to call the music rental company when you phoned. I'm afraid it'll be expensive to order a single part in time for the first rehearsal, especially if they know it's an emergency."

Hoping it would make him more likely to talk to me, I suggested, "Olive lived close to me. Before you contact the music rental company, why don't you let me see what I can do about recovering her music?"

"Thanks, Emily. Don't go to too much trouble. I'll probably have to replace the part. But it would make my job easier if you managed to find it. See you at ten."

I had to find the music right away to get to Joe's in time. Olive's sister, Patricia, had told me she was staying at the Regis Hotel. I called her there.

"Emily! It's good to hear from you. I'm at my wits end. I'm trying to decide what to do with Olive's stuff."

"Don't the police need—"

"The police told me they're done checking out her place. They don't want whatever's there. I've been going crazy trying to screw up the courage to go over. I know she had a ton of sheet music. What'll I do with it all? And her clothes, and shoes, and books, and keepsakes, and kitchen gadgets? I know the police left an awful mess. They recommended a cleaner who specializes in crime scenes, but . . . I don't know . . ." She burst into tears. "What am I goin' to do? I can't even bear to go in there."

"I don't know how much help I can be with the personal things, but I called because I'm trying to find some of Olive's music. The contractor for the musical wants it. How about if we meet at Olive's? We'll figure out what to do with the rest together."

She sniffled. "Oh, Emily, I'd be so grateful."

"Is it okay if we meet pretty soon? I have an appointment at ten."

"Sure. The sooner the better. It'll put my mind at rest."

We said our goodbyes and hung up. Happy to be of help and wondering if I'd find the bassoon part Joe wanted, I gathered my thoughts. If possible, I also wanted to find out about "Vince," Olive's mysterious visitor.

Before I left, KC padded out of the bedroom sleepily rubbing her eyes.

"I'm running an errand. I'll be back before too long."

"Em, I'm sorry to be such a sleepyhead. If you have a few minutes I can make a quick breakfast." She sounded apologetic and sheepish.

"Don't worry about it, KC. I'm good, and you had to get some sleep. See you this afternoon."

Five minutes later, I arrived at Olive's. Patricia appeared shortly after me. She had obviously left in a hurry. Her eyes were red, and smeared mascara streaked her face. Green pants clashed with her navy-blue blouse, and the bun she wore skewed to the left, sending strands of red hair falling into her face.

A yellow police barrier closed off the stairs to Olive's apartment. Patricia met me on the sidewalk, and we exchanged a long hug, rocking together. "Thanks for coming, Emily." She sniffled. "Don't worry about the barricade. We can just step around it and go on up."

"Are you sure?" I didn't want to barge in if it would cause trouble.

"I asked the police to leave the tape up. Hopefully it'll discourage ghoulish lookie-loos for a while."

I mounted the stairs and waited while Patricia unlocked the duplex.

We entered a small entryway covered in dark brown tile. It opened on the living room, which had served as Olive's music room. Furnishings were sparse—a light-blue couch, a few straight-backed chairs, and a sturdy black Manhasset music stand with a chair behind it. Bloodstains covered the carpet next to the music stand and chair, as if Olive had been killed while she practiced. Piles of music were everywhere. Fingerprint powder coated the scene. I hardly recognized the well-kept home Olive had maintained.

Patricia shuddered and turned her back to the bloody carpet. "Everything's got me down—the whole thing. But the music . . . I should be able to do something, but I don't know what. It was important to Olive." Her eyes filled. "I guess I should give it to Gardiner. He's a bassoon player. He'd be able to use it—"

"Don't do that." In my opinion, Gardiner had treated Olive abominably. Might even have murdered her. I didn't want Patricia to give him so much as a broken reed. "Let's see if we can come up with some ideas." I hesitated for only a moment then turned to the pile closest to the music stand.

After blowing off the fingerprint powder, I found the part for *Les Mis* on top of the stack. "The orchestra contractor for the musical will be glad to have this."

"Oh, good. It'd make me feel better if even some of the music went to people who can use it. Do you have ideas about the rest, too?"

I set the *Les Mis* part aside then quickly searched through the rest of the pile. *Daphnis*, Beethoven's Fifth, and numerous orchestral excerpts were in the same stack, along with the Devienne Quartet, the Saint Saens Sonata, and the Telemann Sonata in F Minor. I remembered Olive had been planning a recital. This must be her current practice pile, works she was preparing, either for orchestra or her recital.

Apparently, the orchestra had duplicate parts to *Daphnis* and Beethoven's Fifth, since the sub was already playing from them. I hung onto the music anyway. Joe Rhinehart, the orchestra's music librarian, would know what to do with the parts.

Moving to another stack, I thumbed through. "Wow. Olive had quite an octet library, didn't she?" I found other chamber music, too, for other combinations of instruments. "And look at all these orchestral excerpts." They were everywhere. I began to understand why Patricia felt overwhelmed. She didn't want to sort through all this. Neither did I. It would take forever, and every page would be saying, "Olive will never use this again." It was too sad.

"Why don't you donate it all to the local college's music library? That way it'll be in constant use by people who want it, and you won't have to classify it all," I suggested.

"What a good idea. I knew you'd know what to do."

Olive's reed-making kit had to be here, too. No professional bassoon player could do without one. "Her reed-making equipment might be donated to the college's music program. The director will know some deserving young student."

Having dealt with the music, I thought I'd ask Patricia about my concerns. I considered the best words to use but didn't see any way to handle the situation except to be direct. I took a deep breath and ignored my discomfort. "Would you mind if I look for a couple other things?"

"That's fine with me. The police are done, and Olive trusted you. I don't see what it could hurt."

Unfortunately, the police had pretty much stripped everything. Olive's cell phone and computer were gone. Disappointment overtook me. Then I remembered.

The journals. Olive had fretted over them, afraid a nosy lover would read them.

"If you trust a man enough to make love to him, you should trust that he'll respect your privacy," I'd told her.

Deaf to that line of thinking, she'd hidden the journals in a heating vent in her bedroom floor.

I had worried. "How can you be sure you won't start a fire?"

She'd paid no attention.

Had the police found her journals? The vent cover pushed into a hole cut in the floor. I removed it, fished around, and drew out a journal. Quickly, I felt around in the vent and found another. The first was the most recent. It started three months before Olive's death.

"Mind if I take these?" I handed Patricia the journals.

She looked besieged. I sympathized. Yet another decision. She took the journals and quickly opened and shut them. "I should turn them over to the police." She looked up. "Shouldn't I?"

"I thought you said the police had taken everything they wanted."

She hesitated. "You're right."

"I'm hoping to find out if someone bothered Olive or threatened her."

An awkward silence followed, and I held my breath.

"There might be private stuff in there. I'm sure Olive would rather you read them than Lieutenant Gordon, or even me." She handed the journals back. "And without you, the police wouldn't know they existed. I suppose if you return them quickly, so I can make sure the police have them . . ."

I didn't give her time to change her mind. "Thanks, Patricia. I promise I'll read them right away and bring them back."

I made some sympathetic small talk and then glanced at my watch, concerned about my appointment with Joe. "Patricia, I'm sorry. I have an appointment at ten." I took the bassoon parts for the orchestra and the musical. "I'll take care of delivering these."

"Thanks. I feel much better. I don't know why I worried about the music so, except . . ." Her chin wobbled.

I had to go to Joe's, but I hated to leave her alone in Olive's apartment. "These are terrible circumstances, Patricia, and you're doing the best anyone could do. I know Olive would be proud of you. Let's go for now, and I'll check back and see if I can be of any more help."

"It's alright. The music was the main thing. I'll deal with the rest. I'll call the crime scene cleaners the police recommended and someone who does estate sales. They'll know what to do."

"Well, don't lose touch We can go to breakfast."

"I'd like that. And thanks again."

FOURTEEN

FRIDAY, FEBRUARY 14, 2010, 10:00 AM

I SHOWED UP ON JOE BURKE'S DOORSTEP at precisely 10:00 with Olive's *Les Misérables* part in hand. Because he knew how to stretch a dollar and handle people, he made an excellent living as a music contractor, a business not known for paying big bucks. He had a luxurious house, contemporary, with lots of windows and views of the foothills, surrounded by aspen trees.

His wife, Billie, greeted me at the door with a hug. "It's good to see you." I knew she meant it. White haired, rosy-cheeked, and just a little plump, she glowed inwardly. Her smile would have made an insurance salesman feel welcome. Chatting happily, she showed me to Joe's practice studio in the rear of the house.

He'd told me a builder had soundproofed it, and it overlooked a tree-covered hill with a little stream at the bottom, now frozen. With luxury like this, who wouldn't want to practice?

"I'll tell Joe you're here," Billie promised as she left.

I didn't have to wait more than a minute.

"The prettiest girl in the flute section." He gave me a hug.

The only girl in the flute section, there being only one flute part, and no longer a girl, but I didn't argue.

Also white-haired, but tall, thin, and well-tanned from frequent tennis matches and traveling, Joe's strong hug made me wince.

We chatted for a few minutes before he gestured to the music in my hand. "That looks like Olive's part. Have any trouble finding it?"

I handed it to him. "Luckily, her sister hadn't packed it and given it away yet. She let me have it."

"Well, thanks for bringing it. You know how it goes. That'll save a lot of hassles, plus a few bucks. A penny saved is a penny earned."

Joe's tight-fisted attention to details made him the best. "Glad to help out." I paused, then brought up the reason I'd come. "Who'll replace Olive?"

He'd turned and filed Olive's part in a brown metal file cabinet. "Gardiner'll do it. He already wants the part, so I appreciate you retrieving it."

"Gardiner?" I was puzzled. "I figured he must have turned the work down before you hired Olive."

It would have been logical. The established pecking order dictated that since Gardiner played first bassoon in the symphony, he should have first right of refusal on pickup work, like the musical. Ordinarily, extra jobs wouldn't be offered to Olive unless Gardiner refused them or had done a poor job in the past.

Joe had opened another file drawer and began hunting through, but, at my comment, he paused, turned his head toward me, and glared. "You figured wrong." He sounded unfriendly and hostile.

"But Gardiner played the musicals for so many years. Olive didn't have his experience . . ."

No response from Joe.

". . . and a lot of people found Olive hard to get along with . . ."

No answer.

I sensed I shouldn't press the issue, but curiosity drove me. ". . . so why did you offer Olive the work before Gardiner?"

"Why do you care?"

My face warmed. I hadn't expected a confrontation.

He grabbed a piece of music from the cabinet and thrust it at my chest. Without answering my question, he grabbed my elbow, moved me toward the studio door, and down the hall. In the tiled entryway, he opened the front door.

"I don't understand, Joe. I didn't mean to upset you. What's wrong?"

Just then, Billie appeared.

"Emily!" She called my name just as Joe had almost pushed me out the door. "Do you have to leave already? It's been a long time since I've seen you. I'd hoped to have a chat. I tried a new cranberry-oatmeal cookie recipe yesterday. I want your opinion."

Joe's continued pressure on my elbow made it clear he wanted me to leave.

"How 'bout lunch tomorrow? We can talk," I suggested.

Joe pushed insistently at my arm.

"Oh, that sounds wonderful." Billie smiled broadly, oblivious to everything but her joy at connecting with me.

Joe turned to her. "Remember? We have that thing tomorrow."

Billie frowned. "What thing?"

Joe huffed and lifted his eyebrows.

After a moment, Billie said, "I'm sure I don't have any 'thing.' I must not have been invited." She turned to me. "Where shall we meet? I'm scheduled to volunteer at the hospital in the afternoon. It should be somewhere close."

After a hurried discussion, we agreed on The Articulate Artichoke at noon. Throughout, Joe kept forward pressure on my elbow. Now he pushed me through the doorway and slammed the door quickly, leaving me alone on the doorstep. What was going on?

Joe's behavior puzzled me. Olive's journals might shed some light on the whole situation. Her sister had to take the journals to the police, but I wanted answers. I'd study them now. Hopefully they'd explain Joe's behavior, and her relationships with Red and Vince, too. I pulled into the parking area of a neighborhood park figuring I'd be undisturbed there and opened the first of them. Olive had chronicled every detail of her life. Gardiner predominated, but my name was mentioned often, as well as her professional engagements and relationships. Glad that Olive's paranoid fear of having her deepest feelings read had made her hide her journals, I proceeded to . . . read her deepest feelings. Her paranoias and prejudices were well documented, as well as her humanitarian activities:

Sept. 20: Gave bassoon lessons at the elementary school 'til noon then had lunch with Emily at St. Pierre's.

Oct. 11: Went to Emily's for lunch. Golden kept us company. What a wonderful girl! I'll look into getting a dog.

Nov. 23: Played a Thanksgiving gig with Chuck Holcombe and Phil Gray. Asked them to play my recital. They aren't the best, but they'll do. They both said they'd do it. We'll only have a few rehearsals before the recital, so I'll wait 'til closer to the date to schedule them.

Those entries were from the first journal, before Olive started chasing Gardiner. How she'd loved passing her passion for the bassoon on to kids. And St. Pierre's had been one of our favorite restaurants. Wonderful pastries and great food, too. Called itself a patisserie. I smiled, remembering the good times we'd had there.

But then Olive changed. The changes were reflected in the journals. They were already beginning, toward the end of the first journal. The second journal, covering her last three months, was clearly different.

Nov. 5: Discovered Gardiner went out with Marcie Barstow. Pretty enough, but last stand viola? He can't possibly see anything in her. Only one way to find out. I'll call her tomorrow.

I vaguely remembered that Olive had told me about the phone call. Marcie must have figured Gardiner wasn't worth the trouble of Olive's cross examination. And it wasn't hard to believe she and Gardiner didn't hit it off. Whatever, they didn't go out again.

Under the entry for Nov. 12 I found what I searched for, sort of.

Nov. 12: Joe and I talked about it and decided I should play the musical. It'll be Cats *this time. I'm so excited! I'll be the only bassoon, so I'll have a chance to show what I can do.*

No clue *why* she would be playing instead of Gardiner. Oh, well. Keeping in mind that Patricia had to give the journals to the police, I read on.

Dates with Red Calloway and "Vince Mallone" had been part of a self-deluded scheme to make Gardiner jealous. Olive had met Vince through an online dating service. I had to smile at the account of their date:

Dec. 18: Went to Gardiner's chamber music concert with Vince. Congratulated Gardiner afterward and talked for about an hour. I think he appreciated my comments. When we were done, Vince had left. Why didn't he wait? White trash! It came out OK, though, because Gardiner had no choice but to take me home.

Bet Gardiner loved that.

I don't know why I was hurt or surprised when I read:

December 22: Played a job with Emily today. What a joke. Her vibrato was so wide you could've driven a semi through it and not scratched the sides. No magic in that performance. How long before I can play with real musicians?

I remembered the job she had written about. Trios at a Christmas party. The party was noisy, the acoustics were bad, and we couldn't hear each other very well. Under those circumstances she expected magic? I guessed it's always possible to criticize. But now that Olive's judgements had become personal, I better understood the crowds of people she'd offended.

January 19: Red Calloway hasn't left me alone since I went out with him. Since Gardiner doesn't care, I decided today that Red might as well be of use. I asked him to come over and help assemble my bookshelves. He was awful to me. He had a fit every time I made a suggestion, threw a box of screws at me, and finally came after me with a screwdriver. Imagine. He yelled, "You bitch! I'll teach you to talk to me that way." I had to lock myself in the bedroom 'til he left. He's lucky I didn't call the police. White trash!

Those entries solved the mystery of Olive's connection with Red and Vince. It sounded like Red had a violent temper. Had he killed Olive? I'd move him up on my mental list of possible suspects.

I glanced at my watch. Time to return the journals to Patricia so she could deliver them to the police.

The desk clerk at the Regis said Patricia had gone out, but I left the journals for her so she'd have them as soon as possible.

Turning the problem of Joe and his hiring practices over in my mind, I realized only Gardiner had the answers. Joe was hostile, Olive was dead, and her journals provided no clues. I'd have to visit Gardiner. An unpalatable course of action. I didn't like the man and he didn't like me. I didn't see any alternative, though. He'd be more likely to answer questions face-to-face, where he couldn't avoid me. I looked his address up on the orchestra roster I kept in the glove compartment of my car and headed for his place in search of a solution to the puzzle.

FIFTEEN

FRIDAY, FEBRUARY 14, 2010, 11:30 AM

THE GRAPEVINE SAID GARDINER WAS A night person who avoided mornings. But surely any decent person—not that Gardiner was a decent person—would be up by now. His house was a small white stucco in a neighborhood of immaculately groomed older homes. A flame-shaped entryway led to a covered patio. Evergreens as tall as the house echoed the shape of the entry and flanked the door, their scent welcoming me as I rang the bell.

Gardiner answered the ring in sweatpants and a robe, holding a steaming mug of coffee, heavy stubble covering his face. Handsome enough, with dark brown eyes, a cleft chin, plenty of dark hair, and just a touch of gray at the temples, he'd never appealed to me. The source of Olive's fascination with him mystified me. Besides his unpredictable temperament, male chauvinism, and all the flaws Olive had recounted ad infinitum to me, he was a snob. He looked down his nose at me, a lowly second player, member of the rank and file, often ignoring me entirely, thereby losing points in my book. Our personal history, our one disastrous meeting outside orchestra, lowered my opinion of his morals and decency even further. I expected the worst. He might well be inclined to animosity. As I remembered how rude he'd been at orchestra just a few days ago, anger filled my chest. I couldn't turn back now, though.

"Emily, to what do I owe the pleasure?"

Feigned charm? I hadn't expected to be welcomed. Instead of relaxing me, his friendly greeting alarmed me. I chalked it up to unpredictability or pretense and didn't let my guard down.

"Hi, Gardiner. Can I come in for a minute?"

"Your wish is my command." With a sweeping motion, he moved aside, permitting me to enter. "Welcome."

I paused in the entryway. The chilly dimness of his house contrasted so starkly to the sparkling white exterior, the smell of the evergreens, and the warmth of the morning sun that I had to force myself to enter the living room.

He stroked the small of my back lightly, urging me inside.

His touch reminded me of his baser tendencies, and I arched away from it, hurrying toward a deep, leather-upholstered chair.

Wasn't anyone else home? I'd thought Leanne would have moved in now that Olive was dead. I felt ill at ease, but I didn't know any other way to explore Joe's strange behavior.

"Can I get you a cup of coffee?" He paused in the middle of the room, brows raised quizzically.

"I just finished breakfast. Thanks anyway." I planned to learn the information I wanted and leave as quickly as possible.

"Then, what can I do for you?" He settled on the couch, his left arm along its back, his right hand holding his coffee, and his left ankle over his right knee.

"I thought you might be able to help me figure out an odd experience I had." *Good job. Why in the world should this man want to help me?* I paused, chewing my lip and wondering how to continue. "It's Joe Burke."

Gardiner shifted back against the couch cushions. "How is Joe?"

His sociable answer surprised and relieved me. Maybe this interview wouldn't be as difficult as I had feared.

"Pretty mad. I asked him why he'd hired Olive for the musical instead of you."

"So? Why shouldn't he be angry? You have no right to pry."

I cringed. He was right. But I wanted to discover the relationship between Joe and Olive, if any. I stuck with my question. "Why should he be mad?"

"I'd say that's his business. After all, you don't pay him. Your questions are interference. He doesn't have to justify his decisions to you."

Again, he was right. "I'm interested. I can't ask Olive. Joe's reaction seems so exaggerated. I just want to understand."

"Too bad." Without another word, Gardiner left the room.

The grandfather clock ticked in the hall. It had been eight months since our failed meeting, and I had never been to Gardiner's home. This glimpse of his private life disconcerted me. A faded poster advertising a long-ended opera was the sole decoration. There were no photographs, no mementos, no plants. Just plain beige walls. I hadn't suspected it would be so neat and impersonal. The silence grew longer. The clock ticked on.

The stillness of the room made me uncomfortable. Besides, even if Miss Manners didn't recommend dropping in with questions, uninvited, before breakfast, leaving guests alone for so long without explanation was also not recommended. I went off in search of Gardiner.

I found him in the kitchen. He appeared to be frozen in the midst of pouring another cup of coffee, holding the coffee maker's pot, lost in contemplation of the bland brown face of the cupboard above. He didn't turn to acknowledge my entrance.

I walked up behind him and asked softly, "Gardiner?"

He jumped and coffee sloshed over the side of the pot. "I thought you were in the living room. Why are you here?"

"You were gone for so long I came to see if you were alright."

"I don't like people sneaking around my house," he snapped.

The conversation wasn't going well. It wouldn't help to argue with him. Instead, I told myself the word "sneaking" commented on his feelings rather than my actions, and meekly followed him back to the living room, his coffee forgotten in the kitchen.

We settled ourselves as before, him on the couch, me in the leather chair, but now he leaned forward, alert, elbows on his knees, hands between them.

"What do you want from me?"

So much for his good humor. I had reason not to like the man. He made no secret of his feelings for me, either.

But, in the interest of finding information, I responded as politely as possible. "I hoped you'd tell me why my question upset Joe so. Why should he hire Olive instead of you?"

The silence that followed vibrated with unexpressed . . . what . . . anger?

I finally tried pleading. "Please, Gardiner. You're the only one who can help."

"It's none of your business. Why is it so damned important to you, anyway?" He leaned closer, his hands balling into fists.

My irritation grew. He treated me like a naughty child, now and in all our interactions. His behavior infuriated me. "The question is, why is it so important to you that I don't know?"

He didn't answer.

Besides his personal dislike of me, his professional ego might be outraged. Was that reason enough for his hostility? Cooling a tense situation seemed the best way to get the whole story, so I took a deep breath and swallowed my antagonism. "Look, Gardiner, don't be offended. Olive was my friend. Now that she's dead, I hoped you'd help me. I want to tie up loose ends. I'm curious."

"Curiosity killed the cat," he said, uninformative and unfriendly, almost threatening. "Why should I help any friend of Olive's? She made my life miserable."

True enough. I should have been smarter and not presented myself as her friend. But his statement served to remind me that he had the best reasons I'd so far discovered to murder Olive.

He paused. "I'm not interested in talking about her, or Joe either," he said belligerently. "If you want to know about Joe's concerns, ask him. I'm just glad to have Olive out of my life. Whoever killed her did me a big favor."

He straightened and stood. I immediately stood, too, and left without another word.

Gardiner didn't bother to show me out. How I'd love to prove he killed Olive. He certainly had the character for it. And I owed it to Olive to find her murderer. It was the last service I could do as her sometimes friend.

SIXTEEN

FRIDAY, FEBRUARY 14, 2010, 11:45 AM

I DROVE STRAIGHT HOME feeling that Gardiner's hostile manners were pursuing me. Golden distracted me with an affectionate welcome, jumping and barking as if I'd been gone for years, before she settled down for the obligatory tummy scratch. KC played her flute—scales—in the guest room, and savory aromas filled the air. My home hadn't been this inviting since I'd lived with my folks. I felt tension from the confrontation with Gardiner melt away and my mood shift.

Deciding not to bother KC, I followed my nose to the kitchen.

Sunny warmth greeted me, and everything sparkled. The ivy under the skylight had been freshly watered, and an angel food cake cooled on the counter. Sniffing, I realized that wasn't the source of the scent leading me onward. I picked up a set of cheery blue potholders (where did they come from?) and opened the oven, in quest of the source of the mouthwatering aroma. Pot roast. Just beginning to release its juices. KC knew how to make herself welcome. She must have been to the store with the household budget I gave her and restocked the kitchen.

The mystery solved, I fixed myself a cup of hot chamomile tea and sat down at the kitchen table. A purple African violet, another new addition, beckoned to me. I had a few minutes before my students started arriving to sort my thoughts. As I sipped the tea, I puzzled over my encounter with Gardiner. Granted, I'd shown up unwanted and unexpected, invited myself in, and asked nosy and unwanted questions about him and his friend Joe. But why had he put up such a surly wall? Both he and Joe were hiding something. I was sure of it. But what?

KC's practice session distracted me. For a musician, music is never just background noise. I couldn't help but pay attention.

Scales were the one exercise that made everything else easier, yet most students did anything to avoid them. KC, however, went through them all. Then she played a current popular song, making enough creative embellishments that I knew she was playing by ear. Students usually didn't try playing without a piece of printed music sitting in front of them, afraid they might make a mistake and the music police would arrest them, I guessed. Not KC. I realized she must have a good ear, as well as a spirit of fun and fearlessness. She worked on a Telemann Sonata next and showed a lot of enthusiasm, though her baroque style could use some polishing. Teaching her promised to be a pleasure.

When she poked her head in the kitchen about ten minutes later I said, "Nice work, KC."

"Em." She flushed. "I didn't realize you'd come home." A pause. "I've been having a great time!" She bubbled with delight.

"I heard."

"My mouth is about to fall off, though, and I only played for half an hour."

"Endurance'll come. It smells fantastic in here."

"Thanks. I have to tell you, I—"

The doorbell rang.

"That's my first student. Tell me later, KC."

I taught all afternoon, and by the end of the day my brain was fried. The smell of pot roast had gradually intensified, and I practically drooled for it by the time the last student left at five.

After sending her on her way, I headed for the kitchen but never made it. The dining room was beautifully set for two. KC must have raided the storage closet. Formal china and glasses I'd set aside as too nice to use formed the place settings. There were two tall yellow candles, Barry's yellow roses, and a cherry red tablecloth I hadn't seen for years. My admiration of the scene was cut short when KC entered with an unexpected guest.

"Barry!"

"Hi, Em." He scooped me up in one of his patented hugs.

Over his shoulder, I sent KC a questioning look.

She apparently understood, because she said, "I tried to tell you. I invited Barry for dinner. His number was on the phone's speed dial. I knew you had a concert and couldn't go out. But it's Valentine's Day, you know?"

Now Barry looked embarrassed and spoke to me. "You mean you didn't know I'd been invited? Look, I'm sorry. I—"

I didn't like Barry feeling unwelcome. "KC didn't tell me, but what a wonderful surprise." I startled myself by meaning it, and beamed at him.

Both Barry and KC looked relieved.

"Well, I'll go take care of dinner." KC disappeared.

Barry and I looked at each other.

He said, "She told me—"

At the same time I said, "I'm glad—" then we both chuckled.

Barry said, "I think we've been had."

I suddenly felt the same kind of unease I'd felt with a date as a teenager. "I'd better go see if KC needs any help in the kitchen. I'll be right back."

She took the roast out of the oven as I entered the kitchen.

"KC, I'd already turned Barry down for dinner. What made you invite him?"

KC remained calm. "I know what I know," she said confidently, with a touch of mischief.

"What is it you think you know?" I asked, curious.

"I know he sent you Valentine's Day flowers, and I know it made you happy." She'd maneuvered the roast onto a platter, which I remembered from my marriage—a wedding present from my ex's great-aunt Tillie.

"I—"

KC turned to face me. "I saw the way Barry looked at you just now, and if there's one thing I know, it's when a man is interested. And Barry is interested—in you, Em—you know?"

Her words made my stomach tighten. "But you—"

"Oh, hush. He's alone out there. Go keep him company."

"Aren't you eating with us?" I whined the question.

"Nope. I have plans, okay? They involve a good book and a hot bath."

"But you—"

"Go!"

I did as she told me, taking the roast. In the dining room I said to Barry, "You're right. We've been had."

It was a good thing Barry helped me set it down, or the way I shook with laughter, the platter would have ended up on the carpet.

SEVENTEEN

FRIDAY, FEBRUARY 14, 2010, 7:40 PM

DINNER WASN'T THE IDEAL PRELUDE to a concert. Barry made me laugh, interested me in his opinions, and drew out mine. I'd enjoyed his company immensely, so much so that I'd scared myself. When he offered a ride to the concert, I turned it down. "I'm working." The truth was, if I let him bring me to the concert, he'd have to bring me home, too, and I wasn't ready for the "home afterward" part.

I arrived later than I liked, and I had to park two blocks away. The walk through the cold, clean night air gave me a chance to recover my excitement at playing *Daphnis*, though, and little butterflies began tickling my tummy.

My nose and toes felt icy when I hurried in the stage entrance. Bernie, the security guard, gave me his usual smile and "Fancy meeting you here." All part of the ritual.

Hurrying, I dumped my coat downstairs in the green room and made my way upstairs and through the wings.

On stage, a lone violin played slow scales, the oboe players tried reeds, and the second bassoon sub crammed in some last-minute practice on difficult passages. The symphony's production manager and a couple of stagehands, in emergency mode, whispered together and pointed toward the lights. Not to worry. Whatever the crisis, they'd fix it by the start of the concert.

I sat down and pulled out my flute. The comfort of familiar sounds and movements grounded me and focused my concentration. You were born alone, you died alone, and you prepared for concerts alone, too. Respectful of the necessity for concentration and warm-up, my colleagues entered quietly, one by one. Gardiner conveniently avoided me by entering from the other side of the stage.

With timing born of long experience, I finished my warm-up just as the lights dimmed. The last-chair second violin slid quietly into his seat at the back of the orchestra and, seconds later, the concertmaster, leader of the string section, entered to applause. He nodded to the oboist, soundlessly requesting an "A," and we tuned, first winds, then strings. When we finished, Felix made his entrance, baton in hand. Turning, he faced the audience.

"Ladies and gentlemen, last week one of our beloved colleagues was sadly and prematurely taken from us at the height of her career. Please join us in honoring the memory of Olive Patterson with a moment of silence."

I bowed my head, peeking secretly at my colleagues. Gardiner, slightly behind me and to the left, had reverently closed his eyes from what I could see, as had everyone else in my view. The audience rustled faintly as they settled and bowed their heads. For long moments, the hush was truly soundless. Then, at the first murmurs of discomfort, Felix raised his head, ever the perfect showman, turned around, and stepped onto the podium.

Daphnis had begun.

Whatever the divisions and distractions before a performance, the individuals of the orchestra unite for concerts. The butterflies in my tummy, which had been with me since I arrived and throughout my pre-concert preparations, disappeared, and I abandoned myself to the seamless alternation of my phrases with those of the first flute, as if we were one. I had waited ten years to play *Daphnis*, and I thoroughly and wholeheartedly took advantage of this opportunity. The performance wasn't perfect. It never is. But it was good, and I could look forward to another chance, tomorrow.

Our soloist, an up-and-coming young violinist from New York, played the Sibelius Violin Concerto with passion, according to my colleagues. I found my mind wandering, though. I had been so pumped for *Daphnis*. Now the flash of sequins from the audience distracted me as I performed my part in the concerto by reflex. My mind strayed to the day and its events—Barry's flowers, Joe's mysterious anger, Gardiner's hostility, dinner with Barry. And the questions began. What was with Joe Burke? Why should second-guessing him about hiring Olive for the musical provoke him? Why did Gardiner respond so antagonistically when asked about Joe's decision? Why did I enjoy Barry's company so much? Was I in danger from Joe or Gardiner, or, in a different way, from Barry?

Fortunately, the concerto didn't demand much from second flute. Still in a fog as I walked off stage, I didn't notice Joe Burke until I almost ran into him.

"Emily, good job on *Daphnis*," he said in a loud, cheery voice, taking my hand and putting it between his as he spoke. Then, sotto voce, he hissed, "Stay out of this, Emily. Don't go poking your nose where it doesn't belong." He squeezed my hand hard, until it crumpled in on itself.

"Quit it, Joe. You're hurting me!" I didn't bother with diplomacy as I tried to snatch my hand back.

Joe held tight, though, and continued to squeeze.

Lucky for me, safe and solid, Chuck Holcombe came off the stage right behind me, holding his violin. He had put aside whatever grief he felt about Celia, compartmentalizing it to perform the concert. We all did it. Only the sadness in his eyes revealed his pain.

"Hey, Joe," Chuck said, a warning in his tone. "Watch the firm handshakes. Mustn't harm the lady. She'll need both hands to play the second half."

With a jerk and a quick intake of breath, Joe released my hand and pounded Chuck on the back affectionately. "Chuck. Haven't seen you lately."

Amidst the male greeting rituals, I gratefully took the chance to leave, alternately flexing and rubbing my hand. It hurt. What was Joe thinking? What did he mean? What should I stay out of? At any rate, I would avoid him in the future, even if that meant fore-going the extra work the musicals provided.

I completed the usual intermission chores in a preoccupied haze amidst congratulations for *Daphnis*. Restroom—where I ran cold water over my hand to prevent any swelling and because it was the only first aid available to me—drinking fountain, social chitchat, and back onstage. My hand throbbed. I'd never seen this side of Joe. Was he violent at home? No. Surely Billie would show signs of mistreatment if he hurt her.

The Beethoven lasted fifty minutes. Luckily the piece didn't require a tour de force from the second flute. I don't know if I could have moved my fingers quickly. When it finished, I realized that between my aching hand and questions about Joe's motives, I'd played entirely by reflex. I headed off the stage behind the clari-nets, Janet's floating form gracefully preceding me. I had a sudden inspiration. We could help each other.

"Janet." I knew the lonely feeling of coming back to a newly husbandless house. I bet she longed for some friendly attention. "Can you convince your babysitter to stay late?"

"Sure." She floated into step beside me. "The kids are staying with Mom."

"Even better. Can you leave them until morning? We'll make a night of it. You can stay at my place."

"Good thinking. I could use a drink or ten. I'll call Mom, then meet you at the Blue Dragon."

Backstage, I put my flute away and congratulated myself. The after-concert socializing might comfort Janet. For my part, I felt unsettled. I had enjoyed Barry way too much for my "no more men" rule. And Joe had freaked me out, too. I craved some serious partying.

But speak of the devil, Joe Burke stood beside the exit.

The two blocks to my car abruptly seemed awfully long. Quickly, I looked around and spotted six-feet-two inches of security ahead of me. "Chuck."

He moved slowly down the hall, a long, thin figure in a black overcoat and hat, carrying his violin case.

"Chuck."

He heard my call and waited for me to catch up.

What excuse made sense? "Can you help me? My battery's been acting up," I lied. "I'm afraid it might be dead. Will you go to my car with me? I have cables if the car needs a jump."

Ever helpful, Chuck agreed right away. We arranged that he would drive me to my car and provide assistance if necessary. I looked over my shoulder as we left. Joe Burke followed as far as the sidewalk, then stopped and glared after us.

EIGHTEEN

FRIDAY, FEBRUARY 14, 2010, 10:15 PM

THE BLUE DRAGON WAS NOISY, the service slow, and the corners none too clean, but it was the closest bar open late and serving food. Symphony members hung out there after rehearsals and concerts to unwind in a safe place. Joe Burke's strange behavior had disconcerted me, and I realized that the parking lot, where I waited for Janet, was unlit. Clouds had moved in to cover the moon and stars, and tall evergreens blocked what little light glowed eerily through the clouds. To my relief, she soon pulled into the parking lot and headed for the empty space beside me.

On foot, we threaded our way between parked cars and slivers of broken bottles. Even out here, I heard the rock band, bass thrumming, louder than any music should be.

Janet bubbled excitedly. "This is the first time in six years I haven't had to go home to the babysitter after a gig." She gloated. "I'm gonna rock!"

Sounded like I could prepare for a long night. Okay. Janet would do the same for me.

Inside, the crowded dance floor looked like a mosh pit, as usual. The noise from the band made conversation impossible. Strobe lights created a surreal atmosphere. We checked our coats and Janet pointed to the bar. Perching on adjoining stools, we yelled our orders at the bartender.

"Think we'll hook up with anybody?" Janet screamed.

I figured if we did, he'd be drunk or with the symphony or both, but I only said, "Never can tell." After all, Janet had recently escaped from the prison of her marriage. Let her enjoy new possibilities for a while. The cynicism would set in later. Or maybe not. Maybe it was just me.

Talk wasn't possible, so we nursed our drinks and scanned the crowd. Or rather, I nursed my drink and wished for Barry to appear. He stubbornly refused to be banished from my thoughts, despite my best efforts to forget his existence. The more I told myself not to think of him, the more he haunted my thoughts.

Janet gulped her drinks and put away four by the time I'd finished sipping the first. Her gaze caught that of a dark cowboy-booted muscle-builder, way tall, over six feet and made taller by his cowboy hat. The sultry looks they exchanged should have been X-rated.

Then I noticed his friend. Short—shorter than me—with a paunch that overhung his belt, bald, bearded, also cowboy-booted, with circles of sweat under each arm and headed my way.

"Oh, Lord, I'm too old for this," I groaned to myself.

Janet and the muscle-builder moved to the dance floor, entwined and moving together in a way that looked like pregnancy might result. Where had Janet learned to dance like that? If her soon-to-be ex-husband, Alan, had taught her, he must be more exciting than he looked.

By now Short-Stuff stood way too close to me at the bar. "Hey, babe. Wanna dance?" he roared over the din.

"I don't dance," I shouted, lying.

Looking relieved, he stood on tiptoe and pushed himself atop the stool Janet had vacated. "Me neither."

Figured.

"I'm Bill," he bellowed.

I nodded, without telling him my name, staring into the gyrating crowd and hoping obvious disinterest discouraged him.

"I'm in plumbing and heating supply," he yelled.

I nodded again.

"Own my own store."

I looked him over and murmured "Um-hm."

Thank heaven. Janet headed my way, holding hands with Muscleman and trailing him in her wake.

"Emily, can you believe this?" she roared in my ear. "Isn't he gorgeous? If only Alan could see me now."

Didn't sound like a good reason to get involved to me. Concerned about the dangerous combination of fresh grief and lots of booze, I leaned close, so I didn't have to yell. "Janet, don't do anything you'll be sorry for."

"Why not? I'm doing the time. Why not do the crime? What's Alan gonna do? Leave me?" She cackled—was she laughing or crying?—and staggered backward into Muscleman.

"Janet, come on. Let's go," I begged.

"No. I'm having fun. Leave me alone."

"Hey, sweetheart," Muscleman urged Janet, "let me buy you another drink."

The bartender brought a fresh drink at Muscleman's expense. I pulled at Janet's arm, trying to leave. Then I saw Joe Burke come in. No sign of Billie, his wife. Come to think of it, she hadn't been with him at the concert, either. He looked through the crowd, searching. Gratefully, I realized he hadn't seen me.

"Janet, we have to go. Now."

She must have heard the urgency in my voice. Either that, or second thoughts and sanity took over. Anyway, her smile abruptly disappeared. "Yeah. Yeah. Okay."

"Hey, wait. You didn't finish your drink." Muscleman protested.

Ignoring him, I dragged Janet toward the door. Too late. Joe Burke saw us and headed our way.

"Emily, oh, Lord, Emily, I'm going to be sick." Janet ran for the restroom, and I trailed behind. At least Joe couldn't follow us there.

We were alone. Good thing. Janet threw up messily and noisily while I held her hair and worried. What if Joe waited outside?

The solution came in the form of a gaggle of giggling twenty-something girls. They timed it just right. Janet cleaned up while they preened before the mirror. We made our exit with them. Joe, who waited across the hall, didn't appear to notice.

The girls headed toward the dance floor. Janet and I moved the other way.

I guided Janet to our cars. She was awake and aware but moaning and obviously in no shape to drive. We'd have to leave her car. I opened the passenger side of my Subaru and concentrated on pushing and pulling Janet into the seat. It took all my attention. She couldn't fasten the seat belt, so I located it and buckled it for her. Closing the door, I heard from behind me, "Emily, you're avoiding me."

I jumped, startled.

"I'm hurt," Joe said, in a voice heavy with sarcasm.

Keys in hand, I backed away, feeling my way along the front of the car toward the driver's side until I ran into the bumper of another car, nose to nose with mine. I stopped.

Joe continued his advance until he faced me, inches away.

"Remember what I said, Emily. Mind your own business." He grabbed my arm. "Billie can't know." He sounded angry, and his grip tightened around my arm.

"Know what?"

He ignored my question. "I'm not going to let you screw up my life." He jerked my arm harshly.

I had no idea what he was talking about. Strength favored him, though. He was easily five inches taller than me and far more powerful. So, I tried to appeal to the gentle man inside him—my friend and Billie's husband—with my words.

"Joe, I don't know what you're worried about." I made my voice low and musical like they said you should with the mentally disturbed. It wasn't easy because my breath came fast and shallow, and my teeth chattered. "You know I wouldn't hurt Billie, or you. Billie and I are just having lunch tomorrow. Like we've done a thousand times before." I knew he loved his family and I tried to take advantage of that. "I'm hoping Billie brings pictures of your new grandbaby. I haven't seen Martha since the wedding, let alone her baby. Billie will tell me all about it."

During this speech, he had loosened his grip, but his face contorted with anger. "Go ahead and have lunch, but don't upset Billie. I'm warning you." Then he paused and backed away.

"Emily, you should be more careful." His voice sounded almost normal now. "You shouldn't be out alone so late."

I hurried past him and around the back of the car. When I unlocked the driver's door, Joe, who had followed, opened it for me. I got in, slammed it shut, and locked it.

Secure in my car, I started it and watched as Joe walked across the parking lot. Midway, he paused, turned, and frowned at me.

I rubbed my hand. It ached from Joe's rough treatment at the concert. This man was definitely not the sweetheart I had thought. What was he hiding? Could he be guilty of murder?

I started the car and took off with a squeal of tires. Janet's head lolled back, and she groaned miserably. I only hoped she didn't throw up again. I'd have to help her out of the car and into the house. Then I wanted to ice my hand. And this was supposed to be fun.

NINETEEN

JANET HAD CRASHED ON THE COUCH and still slept when I left at 11:30 the next morning. I jotted a quick note before I took off.

Janet,

Hope you feel okay. I had to leave, but KC is here. Don't be afraid to ask her if you want anything and make yourself at home.

Emily

Leaving the note next to the couch, I headed to lunch with Joe Burke's wife, Billie.

Usually I looked forward to our appointments, but Joe's strange behavior had squelched my enthusiasm. His instruction to "mind your own business" puzzled me. Granted, I had asked nosy questions, but why would my curiosity about Joe hiring Olive for the musical provoke such hostility or affect Billie in any way? I didn't want to put my foot in it, but I hoped to find information to explain it all. I counted on Billie to help me understand.

The Articulate Artichoke was, as usual, quiet. A great place for conversation, but I wondered how they stayed in business.

Billie had arrived before me, and she waved when she saw me come in.

"Emily." She stood and gave me a hug. "It's so good to see you."

We started out with small talk. Billie enthusiastically told me about her role as a new granny and had, as I expected, pictures of her new grandbaby on her cell phone. We ordered, and it wasn't until the waitress brought our meals, a salad for Billie and a sandwich for me, that I mentioned my main concern.

"Do you believe someone killed Olive?" I ventured for openers. "And they haven't arrested anybody. It's scary."

"Oh, I know what you mean. The murderer might be anyone." She put down her fork.

"They've questioned a bunch of the symphony people, me included."

"You're kidding."

I wasn't surprised Billie hadn't heard. She kept too busy with volunteer work to be part of the grapevine.

"What a crazy world." She sounded bewildered.

"I imagine they'll end up questioning just about everybody who knew Olive." I took a bite of my sandwich.

"That means they might talk to Joe and me." Was she excited or shocked?

"You'll have an alibi, of course. Joe always knows where you are," I said.

"Usually, but that weekend Joe's brother had a heart attack. Joe went to New York to be with the family."

So, Joe had been out of town when the murder took place. "Then you *don't* have an alibi," I teased, only half kidding.

Billie chuckled, tasting a mouthful of salad. "Silly. Like I need one."

"Don't laugh." I leaned toward her. "It hasn't been funny for me."

Apparently, she didn't believe I represented a serious suspect. "Well, call if they arrest you. I'll tell them what a sterling character you are."

"I'd appreciate that." I didn't smile.

Billie didn't know how to take that, I guess, because she changed the subject. As always, she wanted to know about my love life. A motherly sort, and happy in her own marriage, she thought everyone should be married.

Knowing her interest would have to be satisfied, I picked up the other half of my sandwich. "If you could guarantee I'd be as happy as you are, Billie, I'd go for it in a minute." I wasn't going to tell her about the side of Joe I'd seen after the concert, or about Barry and his romantic advances. I didn't want to diss Joe or answer questions about Barry that I hadn't answered for myself. Billie would have me married off before lunch ended. I deflected her questions with a question of my own. "Where'd you find Joe, anyway?"

Billie giggled like a teenager. "He spent a summer working for Dad. Construction. You know how music is."

"Tell me about it."

We both laughed.

"One day I brought lunch to Dad at the site. You should have seen Joe without his shirt."

Joe? A sex symbol? Did I want to hear this?

"My folks were pretty worried when I told them I had accepted his proposal. They didn't think he made enough money. And they sure didn't think music provided a steady living. When we married, they gave us half their savings as a wedding gift. I think they were afraid I'd starve."

Wonder how Joe felt about that?

"But Joe works hard and he's smart. He made a killing with the money my folks gave us." Billie reached for a packet of sugar.

"A killing? What do you mean?"

"He has a feeling for the stock market, you know." She tore the packet open and stirred sugar into her tea.

"He loves you a lot," I told her, tentatively, wondering if she would mention Joe's dark side, which I had seen last night.

Billie blushed and laughed. "He never stops telling me so."

"You're very lucky. What's your secret?"

Billie blushed again. "He's just a good man."

Again, I thought of Joe's behavior yesterday and wondered if Billie really knew him. But I kept it to myself. "If that's what it takes, there must not be many of them. Just in the last week Janet Archer and Chuck Holcombe both separated from their spouses."

Billie leaned across her salad. "Oh, no. I'm so sorry. Give Janet my love, will you? What happened?"

I explained how Olive's jealous accusations had been the final chord in Janet's already shaky marriage.

"How terrible. Suspicion is such a destructive thing. You know, last fall, when I came back after visiting my sister, I had three so-called 'friends' phone. They all told me Joe had tied one on and ended up at Olive's."

"Olive's?" Was this the link I'd been looking for?

She went on. "I knew Joe would never fool around, but just hearing their nasty gossip hurt a lot."

"Did you talk to Joe about it?"

Billie chuckled. "No. I didn't have to. I know Joe. He may have ended up at Olive's, but nothing happened. He'd never be able to hide an affair from me. And I didn't want him to feel I don't trust him." She took a bite and went on with her point. "But Janet and her husband have been having problems for a long time. I imagine Olive pushed Alan over the edge. He ran out of faith."

Trust Billie to understand.

"I'm sure you're right."

"And Chuck and Celia Holcombe. They have all those little children. Three? Or four? Tell me it wasn't an affair."

"I don't think so." I explained that I didn't know a lot, but that Chuck had mentioned in-laws and money problems.

"That might have been me if my parents hadn't been so supportive and Joe hadn't been so smart. Poor Celia."

Billie stretched. Taking a last bite of her salad, she looked at her watch and jumped up. "I didn't realize the time. I hate to eat and run, but I'm due to train a new volunteer at the hospital at one thirty. I'll be late." She left money to pay for her meal and hugged me. "Take care of yourself." And she was gone.

TWENTY

BY THE TIME I CAME HOME, Janet had disappeared. She had been worried about having left the kids with their grandma for so long, so KC had driven her to her car.

I'd have to call Janet and make sure she had no regrets.

"Did you have fun at lunch?" KC asked.

"Fun isn't the word."

When she lifted her eyebrow at me, I realized I'd told her everything else, and I might as well talk through my ideas. "Sit down a minute and I'll explain."

"I'll make tea. Let's get comfortable."

Five minutes later, we sat at the dining room table. First, by way of updating her, I explained that the police had found my "motive." The inheritance. Then I recounted everything I'd been through over the past two days with Billie and Joe.

"What do you think all that means?" KC asked.

"I'm guessing it means Olive blackmailed Joe for work."

KC cocked her head. "Why do you think so?"

"Well, Joe 'ties one on,' as Billie says, and ends up spending the night at Olive's. Then suddenly Olive's playing the musicals, even though it doesn't make sense, after all the years Gardiner's played them, unless Gardiner's busy or Olive's a better player than he is. We know neither of those is true. So, Olive must've been blackmailing Joe for work in exchange for her silence about their one-nighter." I paused. "And then I start poking into Joe's hiring of Olive. He feared my questions because he didn't want the truth exposed." I knew I had made a couple leaps of logic, but only that explanation answered all the questions.

"But why would Olive do that? Why would playing the musicals be so important to her?" KC asked.

I thought a moment. "I guess you'd have to know Olive and her feelings about music. Gardiner had rejected her and hurt her feelings, both with words and with his behavior. She wasn't taking it well. I know that for a fact. It wouldn't surprise me if she wanted to embarrass him professionally in return for the way he'd embarrassed her personally. Or she might have been trying to attract his attention, hoping he'd be impressed by her performance. Olive measured her worth by her playing. It's possible she thought that if she stirred him with her performance, he'd finally love her. I know it doesn't make sense to you and me, but to Olive . . ." I shrugged. "Then too, she probably couldn't stand seeing another bassoonist hired in preference to her, even Gardiner, whom she respected and supposedly loved." I paused and thought for a minute. "Assuming all that's true, though, there are a couple things I don't understand."

"Tell me." KC leaned forward. "We can figure them out together, you know?"

"Well, for one thing, Billie knows all about it, and so does most of the Western Hemisphere, apparently, or at least Janet does, Billie's friends do, and probably Gardiner does, too. Why would Joe submit to blackmail if everybody already knows about it?"

"Ah! But *Joe* doesn't know everybody knows." KC's voice rang with confidence. "I bet he thinks he succeeded in keeping his little fling secret."

"But Billie doesn't think he did anything to be ashamed of. She says he'd never be able to hide it if he had. If he'd only had too much to drink and Olive drove him to her place to sleep it off, perfectly innocently, why should he worry?"

"Em, I doubt it was innocent. When there's a man, a woman,

and a few drinks involved, it usually isn't." She shook her head and smiled, apparently amused at my naiveté.

Well, fine, I'd bow to her expertise.

"Even if nothing happened, Joe undoubtedly doesn't think Billie'll buy it. I wouldn't. And even if she pretends to laugh at the idea that Joe had an affair, maybe Billie's not as sure of him as she pretends to be."

"Billie . . ." I didn't finish my thought.

"Billie could have murdered Olive out of jealousy."

Billie? The gentle grandma? With the passion to be a murderess? "You think?" Billie *hadn't* told me where she'd been that day. I considered that. "Okay. Let's assume all that's right." I reviewed the theory for my own clarity of mind. "Joe has too much to drink, spends the night at Olive's, and doesn't want Billie to find out about it, for whatever reason. Olive wants to play the musical and embarrass Gardiner, who has, by this time, rejected her. Or let's say she plays to attract his attention. Either way, she blackmails Joe for the work. That gives both Joe and Billie motive to kill Olive. Billie to dispose of the 'other woman' and Joe to end the blackmail. But Joe was in New York the day of the murder, with his brother, apparently. That leaves Billie. What I don't understand is how Gardiner fits in."

Leaning her elbows on the table, KC thoughtfully steepled her fingers. "Well, Gardiner probably knew Joe and Olive spent the night together. Everybody else knew, including his friend Janet, who told you Olive 'lied' about Joe. She may have said something to Gardiner."

KC sounded sure of herself, but I didn't understand. "So?"

"So, if Gardiner knew Joe had spent the night at Olive's, Gardiner must have figured he didn't get hired because Joe and Olive were sleeping together, you know?"

"Why would that make Gardiner threaten me?" If there were dots, I couldn't connect them.

"What if Gardiner killed Olive to reclaim the work?"

"Murder? To take back work? Isn't that a bit extreme?" I sipped my tea.

"Murder is always extreme. But maybe he didn't plan to murder Olive. Only scare her off. Things spun out of control when he hit her, and he accidentally killed her. He wouldn't want you to know Joe didn't hire him because of Olive, would he? That would lead you to suspect him."

"Gardiner had so many reasons to kill Olive. What would I care if he had one more?" My brain had gone into overload. "What a mess." I expressed my frustration. "Is there anyone who *didn't* want to kill Olive?" The suspects stacked up like music to prepare, with no practice session in sight.

"Just you." KC stopped me mid-tirade. "You stuck around even after Olive went crazy. You tried to help her."

KC's faith touched me. Only she and Barry believed in me.

"But the trouble is, Em, you have a motive—the inheritance—plus you were seen near the murder site. Someone else was there. Who? That's the question we have to answer."

KC was right, but I didn't know what to do next. I decided to think about something else, hoping the solution would come to me later. "What about you? Make any progress with Curtis, the Board member?"

"I don't know about progress. I saw him yesterday. It didn't go well. I tried to persuade him to talk about music and being on the Board, and how he felt about musicians. He told me quite a bit about how wonderful classical musical is. How it soothes worries, unites people, and raises them to a different level." She poured a fresh cup of tea. "But then we brought up the topic of musicians. He resents paying them." She imitated a deep, male voice. "'They play for a living. I do *real* work. The symphony is expensive to run. We can't afford higher wages for people who only work three days a week. Higher wages would be nice, but nice doesn't pay the bills. I want to protect the symphony.'" KC's voice returned to normal. "When I pointed out that musicians *are* the symphony, and they have to pay their bills, too, that they practice individually and rehearse with the group, besides playing concerts three days a week, he started to raise his voice. And he told me about the petition Olive circulated demanding higher wages."

I remembered that. As if her activities could make any difference. Olive only infuriated the union's negotiating committee for stepping on its toes.

"He sounded more and more upset, so I thought I'd better change the subject."

"KC, that's great. You can't be too pushy, and you persuaded him to talk."

"I'm supposed to see him again on Tuesday, the eighteenth."

"It's wonderful what you're doing for me." I paused, moved by her support. "But be careful. He might be a killer. Protect yourself." The safest thing would be for her to stay completely away from him.

"Oh, I can take care of myself." She waved her hand, pushing my worries away. "I have experience with guys like this."

Hoping her experience justified her confidence, I approached a related subject. "Have you given any thought to a new career?"

KC laughed. "Yeah. I applied for a job as a receptionist. They even had me come in for an interview. Turned out the boss had been a client. He pushed me out the door so fast I broke the sound barrier. Just as well, I guess. Working together would have been awkward, I've gotta think. Not a great start, huh?"

I chuckled, too, but not from amusement, although I tried to stay positive. "Well, it can't get any worse, can it?"

I TAUGHT FLUTE LESSONS FROM 2:00 UNTIL 6:00 and ended up mentally and physically exhausted. As I said goodbye to my last student, KC announced dinner in the dining room and did her best to revive me. She'd made some kind of scrumptious chicken thing. Once, I would have eaten fast food, alone, at Lundy's. Thanks to KC, I had time to inhale dinner and work in a quick nap before I left. What had I ever done without her?

I felt almost human again when the security guard greeted me for that night's concert with the familiar, "Fancy meeting you here."

But none of it helped, and my warm-up felt scattered.

I kept seeing Olive's mistakes. Beside me my section leader, Sandy Baines, warmed up. Olive had publicly embarrassed her with insensitive comments. Behind me in the clarinet section sat

Janet, whose shaky marriage fell apart under Olive's paranoid suspicions. In the same row Gardiner presided over the bassoon section. Olive had stalked him, stunted his budding relationship with Leanne, and tried to humiliate him professionally. In front of me, in the first violin section, Gardiner's ex, Clara James, prepared to perform. Olive had continually poked and pried into her already painful divorce wounds. Billie and Joe Burke were in the audience, taking the opportunity to hear Beethoven's Fifth together. Their blissful, years-long union was marred with secrets, thanks to Olive, and Joe had been victimized by Olive's blackmail-for-jobs scheme, if KC and I had guessed right. And what about the people who weren't here? Sometimes self-centered and thoughtless, Olive had ignored the needs of David O'Malley's children and overlooked his kindness. And who knew how many assorted petty wounds she'd delivered, like tactless comments and blistering musical critiques?

But by the time the concert started, thanks to practice and training, I had compartmentalized, put my thoughts aside, and shifted my concentration to *Daphnis* and the concerto. It wasn't until intermission, knowing I had to talk to Clara James, Gardiner's ex-wife, that I thought about the murder again. I hurried out with the strings. Clara walked just ahead of me.

"Clara." I called.

She turned and waited at the side of the stage. "Great job on *Daphnis*, Emily."

The compliment startled me. It's true, I had put my questions aside and concentrated when the concert started but, judging myself, I hadn't thought my playing better than average. Clara said, "I haven't had a chance to talk to you since Olive died. How are you doing? I know you two were friends."

We walked through the dark, crowded wings of the stage and out into the florescent lights of the backstage area, where crowds of symphony musicians chatted noisily.

"Oh, fine, I guess." Fine didn't cover anything at all—not my guilt at having lost patience and hung up on Olive, not my grief at having permanently lost her unique outlook on life, and not my sadness at the waste of her potential. Instead of mentioning my feelings, I turned my attention to Lt. Gordon. "The police investigation has pointed a finger straight at me, so I'm a little stressed."

"You? Why?"

"Well, I don't have an alibi, I've been seen near the scene at the time of the crime, and I benefitted from Olive's will. It doesn't look good, but I didn't kill her." Saying it out loud made me feel better.

"I know you didn't kill her. You couldn't." Clara staunchly defended me. What if she knew I thought of her as a suspect? Clara had a good motive, and *someone* had murdered Olive.

"What about you? How are you doing?"

Clara hesitated. "I don't deny I'm relieved to be free of the problems Olive caused for me, but nobody deserves to die the way she did."

Finally. Someone who expressed something other than glee at Olive's death.

I continued. "I have the feeling the police are suspicious of everybody. I guess it's their job. Have they questioned you?"

"They did. It's possible I'm a suspect, but I went out to dinner and a movie the day of the murder. My companion can vouch for me from five PM, when he picked me up, until eleven. By that time, I guess Olive's body had already been found."

Her alibi left an hour and a half unaccounted for. Did she kill Olive during those ninety minutes? Possibly. I made a mental note. But Clara seemed so kind. Surely, she wasn't a killer. "Companion? He? Give."

Clara blushed. "He's a guy some friends fixed me up with. It's way too early to get excited."

"Well, keep me posted. You know I wish you the best." By then we'd gone down the stairs to the green room. Clara stayed there and headed for an armchair, while I left for the restroom.

I had hardly latched the stall when I heard the main bathroom door open and a voice say, "Yeah, Olive and I hung out together for a while, but she was too high maintenance. I couldn't take it." I recognized the voice of Hester Crabbe, second oboe.

"High maintenance how?" That voice I didn't know.

"Everything always had to be just so, her way. The last straw came when she accused me of stealing some money she'd withdrawn from the bank. Later, I heard she found it under a stack of music. But did she apologize? No. Life's too short to put up with that kind of stuff."

I remembered Leanne had hinted at the funeral that Hester had some problem with Olive. Hester's story explained Leanne's comment.

Embarrassed, I didn't want Hester to feel like I eavesdropped on her conversation, but I couldn't avoid it. I had to return to the stage. Besides, I wanted to find out the identity of Hester's friend. I flushed the toilet then emerged from the stall. One of the newer string players exchanged a distressed look with Hester before disappearing into the stall I had just vacated.

I said, "Hi," to Hester.

She responded, "Hi," but didn't say another word.

I washed my hands in awkward silence and left.

Great. Another ex-friend who didn't have much of a motive but didn't mourn Olive, either.

I started the Beethoven relying on muscle memory built up from my practice sessions. That reserve was the reason I practiced, and it took me into the music, where I found refuge and familiarity. But by the time I reached home adrenaline oozed away, and I welcomed Golden's enthusiastic "hello." I rubbed her ears and found myself wanting to be enveloped by one of Barry's hugs. He wasn't there, though, and I had no one to blame but myself. Even KC had turned in. The letdown was total. No one to talk to, no one who understood, and no one who cared. Just Golden. I went to bed glad for her company, at least, but feeling lonely and sorry for myself. Sleep didn't come easily.

TWENTY-ONE

I PLAYED AN EXCELLENT *DAPHNIS* Sunday afternoon. On the last concert of the series, and my last chance at *Daphnis*, I'd been able to immerse myself in the music, oblivious to all other concerns. "After all," I told myself before the concert, "I didn't kill Olive. There must be clues pointing to the real murderer. Lieutenant Gordon will find them. He's a professional." In other words, I'd gone into denial, forgotten everything but the music, and played a great concert.

Drained, but pleased with my performance and in a celebratory mood, I arrived home ready to relax. Golden danced her welcome and again, the house radiated wonderful cooking smells. Chicken Marseilles? Mmmm. Yum. My mouth watered. KC practiced in the guest room, adding to my feelings of well-being.

She must have heard me come in because she appeared on the stairs a few minutes after I arrived. Stopping before she descended the last four steps and leaning over the bannister, she asked, "Em, how'd the concert go?"

"Great!" I put my keys into my purse. "I finally played *Daphnis* the way I wanted to, the soloist outdid herself, and the Beethoven moved me, even as many times as I've played Beethoven's Fifth."

"I'm so glad. You deserve it." She danced down the last four steps and followed me into the studio, where I put the satchel that held my flute, purse, and music stand into a cupboard.

"I got the nicest call from Barry while you were gone." She reminded me of a happy, wiggly puppy, bubbling with joy.

"Am I supposed to phone him back?"

"Actually, he called to talk to me."

A prick of jealousy disturbed my glow, surprising me.

She hurried on. "He wanted to thank me for dinner Friday. He appreciated that I found a way for you two to be together on Valentine's Day, okay? He cares about you, Em. I can tell, you know?" Her sincerity couldn't be mistaken.

I didn't argue, but the tender side of her surprised me, to say the least. You'd think what she did for a living would trounce all the romance from her soul. But I'd caught her mooning over a book with a scantily clad, curvaceous woman and a bare-chested, well-muscled man on the cover.

She continued. "How come you won't give him a chance?"

"How come you're meddling?"

She looked so upset that I felt guilty.

"KC, men are a pain." I tried to explain myself. "Surely you've noticed that in your line of work?" I didn't give her a chance to answer. "They complicate things. They expect you to live their life, not your own. They demand it, never appreciating what you do for them. Life is a series of compromises, trying to please them, with only occasional happiness. I don't want it. My friends care, they're considerate, and I have my freedom. It's all a joy."

"Sounds like you've been hanging out with the wrong men. Barry's a sweetheart. He's real. He only wants your company."

I didn't reply.

KC took a step toward me. "Come on. Be honest with yourself. I saw how glad you were to see Barry Friday night. You're just fooling yourself. Don't throw it away."

Okay, I had to admit she was right, but not out loud. "He'd be the last person I'd date. He's my lawyer, KC."

"So? You're on the same team, looks to me."

My post-concert highs completely destroyed, I felt upset, but unsure at whom. Barry, KC, or myself. Despite the mouthwatering smells, my appetite deserted me. "I don't want to talk about it. I'm taking Golden for a walk."

KC laid her hand on my arm. "Just give Barry a chance to show you he's different. You won't be sorry."

I shook her hand off. "What I'm sorry about is that no one believes anything I say, whether it's about love or murder." I hurried out of the room before she, or I, could say anything more.

Golden and I had a long walk, and by the time we returned, the chicken was cold. KC practiced in her room, my arrival unnoticed. I made up a plate and, like old times, ate cold food with only Golden for company.

TWENTY-TWO

MONDAY, FEBRUARY 17, 2010, 8:05 AM

THE NEXT MORNING, KC made a wonderful breakfast of fruit, eggs, and hot oatmeal. Comfort food with fiber. I took it as an apology. She didn't want any hard feelings between us. Neither did I. I had decided I was in the wrong. She had been trying to help and had no idea I would react so strongly. "KC, I . . . that is I . . . I'm sorry. About yesterday, that is."

"It's okay, Em. I shouldn't have questioned you."

I hugged KC, relieved she'd forgiven me. I'd eaten my fill and put on my coat to take Golden for a walk when the phone rang.

"Barry." My face burned as I thought of yesterday's conversation with KC.

"Hi, Em. Sorry to call so early, but I'm afraid I have bad news."

Those were words you didn't want to hear from your lawyer. My stomach instantly threatened to lose the breakfast I had just finished. I let go of Golden's leash, sat abruptly in the nearest chair, a cane-bottomed heirloom that had belonged to my grandfather, and waited silently.

Barry didn't say anything for a few seconds. "I heard from my source at the MPD."

My arm and shoulder tightened as I clutched the receiver "And?"

"Em, the police are issuing a warrant for your arrest in Olive's murder. My source didn't know exactly know when, but Lieutenant Gordon will be coming for you. It's step one. When he arrests you, call me. I'll come. It's what lawyers do. Besides, I'm your friend. You're not alone."

I went numb for only a moment before hope reasserted itself. "But I didn't do it. You'll get me out, right? You won't leave me in jail?"

I had a feeling the long silence that followed didn't bode well, and I was right. "Em, I didn't want to worry you. It was such a long shot they'd arrest you that I didn't tell you before . . ."

"What?" How could it be any worse?

"There's no possibility of bail on a homicide charge." His words numbed me all the way from my stomach to my brain, so I barely understood. "The DA got elected with a get-tough-on-crime campaign. The cornerstone is no bail if the charges involve violent crime. Once they arrest you, you'll be in jail 'til you're acquitted."

Well, at least his scenario called for acquittal. "Barry, I can't go to jail." I turned to denial. "They can't have any evidence. I didn't kill her." Every made-for-TV prison drama I'd ever seen came into my head. Near panic now, I hugged myself and rocked. "I won't go to jail. Somebody has to find the real murderer."

He didn't respond.

When he spoke again, he summed up the police case in a calm, low voice, like any professional person talking to a crazed client. "You were seen near the murder scene walking Golden during the right time frame. Olive made you a beneficiary in her will." He cleared his throat. "What you don't know is she made an appointment to change her will, with the specific intention of removing you as a beneficiary. In addition, your fingerprints were all over her apartment, and they found gold canine hair at the murder scene."

"Barry, I visited Olive a thousand times, with and without Golden. The hair and the prints must be from those visits. And I didn't know about the will . . . the original or the changes."

"Em, you're preaching to the choir. I believe you. But there's enough evidence for probable cause."

Panic had taken control of my brain. My thinking was confused and chaotic, but I trusted Barry. This was his business, after all. Barry would help me out of this mess. As if I hadn't heard the beginning of the conversation, I asked, "What should I do?"

Patiently, Barry spoke, sounding gentle and sorrowful. "Do as much as you can to arrange your affairs."

"That's your advice?" Unbelievable. Stunned fear turned to adrenaline, anger took over, and I shot out of my chair. "You want me to sit here and wait to be arrested?" I paced. "Trust that the police will keep looking for someone else after I'm in custody?" I felt tears fill my eyes. Angrily I brushed them away. I was alone. Again. "It's obvious I'm going to have to find the murderer myself."

"Em, I know you're upset, but being cooperative at this point could—"

"Don't tell me not to defend myself. Or to let the real killer go free." I hung up before he finished.

TWENTY-THREE

MONDAY, FEBRUARY 17, 2010, 8:15 AM

KC APPEARED AT MY ELBOW as I hung up. "Em?" The worried expression on her face did nothing for my mood, except add guilt to anger and fear.

I knew taking my feelings out on her was pointless. "That was Barry." I took a deep breath and tried to calm down and think.

"What's wrong?"

"Not a thing, except that Lieutenant Gordon is due to show up with a warrant for my arrest, Barry wasn't sure when, and he not only can't keep me from going to jail, but once I'm in, he can't get me out 'til I'm acquitted. *If* I'm acquitted!"

"Em, I'm sorry—"

"I don't have time to talk right now. I'm bolting before Lieutenant Gordon comes." Then I had a thought. I hadn't known her long, but KC routinely avoided the police. "Can you help me?"

"Help you how?"

I headed upstairs to the bedroom, pulled out my only suitcase, and began packing as I talked. "I'm going to Mom's." Mom disliked dogs, and she made no exception for Golden. "Can you take care of Golden?"

"Sure. I can do that, but have you thought this through?" Concern shone in her eyes.

"What?"

"Your mother's house is the first place they'll look."

She was right, of course. Dodging the law wasn't my forte. "All right, where should I go, then? They'll check all my friends, too." I tried to think like a law enforcement agent. I remembered all the TV shows I'd seen and the books I'd read. "And if I use a credit card, they'll be able to trace me through the charges." We were both silent a moment. I brainstormed. "What if I check into a motel? Pay cash?"

"You have that kind of cash?"

"I'd have to go to the bank. I have enough money to stay . . . six days if the motel's cheap enough."

"Em, it can't look as if you cleaned out your bank account and took off. If there's any suspicion that Barry advised you to run, he could lose his license. His friend at the MPD might put it all together."

"*Barry* advised me to turn myself in," I said. "I'll swear to it."

"And why should they believe you, an accused murderer?" If KC aimed for humor, she made a poor job of it.

"What, then?" I had been throwing random articles of clothing into the suitcase, which balked when I tried to close it.

KC pushed me aside, tucked a stray hem inside, and closed it easily.

We both sat on the bed and looked at each other.

An idea occurred to me. "I have a student, Jenny Kennedy. Her parents—she's a teacher and he's a principal—have a cabin in the mountains. I've been there in the summer. They don't open the cabin 'til spring break, so they won't be there. If you're willing to help, I'll leave my car there so it won't be in the city. It'll look like I'm gone. Then you can bring me back. It'll buy me some time to look for the real killer."

She responded immediately. "Tit for tat. You helped me when I needed it, so now I'll help you. What do you want me to do?"

"I'll drive up to the Kennedy's cabin. Can you follow me?"

"Sure."

I grabbed my suitcase and led the way downstairs, planning as I went. "I'll leave my car there and you can bring me back." I thought a few seconds. "But what about you? I don't want to involve you with the law."

KC laughed. "It's nice of you to think of me. But I'm not a lawyer, so I can't lose my license. And I'm a good liar. Much better than Barry. I'll tell Barry and the cops that all I know is you asked me to take care of your dog." She paused. "I do think it's important to be careful, though. We don't want any of the neighbors to catch on."

I thought of Mrs. Jensen. KC was right again. "Okay. I've told you I'm on vacation in the mountains. You're not sure exactly where. The police don't know Barry talked to me. His source at the MPD doesn't know Barry talked to me either, so he should be alright. Hopefully he's smart enough not to volunteer any information. If the cops happen to find my car, I can claim I left in all innocence on a cross-country skiing vacation not knowing they wanted me." I thought for a minute. "For right now, drive to the Pic-n-Run down Lake Street and wait. I'll head out of the driveway the opposite way. Watch for me. I'll circle around. As I get close, I'll call. When you see me, follow. I'll lead the way to the cabin." I thought about it quickly and decided I couldn't do any better on the spot. "I think that'll work."

I entered the studio. Thank goodness my satchel remained packed from yesterday's concert and held my flute, folding music stand, and purse. Setting the suitcase down, I grabbed the satchel and put it over my shoulder.

Then I knelt and did my best to say goodbye to Golden. She knew something was up and had been following me everywhere as I packed. "Bye, bye Love-dog. I'll come back as soon as I can."

She looked into my eyes, put her paw on my shoulder, and whined.

How long would it be before I saw her again? What if I didn't come back? But I had to go. Tears in my eyes, I hugged her. Then, wrenching myself away from Golden, I grabbed my suitcase.

Outside, I handed it and the satchel to KC. She put them in the back of her maroon SUV.

"OK. Let's go." I climbed into my ancient green Subaru, lowered the window, and gave her one last chance to back out. "You're sure you want to help?"

For answer, she opened her car door. "I'll wait at the Pic-n-Run. How long'll you be?"

I leaned into the open window. "Just a few minutes. See you soon."

And so I started my life as a fugitive.

TWENTY-FOUR

MONDAY, FEBRUARY 17, 2010, 8:30 AM

KC FOLLOWED ME WEST FOR AN HOUR, winding up into the mountains on a road which started as a four-lane divided highway, went to two lanes, then developed so many cracks and potholes I hesitated to call it a paved road. Increasingly spectacular scenery welcomed us, and when at last we turned right onto a dirt road, we were at the top of the world, as far as I could see. To the left, the ground dropped away and across a wide valley another mountain range was the only thing blocking a view to land's end; one of my favorite vistas.

We followed the ridge for a mile or two then made another right and dropped back into the shelter of the hill we'd just come up. At first, the road was well maintained—graded and leveled. As we descended, evergreens grew more abundant, and we ran into patches that were icy in the constant shade. We turned left, down into a wooded valley bisected by a frozen stream, and the road became nothing more than a couple of rutted tracks. I'd never traveled this route in the winter before, and I gave thanks for my all-wheel drive. KC had no trouble, either, in her SUV, but this place was so out-of-the-way God had forgotten it. It had to be well out of Lt. Gordon's reach.

After several miles of ever-deepening snow and ice, I wished my car had higher ground clearance. Finally, I saw a wide place in the road, big enough for two to three cars. I pulled over and parked. I couldn't see the cabin, which lessened my anxiety.

As I exited my car and began locking doors, KC climbed out of her BMW. "What a beautiful spot. I didn't know places like this existed anymore. Who did you say owns this?"

"The family of a student. The family's cabin is in that clump of trees." I pointed up the hill in front of us and to the right.

Nothing was visible except evergreens.

My fantasy home in the mountains, just for me, was totally away from everything except rabbit trails, the scent of pine, and the sound of wind in the trees. But now that I had found the ideal location, I daren't stay. I had to find out who killed Olive or I'd never be able to go home again.

I finished locking my car and settled into KC's SUV. The silence and peace were just what I needed. As we left, KC loaded a CD— soft, soothing jazz—and we listened in companionable silence as the clouds rolled in and snow began to fall.

I thought about what to do next. Thankfully, this series of concerts had ended and the symphony had a week off, so I didn't have to worry about that, but there were other things to take care of. I decided I'd better contact my students.

Pulling out my cell phone, I texted each of them and cancelled for the upcoming week, telling them all I'd be taking a skiing vacation during the orchestra's week off. The loss of income would be a major blow to my budget, but I didn't see any way to avoid the hit.

Calling my mom was next. If she failed to reach me, she could very well do any number of crazy things to find me.

"Hi, Mom."

"Emily. I was just about to call you. Like minds have great thoughts, I guess."

A little convoluted even for Mom, but I got the gist.

"I'm going on a cruise. Can you take care of Harriet while I'm gone?"

Harriet was Mom's parrot. The bird owed her entire stock of phrases and communication skills to Mom. I tried, but Harriet never learned a word from me and never accepted correction. When she came out with phrases like, "Flocking birds feather together," I wondered what sort of deviant "fowl" play she engaged in.

"Actually, I called to tell you I'm going to run up to the mountains for a few days. Cross-country skiing." I'd keep my story consistent.

"Well, thank heaven. It's about time you had some fun. But the mountains in February? And it's not like you. Who persuaded you to leave your students for as long as a few days? It's not that sexy lawyer you told me about, is it?"

A problem I hadn't anticipated. "Mom! I never told you he was sexy."

"So, he *is* sexy?"

I pointedly ignored her. "And . . . the parents of one of my students offered me the use of their cabin."

"Really? Anybody I know?"

The woman had zillions of questions. "No. No one you know."

"Who, then?"

"I . . ." Why hadn't I foreseen this inquisition? I didn't want her to be able to tell Lt. Gordon anything concrete, but I didn't want her to have to lie, either. "Heavens. I've forgotten the name. Isn't that awful? And they're being so nice to me, too."

A short pause followed. "Emily Lynn, you're lying to me." Since age five, she'd called me by both of my given names when I was in trouble.

I should have known this would happen. I'd never been able to mislead her, undoubtedly the reason our relationship had remained as strong as it had over the years. Once Mom's antennae alerted her, she couldn't be stopped until she discovered the truth. I'd learned confession was the simplest way out. "I'm sorry. I didn't want you to worry or have to lie to the police."

"The police!" She seldom lost her good humor, but this was one of those times. "What have you done?"

"I haven't done anything. It's about Olive."

Mom knew all about Olive's murder. She had to hide under a rock to miss it in the papers. Besides, she'd been to the symphony concert yesterday. "What does that have to do with you?"

I hadn't told her about Lt. Gordon or his suspicions. If I had, based on past experience, she'd have called him, and his superiors too, and given them a piece of her mind. Mother bears had nothing on Mom when it came to defending their offspring. Now I had to fill her in on everything that had happened since Lt. Gordon first appeared on my doorstep.

Her reaction was, as always, unpredictable. "That's ridiculous. You're not organized enough to kill anyone."

"Thanks for the vote of confidence, Mom." I rolled my eyes.

She hadn't lost the thread of the conversation. "Where are you staying, then?"

This was about to be a problem. "It's better you don't know."

"Don't know? What if I need to reach you? What if my heart acts up?"

Mom had a healthier heart than mine. She walked two miles a day and ate vegan, constantly nagging me about the animals I "killed."

"I'll just be out of touch for a few days." I hoped that was true. "And if Lieutenant Gordon asks where I am, you can honestly say I told you I left for the mountains to use a student's cabin, but you don't know exactly where."

She mumbled something I didn't catch but returned to the original subject. "Then you'll take care of Harriet?"

She wasn't leaving for a month yet, so before we said goodbye, I agreed. I'd be home in my own bed by then. Surely. I put the phone away.

Taking her gaze off the road momentarily, KC glanced at me. "Better take your SIM card and battery out."

"Why?"

She raised her eyebrows. "You don't want the police to be able to track you via your phone." She pursed her lips. "I think we'd better buy you a burner phone, too."

That didn't make sense. "Why disable my phone and then buy a new cell phone?"

"I'm sure you'll want to use your phone again. The police can use the GPS on your cell to track you down. That can't happen if you take the SIM card and battery out. Burner phones can't be traced, since the cops don't know who they belong to. They're cheap and totally private. If you make any calls you don't want the police to know about, you won't leave a trail because everything's anonymous."

"But what about the texts and calls I've already made? I used my personal cell phone."

"That should be okay. You texted your students and called your mom from the mountains. You're on vacation in the mountains. Everything is consistent, so far."

"Okay." I took the back off the phone, removed the SIM card and battery, and put all the parts back in my purse. "How do you know all this stuff?"

KC coughed. "You pick up these things. I don't always want the police to know where I am, if they're paying attention."

Deciding I didn't want to know any more, I let the subject drop and returned to my thoughts. Where should I stay? My thoughts chased each other round and round, but I couldn't make a decision. Feeling safe for the moment, and soothed by KC's jazz, I did what I always did when suffering unbearable stress. I fell asleep.

TWENTY-FIVE

MONDAY, FEBRUARY 17, 2010, 1:00 PM

I WOKE AS WE APPROACHED THE CITY LIMITS.

In agreement about the necessity, KC and I headed for the nearest MegaMart. She knew all about burner phones, so I bought what she told me to, one for her and one for me. Fortunately, several of the weekend students had paid their monthly tab in cash. I hadn't gone to the bank yet, so, even though it took most of the money I had on me, I used that cash for the phones, leaving no credit card record.

Back in the car, we traded cell numbers, and KC told me, "That way we'll be able to stay in touch without leaving a record for the cops."

I followed printed instructions to switch on the phones, while KC started the BMW and asked, "Where to?"

Amazingly enough, my mind, refreshed from a nap, had found the answer.

My first house had been a condo in a not-so-good neighborhood. I moved into my husband's house when I married but kept my place as a rental. During my marriage, the condo provided a monthly income that helped me build up some savings. After my divorce, I stayed in it for a while, then used the accumulated savings for a down payment on a house in a better neighborhood. Now the condo provided extra income when I could keep it rented, though that wasn't easy. Unfurnished and, fortunately for me, empty right now, it would serve as a hideaway. I figured the neighbors were too mistrustful of cops to call them, even if they did suspect the new building resident was wanted.

On the other hand, my ownership was a matter of public record. Even though the condo had been purchased under my maiden name, sooner or later the police would discover it. It would only buy me a couple of days, but it would serve for now.

When we arrived, KC helped me carry in the few things I'd brought, then said she'd buy groceries while I "settled" my things, as if there was much to settle.

After she left, I succumbed to the luxury of feeling sorry for myself. How had a nice, quiet second-flutist gotten into this position? It could be worse, though. I felt safe for the moment. And I'd cared for the condo, making repairs after the last tenant moved out. Now everything functioned. I'd left the electricity on to keep the fridge working, and the furnace on low so the pipes didn't freeze. I turned up the thermostat to take off the remaining chill and relaxed, soon to be warm.

I'd plopped my suitcase in the middle of the bedroom and decided not to unpack. I hadn't brought much. Besides, there wasn't any place to put my stuff, and I wouldn't be here long. *God willin' and the creek don't rise.* On the other hand, I'd packed in a hurry and my underwear lined the bottom of the suitcase. I repacked, moving my underwear, jeans, and . . . no socks. Even when I packed carefully, I usually forgot something. Hurrying as I had, I'd forgotten not only socks, but also jammies, jewelry, and pantyhose. Well, I wouldn't use pantyhose or jewelry. After all, dressy affairs weren't on my agenda. But I made a mental note to have KC bring me socks and PJs.

Then, feeling guilty at the way I had left things, I called Barry on the burner phone, taking the extra precaution of using star sixty-seven to block the number. I wanted to talk to him, but if the police checked Barry's phone records, I didn't want them to know the new number. I didn't want Barry to know the new number, either. Mostly, I didn't want to put him at risk professionally. Besides that,

I didn't know if he'd lie for me or not, and I didn't want to find out. Mentally, I blessed KC for insisting on buying the phone.

Barry's landline answered with a message, but when I started to record, he picked up.

"What's with the new number? It came over the caller ID as 'blocked call.' I never answer those."

"I bought a phone that couldn't be traced." I explained I had blocked my new phone number for his protection. "That way you can honestly say you don't have my new number if anybody asks." Knowing I owed him an apology, I rushed to clear the air before he said anything else. "I'm sorry for shouting when we last talked."

"Don't worry about yelling. Anybody would have been in a state. But you shouldn't have taken off."

"I had to. Olive's killer is loose, and the police are focused on me. I can't sit and do nothing."

"I gave my word you'd be available. Your actions hurt my credibility."

I didn't know what to say. I felt bad, but I had to take care of myself. Nobody else was. "Barry, I'm sorry but I just didn't have a choice."

"Emily . . ."

Uh-oh. I was in more trouble than I thought. He wasn't using "Em."

". . . when Lieutenant Gordon brought you into the police station for questioning, I assured him you'd stay in town. That's part of the reason he let you go home."

"Sorry. I can't help it."

Barry sounded angry, and he kept calling me "Emily." But I'd apologized and explained about the new phone number. What more could I do? Then, sticking to the same story I had told everybody else, I explained I was taking a skiing vacation in the mountains during the symphony break.

Of course, he knew I lied. "Fine. But I can't agree with the course you've taken. You're ignoring my advice. Officially, I don't know anything about it. Don't tell me where you are. I won't be a part of it." Then he hung up without so much as a "goodbye."

Barry's disapproval bothered me more than I expected, but I couldn't do anything about it. Despite his displeasure, I had to clear myself. I couldn't risk being noticed and arrested, though.

If I had an assistant on the "outside," one I trusted, it would reduce my risk. KC was the obvious choice. She already knew the situation, had access to the things I'd forgotten from home, and, as she herself pointed out, had every reason to help me. She depended on me for a place to stay. Besides, she had her own reasons to distrust the legal system.

Speak of the devil. KC chose that moment to arrive back from her trip to the store. I opened the front door and took the grocery bags she'd brought to the kitchen, while she went back to the car to fetch the others. I left the door unlocked, and a couple minutes later she let herself in, bringing in more bags.

"Em. Look what I found."

A sleeping bag and a camping chair. Comfort.

"They're out of season, you know. They were on the sale rack," she gloated.

"I wouldn't have thought of it. I'm glad you did. You're a marvel, KC."

She flushed then looked at me. "Em, I've been thinking . . ."

A long pause followed. "What? Spit it out."

"We have to keep you out of jail. You never know what'll happen there."

It made me wonder what had happened to her there.

Correctly interpreting my expression, she answered my silent questions. "It's just that people aren't kind to each other in lockup."

That wasn't exactly news. "How so?"

"Just take my word for it. I know."

KC had only heightened my fears, while leaving me unenlightened. In the interest of self-possession, I ignored my feelings. "It'll be okay. This nightmare has to end sometime. You've already been a big help." I paused. "But I'm concerned about Golden. She's not used to being left behind."

KC didn't hesitate. "Don't worry. I'll take care of her."

Golden. She cheered me up when no one else did. I couldn't

avoid the separation, but it comforted me that she liked KC. Arranging her care with a person she approved by tail wag made everything else easier.

"And I left a few things at the house. I want to talk, too. I can take care of myself while you bring my things. Come back at dinnertime and we can eat together." I hoped she'd offer to cook. My rumbling tummy already missed her meals.

"Don't worry. I'll get your stuff then cook a dinner that'll make us both feel better. We'll figure it all out."

I gave her a list of the things I'd forgotten—a nightgown, socks, my toothbrush—and, though I'd brought my flute and a music stand, I hadn't thought to bring music. She promised to come back as soon as she'd collected everything.

"I could use your help with one more thing."

She'd been about to leave and paused with her hand on the doorknob. "Sure. What?"

"I'm not sure how to proceed with an investigation. It's a risk for me to leave here. I don't want to be seen and picked up by the police."

"I hear you. Where do I come in?"

"Good question. I want to start finding people who might have been at Olive's." I paused. "Gardiner was supposedly in his studio during the time she was killed. But nobody saw him. He might have left by the side door. What was he doing? And there's something else that's bothering me."

"What's that?"

"Olive's journals said she used a man named Vince and my adult student, Red Calloway to make Gardiner jealous. What I don't understand is why she never mentioned either of them. She told me everything else."

KC opened her mouth to say something, but I cut her off.

"And I'm frustrated. How am I going to look into those things if I can't leave the condo?"

KC stared at me silently.

Sooner or later I'd have to go out. KC's help could minimize the risk. "Can you pick up some stuff so I can disguise myself? You know, hair dye or a wig, sunglasses, whatever you can think of."

She grinned and flipped a strand of my hair. "You're talking to the right girl. When I'm done, you'll be a new woman, or women. I know just what to bring."

TWENTY-SIX

MONDAY, FEBRUARY 17, 2010, 4:00 PM

WHILE I WAITED FOR KC TO RETURN, I finished putting away the groceries, ate some cheese cubes and crackers she'd brought, then fidgeted and paced. I wanted to check the burner phone for news, but the simple phone wasn't able to access the internet. Practice appealed, but sounds of the flute would advertise my presence to the neighbors. Nothing left to do but doze. I tossed and turned, unable to get comfortable in the sleeping bag. I ended up sitting in a corner in the camp chair, staring at the ceiling. *This is how it might be from now on.* Besides all the other scary things about jail—creepy cellmates, threatening prison guards, intimidating inmates—I wouldn't be able to practice. Even worse, there'd be no music at all.

Whether accurate or not, my fears shot me out of my chair. I started pacing again. Alright. I'd amuse myself by singing the music. I hummed a few bars of *Daphnis*, but missed the magic of the orchestra, with all its different instruments and lines. My singing voice sounded thin and wavery and out of tune. *Oh, this is awful.* I resumed pacing.

Thankfully, at 5:30 p.m., KC showed up with everything I'd asked her to bring.

"I paid cash, so there's no trail."

I didn't like having her spend her own money, but I didn't know what to do about it since buying the cell phones had seriously depleted my cash.

KC had also brought some utensils she said we'd need to cook dinner—pots and pans, dishes, silverware—as well as another camp chair, a blow dryer, styling wand, and more.

Paranoia made me ask, "Were you followed?"

KC sounded amused. "No way. I know my way around."

Of course she did. I relaxed.

"I grabbed some books, just in case you're bored."

I had no intention of spending my time reading, but I gave her points for the thought and hugged her. She continued to prove her worth over and over. "You think of everything."

She blushed, then proceeded to mix ingredients for a quiche while she talked. "The cops were watching the house. They wanted to know where you were. I told them you were skiing in the mountains and that you asked me to take care of the dog. Like we agreed. When they asked for how long, I let them know you asked me to stay for a week. I hope that's okay."

"That's great. Thanks." Hopefully that would take care of any concerns they had.

She put me to work cleaning and chopping mushrooms. I risked my fingers, trying to chop and think about anything else at the same time, but I started a conversation anyway.

"What about you? Your date with the Board member, Curtis, is tomorrow, right?"

"Yeah."

"I've been worrying about it. Are you sure you want to go through with it? I don't want to put you in any danger."

KC came the closest to sounding annoyed I'd heard her. "I told you. I can handle myself. Now drop it."

Guess I'd been told. I searched for another topic. "How's your job search going?" My demand that there be no clients at my house practically forced her to find an alternate profession. I hoped she would find a job she enjoyed, that didn't threaten her safety, yet paid well.

She snorted, furiously chopping onions. "They expect me to

know everything about computers—word processing, spread-
sheets, databases—and for all this they pay a pittance." Her voice
rose and she talked faster. "It'd take a whole day's work to earn what
I made in fifteen minutes as an escort. And not even a nice dinner
or an art exhibit in the bargain."

I felt bound to provide a balanced point of view. "On the other
hand, administrative assistants are rarely attacked by their bosses."

KC responded by stirring the quiche mixture with a vengeance.

I wanted to make a point. "The only people I know that make
the kind of money you're used to are doctors, lawyers, and mob-
sters. You'd have to go back to school. Or learn to shoot. "You need
to find something you can feel safe doing."

KC poured her mixture into a baking pan and slid it into the
oven. "It's back to school for me, then. I won't work for so little
money. And at a job I don't like."

She said the concoction took forty-five minutes to bake. "Now
for the fun part. The disguise."

To my surprise, it consisted solely of makeup, eyeglasses, temporary hair tint, and some of my own clothes and jewelry. "Em, what
you look like to people is mostly attitude. You wait. I'll show you."

The hair color came first. "It's a shame to hide that rich brown
hair of yours with this stuff, but you wanted a disguise."

Rich brown hair? Me? KC naturally saw the bright side of
everything.

She had two boxes of temporary dye. The first was a silver color
I wouldn't wear to a carnival. Looking at it made me feel a little sick.

"First we have to cover your dark natural color. After it dries,
we'll use the second package. Technically you're not supposed to
use one color after the other, but I've done it lots of times."

The second package appealed more, and I recognized the color
the popular girls in high school used to wear.

"The package says it's temporary, but it'll be six weeks before it
comes out."

All this didn't inspire my confidence. There wasn't any choice,
though. I had to try it if I wanted to find out who really killed
Olive, so I pretended to be happy and positive as KC applied the

silver dye and conditioner. As she cut my shoulder-length locks into a face framing geometric wedge, I heard approaching sirens. Oh, great. I pictured myself being arrested now, with only the gaudy tint in, and a half-cut head of hair. To my relief, the sirens passed by and faded into the distance. KC finished the cut and patted my hair with a towel until she'd dried it as far as possible, then suggested a dinner break.

BY THE TIME WE WERE DONE with dinner, my hair had air dried, and KC applied the second box of dye, then conditioned my whole mane again. Two hours later, my hair was dry, styled, and what the box called "Honey Blonde." KC wasn't happy. She tsked and said she had hoped for a lighter shade.

I wasn't complaining. I eyed the glamorous blue-eyed blonde in the mirror with amazement.

KC proceeded to make me up like a high-fashion model and demonstrated a runway walk, then had me try it. Who knew I could be so striking?

"Now, put on a slinky knit dress, pull your hair up high with a few strands escaping, mince along, and people see a trophy wife." She demonstrated the walk as she spoke. "Or pull your hair into a bun, put on the eyeglasses, wear a dress-for-success suit, and stride quickly and confidently, and people see a successful business-woman." She held up the suit and the glasses. "Leave on the glasses, pull your hair back in a ponytail, and wear some jeans and a sweat-shirt, and you're a college student. A book would be a good prop, too. You could hide behind it." Next, she patted on some heavier base, added bright blush, took off the eyeglasses, added two more coats of mascara and eye shadow, and made the lipstick bright red. With the air of a magician she said, "Voila! A lady of the evening, if you use your hips and dress the part."

Did I have the wardrobe? Had she bought me fishnet stockings?

"And if you feel too recognizable, you can wear your sunglasses and a scarf."

I'd seen the difference attitude made in students and how they learned, but I didn't know it could make a sudden concrete physical transformation. It turned out on top of all her other emerging strengths, KC's imagination found possibilities in the unexplored.

"Okay, I'm convinced." I felt wholly different about myself. Who was this woman in the mirror?

Despite my pleasure at my transformation, I was exhausted by an emotional day. About to suggest we end the evening early, I considered how to broach the subject when KC excused herself. "It's better if I don't visit again. I'm pretty good at shaking tails, but no sense tempting fate."

I hugged her, grateful for all her help. She assured me again that she'd dog sit until I came home, then left to tend to Golden. I just hoped it wouldn't be long before I saw her again.

TWENTY-SEVEN

MONDAY, FEBRUARY 17, 2010, 9:30 PM

AFTER KC LEFT, DRAINED AND WEARY, sleep nevertheless eluded me. I tossed and turned. The sleeping bag wasn't comfortable and, feeling like someone else, someone with blonde hair and confidence, I gave up on sleeping and called Barry on the burner phone, again blocking the number.

"Hi. It's me."

Without preamble he told me, "I heard from Lieutenant Gordon."

"Oh?" I braced for bad news.

"It's official. He has a warrant for your arrest." He sounded way too cheery for the information. "He started the search with me."

"What did you tell him?"

"Exactly what I knew. That you'd mentioned a lull in the symphony schedule and told me you'd be going to a friend's cabin in the mountains. I said I didn't know if you could get cell phone reception or not, gave him your cell number, which he already had, and assured him you wouldn't be gone more than a week."

"That's what KC told him, too."

"That's good. If he thinks you're on the run, he'll start a manhunt. This way, he thinks you left town, if not innocently, at least without knowing you're a suspect. I promised you'd come in as soon as you came back." He paused. "At least it's giving you some breathing room." He paused again, I guess hoping for some reaction from me.

He didn't get one.

"And I didn't tell him about your new cell."

I should hope not, considering I used the disposable as much to protect Barry as to safeguard myself.

After an uncomfortable silence, Barry said, "Emily."

Uh-oh. No affectionate nickname.

"I'm doing my best for you here, but I'm already arguably guilty of aiding a fugitive. I'd like to come out of this with some possibility of continuing to practice law."

He was right. He'd done his best, and I hadn't shown much appreciation. "Sorry, Barry. I know you're trying to help. But I wish it was all over."

"I know, Em."

I took the nickname to mean "apology accepted."

"It will be. Soon. You'll see. A week will be plenty of time." Barry paused. "There's . . . something else." He sounded as if he walked on eggshells, now. Regretfully, I realized no trace of the happy mood he'd shown at first remained. "The police want a sample of Golden's hair."

I hugged myself. No end to the bad news.

He continued firmly, "I told the lieutenant we'd be delighted to cooperate."

Unsure of how to respond, I didn't say anything.

As if he expected an argument, Barry explained, "I wanted to show some spirit of cooperation. He could get a court order, anyway. I assured him the hair at Olive's most likely belonged to Golden—that she'd been there a lot. That way he knows he'll have to work harder to prove his case."

"You're the expert, Barry. Thanks for handling it."

The return of Barry's support was a physical sensation. It felt good to have at least one source of stress removed. Now, I only had to resolve about a thousand others.

TWENTY-EIGHT

TUESDAY, FEBRUARY 18, 2010, 8:00 AM

BARRY'S GOODWILL COMFORTED ME, and, in the afterglow of our conversation, I hadn't felt so alone. This morning, though, it had all worn off and it was me against the world, or at least against the Monroe Police Department. Ignoring my discouragement and putting one foot in front of the other, I busied myself with my list of follow-ups.

Neither Red Calloway, my adult student, nor Olive, had mentioned the other to me, even though they'd been seeing each other, according to Olive's neighbor. Also, Red had threatened Olive with a screwdriver, according to her journal. That put him at the top of my list of possible suspects. I called him, blocking the number.

"Hey. It's Emily. Listen, I had to come back early from my vacation, so I can give you a lesson tomorrow after all. Will that work?"

"Sounds good."

Meeting at my house was impossible. Sure the police would be watching it, I improvised. "The problem is that repairmen will be working at my house, and they'll be bumping and banging. I hoped we could have the lesson at your place."

"Sure. Same time?"

"That'll work."

After we hung up, I thought about Red and our upcoming

meeting. How could I best slant my questions and protect myself? I'd have to think about it.

I SPENT THE HOURS AFTER LUNCH EXPERIMENTING with disguises, matching makeup to eyeglasses and outfits. The "successful businesswoman" persona most suited my personality, and the clothes were, by far, the most comfortable. It had the added advantage of not being outrageously out of character for me. Hopefully, Red wouldn't think it strange if I went that way to our lesson.

Having made a decision, I washed the makeup off and gave the burner phone a frustrated glance. I wanted to check the news for the status of Lt. Gordon's investigation but couldn't because of the phone's limited capabilities. I resisted the temptation to turn on my personal cell, even for just a few minutes, though. The reward wasn't great enough to justify the risk. I drummed my fingers in irritation, imagining first that all was calm, then that a massive manhunt was underway for me. Which was it?

I could have called KC, but I suppose I wanted an excuse to phone Barry. Making sure to block my number, I phoned his cell.

I started with pleasantries, but Barry wasn't interested in rehashing his day. "It's bad enough to have to go through it once. If people interacted with an ounce of common sense or kindness, lawyers couldn't stay in business. What did you do today?"

My account of experimenting with the disguises made him laugh, and that made me feel good. He had no news on Lt. Gordon's investigation, which I guessed meant that he and KC had been convincing, so I told him about the planned lesson with Red Calloway. I got no further.

"You what? You're in hiding and you schedule a music lesson with one of your students? Are you nuts?" So much for interacting with kindness.

I patiently explained. "A couple of people knew Olive dated Red. It's strange that Olive didn't tell me, too. I want to find out more." I didn't tell Barry about Olive's journal entry. The conversation wasn't going well anyway. In my mind, though, the fact that she kept the incident with Red secret raised questions that were important to answer.

Barry did listen. I'll give him that. He listened and then quietly and patiently let me have it. "Emily."

His use of my full name signaled trouble. "Em" had disappeared, along with his good nature.

"It's completely up to you if you want to risk your freedom and physical safety," he said coldly. "However, as I have told you before, my livelihood depends upon being free of a criminal record. I could, as of today, legitimately be prosecuted and found guilty of aiding a fugitive, obstructing justice, and several other minor crimes. I have undertaken all this to protect you, because I care for you. If you don't care about yourself, at least care enough about me to make some effort to protect me from exposure."

"It's not all about you, you know. Olive's killer hasn't been found, and he . . . or she . . . mustn't get away with it. On top of that, I have to prove my innocence or spend my life in jail, where who knows what might happen. Besides, I've been careful to use the burner phone whenever I call you, to block my number, and I plan to disguise myself whenever I leave the condo."

Barry listened, and then snorted. "A disguise. You're going to teach a flute lesson to someone who knows you well in a disguise. What sort of impression is that going to make?"

I wasn't that stupid. "I'll take off the glasses and the scarf before I go in. I'll just have to make it between the bus stop and the front door. Red'll never see a thing. He'll think the hair color and cut's some female thing."

"Emily, I can't stop you from doing whatever you decide to do, but please be aware that I feel you have betrayed both my trust and your own good sense." His voice chilled the air enough to turn antifreeze solid, and our connection abruptly cut off. He'd ended the call.

What? He wanted me to sit, quietly reading books, until Lt. Gordon decided the time was ripe to haul me off to jail for the rest of my life? Let Olive's killer go free? I don't think so.

Without thinking, I took refuge where I always did, in practice, angrily running through scales. As I calmed down, I realized

I'd forgotten about the neighbors. Well, too late now. Either they'd turn me in or, if I lucked out, they weren't at home. Since the flute wasn't that loud and the damage, if there was any, had already been done, I decided to keep playing, albeit sotto voce.

My mood became sorrowful and guilty. Feeling the need to switch to Bach, I dug into the pieces of music KC had brought me, searching for the "Unaccompanied Flute Sonatas."

I mournfully started the A minor, feeling caught between a rock and a hard place. Barry'd been so kind to me. I'd like to respect his wishes, but what choice did I have? I wanted Red to explain some things. I didn't think of him as a violent man, but his behavior to Olive said otherwise. I couldn't remove him from suspicion unless I visited him, asked questions, and received suitable answers. How else could I find out if he'd killed Olive?

After about ten minutes of Bach, my mood shifted enough to phone Barry again. "Barry, I—"

"Em, I'm sorry." He interrupted me. "I shouldn't be surprised you're looking for Olive's killer. I guess I didn't expect you'd put yourself at risk. I know you have to do what you feel you have to do. Please, though, for goodness sake, be careful."

After a short conversation, I had no appetite for dinner. Instead of eating, I spread out my sleeping bag in the dusky twilight feeling forgiven, but squelched. I wasn't concerned for myself. After all, my alternative was spending my life in jail. But if the police caught me, I might very well ruin Barry's career and put him in prison. That was the last thing I wanted to do. I couldn't give up now, though, Barry or no Barry. The stakes were too high. For his sake, in an effort to protect him, I resolved not to call him again. I didn't want him found guilty of aiding and abetting a fugitive.

My world, which had shrunk so fast, had become smaller yet.

THIRTY

I ANXIOUSLY AWAITED KC'S CALL. First AND most important, I wanted reassurance she was all right. Assuming the date between her and the Board member, Curtis Strange, had gone well, I also wanted to know what she had learned from him. Unable to wait for her to call me, I phoned on the burner.

"Sorry, Em. I'm just getting up." Sleep deepened and slowed her voice.

In response to my question, she said, "Curtis and I had a late night. We went to the O'Neil Gallery and dawdled over a late dinner."

I heard the scritch of sheets and blanket.

She continued. "I didn't have a chance to bring up the subject of Olive casually 'til the end of dinner. When I finally mentioned the police hadn't arrested anyone for her murder, Curtis grunted and said, 'She deserved what she got.'" KC spluttered. "I asked why anyone would deserve murder, but he didn't answer me and then changed the subject. Sorry."

"Sorry? That's the one of the best leads we have so far. Are you seeing him again?"

"Yeah." KC sounded disgusted. "He's going to be out of town the next few days, but I'm seeing him Monday, the twenty-fourth."

I did the math. Five days.

After a moment's silence she said, "I hope this is worth it, because I don't want to see him again." KC's voice elevated. "It's not enough to go to galleries or to eat at nice places. I don't like this guy. There's just, I don't know, something about him. He's a jerk. It's hard to force myself to keep seeing him without a paycheck."

I already felt guilty. Now I felt heat rise in my face. "How about we agree that if you don't find out anything concrete on your next..." I didn't want to say "date," knowing how KC felt, so I said, "... appointment, we'll find some other way."

She cheered up at that, and we said our goodbyes.

I couldn't predict whether the upcoming lesson with Red might expose me to danger. My good sense urged me to protect myself, so I packed one of the kitchen knives KC had brought into my purse, then boarded the bus. Red made an abundant living as some kind of classified high-tech computer guru, set his own hours, and lived in a contemporary two-story frame house right on the bus line, so surrounded by evergreens it couldn't be seen from the street, which couldn't have been more than twenty feet away.

Red smiled enthusiastically and gestured me inside. "Hi, Emily. It's nice we didn't have to miss our lesson." He nodded toward my hair and asked, "New look?"

I shrugged. "Time for a change."

He'd brewed coffee and put out cookies and Danishes. At my house, students get water, and then only if they ask for it. I'd never stay on schedule if I provided this kind of feast.

As we put our flutes together, I said conversationally, "I guess you've heard about Olive."

Red didn't so much as twitch. "Yeah. I went to the concert last Saturday. Terrible thing, isn't it?"

I stretched the truth a little. "She happened to be one of my closest friends. You knew her, too, I guess."

His eyes narrowed and he spoke more slowly. "Not very well."

"She made me laugh." It had been true, for at least a while.

Red made no comment and started blowing long tones, making it tough to continue the conversation.

I went for shock value. "She told me you two were dating."

Red put his flute in his lap. "Look, Emily, we went out once. That's all."

"Really? I thought she mentioned something about you helping her with some bookshelves."

Slowly, he responded, "Well, yeah, I did that, too. But those were the only two times I saw her." He picked up his flute, indicating the subject was closed, for him.

I ignored the hint. "Didn't you like her?" You had to hand it to the guy. He hadn't told a lie yet.

Red slammed his flute into his lap, more roughly than his flute teacher liked. "Geez. What are you, the cops? I saw her twice, okay? We didn't enjoy each other. Why else would I only see her twice? What do you want from me, anyway?"

"The truth is, Red, she told me all the details." That wasn't a lie. He didn't need to know it had been posthumously, in her journal.

Red held his breath, and his fair skin began to turn the color that had given him his nickname. After a moment, he spoke again, very calmly. "Tell it to the cops."

His answer surprised me. He didn't sound worried.

"I didn't want to waste their time, or yours. We know each other pretty well. I didn't want to make trouble for you."

Under complete control now Red said, "You couldn't make trouble for me unless I'd done something wrong."

"I'd call threatening Olive with a screwdriver wrong."

I'd been hoping to startle a reaction from him, but Red just laughed. "It may have been wrong, but it sure satisfied me." He smiled at the memory.

This wasn't the response I expected. "Satisfied you?" I sounded puzzled, even to myself.

"She richly deserved it."

"What does one do to deserve being threatened with a screwdriver?" I couldn't imagine what his answer would be.

He looked sideways at me. "I thought she told you all about it?"

"According to her, she made a couple comments and you came after her like a madman."

Red chuckled. "I did lose it. It's kind of funny, now."

"I can see that," I said dryly.

"It's just that she used the same words as my ex-wife." He smiled. "That pushed my buttons."

I raised my eyebrows in a question.

"You have to understand," he began, with the air of a man with a long story to tell. "She asked me to help her with these bookshelves. I was glad to. But the whole thing was a fiasco. First, she didn't have the right tools, so I had to go to the hardware store to buy a Phillips head screwdriver, if you can believe it. Then she hung over my shoulder and picked away at me for two hours. 'Is that tight enough? Isn't that backward? Why'd you do it that way?' Stuff like that. When I finally put it together, despite her interference, she found this minuscule scratch in the wood and ordered me to take it all apart and turn the scratched board to the inside. That would have been okay, but then she said, 'Can't you do anything right?'" He laughed again, a real belly laugh this time.

Was I being dense, or was this not particularly funny? "I don't understand."

He wiped his eyes and took a breath. "You don't know how many times my ex said that to me. Olive hit me where I live. I threw the box of screws down and grabbed the flathead screwdriver. She backed away. I followed. She turned and ran. I chased her with the screwdriver, yelling, 'You bitch! I'll teach you to talk to me that way.' It wasn't funny at the time, but I wouldn't have hurt her, probably couldn't have even if I'd wanted to. A screwdriver, after all, and a small one at that, is not a vicious weapon." He smiled. "You should have seen the look on her face. She ended up locking herself in the bedroom. I gave her a good scare, which she richly deserved."

I guessed I appreciated his laughter. A mental picture of Olive running, hair flying, from a wild-eyed madman armed with a screwdriver flitted by on my mental screen. And, I had to admit, few of her acquaintances remembered Olive with this much joy. I didn't agree she deserved to be so frightened, though.

When he had laughed himself out, Red wiped his eyes again. "'Course, I don't suppose I'd be laughing unless I had proof I didn't kill her."

"You can prove you didn't do it?" I listened carefully.

"Yeah. Cops have already been here. I guess her neighbor told 'em I'd visited her, and she'd noted our date on her calendar. When they asked my whereabouts on the day of the murder, I checked my calendar. I'd been in Boise on a business trip. Had all my receipts, all with times and dates stamped on them, and my signature to prove I was there, six hundred miles away."

Relief replaced my nerves. The kitchen knife I'd brought for protection would stay in my purse. And I could cross one name off my mental list of suspects.

Red and I finished the lesson in good spirits and feasted on coffee and Danishes. I came away feeling a strange sense of camaraderie, as well as a conviction Red had an extremely odd sense of humor. But we'd built a bond together. I don't suppose either one of us would call it a conventional good time, though.

My worries rekindled on the bus ride home. What if I saw a cop? Hoping I looked inconspicuous, I hid behind a book I didn't read. Fortunately, the trip proved uneventful. I walked through the door of the condo and collapsed into the nearest chair, relieved and safe, for the moment.

THIRTY-ONE

THURSDAY, FEBRUARY 20, 2010, 8:30 AM

I'D SPENT THE EVENING THINKING ABOUT VINCE. I wanted to find out more about him but had been nervous riding the bus to and from Red's. I didn't want to go out again unless I had to. This morning, I considered a plan that didn't involve leaving the building.

The first step was obvious. I phoned KC. "I'm sorry to bother you, but I need help, once again."

"Don't worry about it. I told you, I appreciate staying here, and I appreciate the flute lessons. What can I do for you?"

"I can't use my phone, the burner phone doesn't access the internet, and the condo doesn't have a computer. Can you check the listings for a Vince Mallone? David, Olive's neighbor, said she dated Vince, but she didn't tell me a thing about it."

"Sure." A longish pause followed while KC looked up the information on her phone. "There are two in Monroe."

Fortunately, I kept a pencil in my satchel so I'd always have one in rehearsals. I used it to jot down the numbers she gave me.

Using star sixty-seven and my burner phone, I called the first number.

A woman answered. "Hello?" She sounded like my great-aunt Violet. I pictured her with white hair, a pronounced stoop, and a cane. Vince's mother, perhaps?

"May I speak to Vince Mallone, please?"

"I'm sorry, dear. He's at the VA. He usually plays Bingo on Thursday mornings. Can I give him a message for you?"

"That's okay. I'll call back later."

"I'd be glad to take a message."

"I'll just try back. Thank you." I hung up before things got awkward.

I tried the other number. A sleepy-sounding male answered on the fourth ring.

"May I speak to Vince Mallone, please?"

"Speaking."

I wanted to see him in person, observe his body language, so I could use all my senses to help me gather information. I thought fast. "This is Meg with Leonard and Leonard." They were a large legal firm in town. "I'm phoning friends of Olive Patterson in connection with her will."

"Yes?" He sounded cautious.

"Can you give me your address? I want to send you a copy."

"Two oh four Glendale Avenue, apartment 2B. But there must be some mistake. I wasn't close to Olive. I hardly knew her."

"It's routine."

"But—"

I hung up before he asked any more questions.

Despite my reluctance, I had to leave the condo if I wanted to meet Vince. Figuring procrastinating would only make my fears worse, I donned the "successful businesswoman" costume. Not forgetting my book, sunglasses, and scarf, I checked for the kitchen knife in case I had to defend myself and walked to the bus stop. After two buses and a hike of nearly a mile, I finally arrived at Vince's, bedraggled but curious.

He lived in a neighborhood of apartments that had seen better days. His building, 204, sported two wilted sycamores at opposite ends of a two-story brown frame structure. Dog feces littered the parking lot. A rickety handrail, its paint peeling, ran along the second floor and protected the outside of the doors and a walkway. Names of the residents were on rusty-looking mailboxes in front of the building. "Mallone" appeared on 2B. I looked up. The second apartment on the second floor. A stained-glass woodpecker hung in the window, shattered, like it had been struck by a hammer.

I climbed the stairs. Knowing this man could be a murderer, I took my knife out of my purse and tucked it into a pocket. Keeping my hand in my pocket, I knocked.

"Just a minute."

An inoffensive-looking sandy-haired man in a plaid flannel shirt and khaki slacks opened the door. I used the direct approach.

"Are you Vince Mallone?"

At his affirmative nod, I said, "Hi. I need to ask some questions about Olive Patterson. May I come in?"

"Again? Does this have anything to do with the will?" He must be thinking about my recent phone call and didn't hesitate to step aside and admit me. I entered a living room covered in olive green shag carpet beginning to shed, and sporting a Formica wood-grain coffee table, and two mismatched Early American-style rockers.

He didn't wait for me to answer his question. "Can I get you something? Water? Tea? I'm sorry. I don't drink coffee."

"Thanks. Water's fine." I wanted a few minutes to look around, so I had to ask for something. I would have preferred tea, but it didn't look like Vince had a lot of money to spare, so I asked for water to avoid depleting his supplies. Tea might be his only luxury.

He left the room via a doorway at the back left. The room felt temporary, like no one had put any effort into making it pleasant. Minimally furnished, no decoration relieved the stark white of the walls, and the two clashing rockers, one plaid, one floral, were the room's only seating. The coffee table offered a flat surface, but nothing provided comfort or interest—no magazines, no computer, no pillows.

Vince returned carrying water in two jelly glasses. He handed me one, then took the second and parked himself in a rocker. I sat in the other.

"Thanks for being good enough to talk to me," I said.

He hadn't asked me a single question, except for the rhetorical one at the door. "No problem. I'm getting used to talking to people about Olive."

"Oh?"

"The police have been here, and, of course, I talked to my therapist about her, too."

I wondered briefly how Lt. Gordon had found Vince's name and number, then remembered he had Olive's phone and computer. I did a mental double-take as the word "therapist" registered on my consciousness. "Your therapist?"

"Well, yeah. I'm trying to get my life back in order after the divorce and the bankruptcy. I'd tried to find some female companionship for the first time. My therapist applauded me for having the courage to go to the dating site and go out with Olive. The date was unsuccessful enough, though, that when I didn't have any particular motivation to try again, my therapist worried."

I remembered the journal's account of how Olive had left Vince waiting while she spent an hour talking to Gardiner. I'd been amused when I read it. Now I felt sorry for this poor man, gentle and innocuous. I knew about post-divorce vulnerability and the fear of being abandoned again.

I gave him my most sympathetic "Unsuccessful?"

"I told the detective all about it."

I tried to be vague. "I just have to corroborate a few facts." I wanted to hear the story from him, but the account he gave me agreed exactly with what Olive had written, except for the end.

"I didn't know what to do. We'd gone to this chamber music concert. Who listens to this stuff, anyway? She goes in to see this other guy. What was his name? Something strange. Gardiner. That was it. Anyway, they disappear into this tiny little room with one chair and no exits. Then Olive shuts the door. I waited for almost an hour. Well, you know, obviously she didn't want to be with me. At first I felt funny leaving her with no car, but, after that long, I decided her transportation wasn't my problem. I left."

He'd put himself out there and Olive had treated him thoughtlessly, as she did so many others. He shouldn't suffer for it, so I gave him my support. What could it hurt? "How rude, to say the least. Did you call? Try to find out what happened?"

His gaze didn't meet mine as he looked at his shoe and used

it to roll an imaginary something. "Nope. I don't pester women. I know when I'm not wanted."

I wasn't sure what to do with that, so I changed the subject. "You must be wondering why I'm here." Really, his lack of curiosity was unnatural. He hadn't even asked my name.

"When you didn't mention the will, I just assumed it had something to do with the investigation."

"You're right about that." If he didn't care to ask any more, I wouldn't volunteer information. "If you could confirm your alibi for the day Olive died."

"I told the first detective I'd been at the shop until late. It's open 'til nine."

Sounded like he assumed I worked for the police. Well, let him. That made my questions easier.

"He promised to check with the late customers. I gave him the receipts."

It sounded like Lt. Gordon might actually have pursued some different leads, at least before he focused on me. "I didn't realize. We haven't talked recently." I congratulated myself on a true statement. "I'll ask him about it."

"If he doesn't have them, I don't have copies. I gave him the originals. He said he'd return them." For the first time, his voice showed some sign of concern.

"I'm sure it's okay. The lieutenant and I crossed wires." Time to make my exit before I annoyed him enough that he called Lt. Gordon. "Thanks so much for talking to me."

THIRTY-TWO

FRIDAY, FEBRUARY 21, 2010, 10:30 AM

MY LIST OF POSSIBILITIES HAD SHRUNK. After an absent-minded dinner of cold leftovers and a night spent tossing and turning on the hard floor in my sleeping bag, I'd concluded one suspect had unlimited motive. Gardiner. Furthermore, his so-called "alibi" explained nothing. He might have left his studio by the side door at any time during a three-hour period and murdered Olive; time to push him. I wanted to hear his explanation, or lack thereof.

I waited until 10:30, when I figured he'd be up, checked for my knife, then headed straight to his place. No reason to phone ahead. I already knew he wouldn't want to see me.

Gardiner answered the doorbell's chimes as he had before, in bathrobe clad, unshaven splendor, coffee cup in hand. Didn't the man ever dress? This time, though, Leanne joined him, also bathrobe clad. Did I know how to make myself welcome, or what?

"What do you want?" A surly greeting if I ever heard one.

Leanne approached from behind him and began lovingly rubbing his back. "Emily. What a surprise." She sounded sleepy and friendly.

"Can I come in?" This wasn't something I wanted to discuss at the door.

"No." Gardiner said at the same time Leanne said, "Of course."

I decided to listen to Leanne and pushed my way past Gardiner, who scowled at Leanne.

I led the way to the living room and seated myself, without invitation, in the leather chair. "I want to talk to you about Olive."

Leanne frowned. "What do you mean, disturbing us with something like that? Haven't we been through enough with the cops? Why don't you just leave, and take that fakey blonde dye job with you?"

She'd insulted my hair and offended my womanly vanity. I ignored her. I had a purpose, and understood I'd come at a very bad time. "I'll leave as soon as I can, Leanne."

Gardiner apparently didn't have any qualms about unnecessary nastiness. "I'll handle this. Go find something to do, Leanne," he said, dismissing her. I wanted to smack him on behalf of women everywhere, but I managed to restrain myself. Gardiner's chauvinism only affected Leanne, after all. She left immediately, and I wondered again why a beautiful, talented, intelligent woman puts up with a man like Gardiner.

As soon as she left, he advanced toward me and leaned one of his hands on each arm of my chair, effectively trapping me. "I thought I told you I wasn't interested in talking about Olive."

"You did, but—"

"I'm. Not. Interested." He emphasized his words by lunging suddenly closer.

Instead of giving him the satisfaction of scaring me, I leaned toward him, so we were nose to nose.

"Unfortunately, Gardiner, your desires are unimportant to me now. I want to know what you were doing when Olive was killed."

He reared back, and the pause that followed lengthened. I worried he might not answer.

I leaned farther forward. "She looked for you, you know, before she was killed. Did she find you?"

"Damn you, Emily!" He whirled away from my chair, falling into the couch and jamming his fist into its arm. His eyes narrowed and he leaned forward, toward me, hands between his knees. "I can't be responsible for what she did. I was in my studio, reorganizing my music library."

"Prove it to me, and I'll leave you alone."

"Leanne can vouch for me." He smiled tightly. "She knows."

"Did she help you?" I already knew she hadn't. "Should I ask her?"

"She didn't help, but she saw me go in the studio. She knows I was there." His gaze moved to the door she had disappeared through.

"And *I* know the studio has a side door."

At that, the bluff and bluster went out of him. He said quietly, "Emily, you're too nosy for your own good."

I let him stew a minute.

"Don't you think that's the first thing the police saw?" he whined.

"I haven't any particular reason to trust the police investigation." A tactful understatement.

"Well, I explained it all to them, and I *don't* have to explain it to you."

True. I decided to try charm. "I know, but can't you help me out? I didn't kill Olive, but they're determined to throw me in jail."

"If I didn't think half the orchestra'd know all about it within fifteen minutes of telling you, I'd explain. But I'm tired of everybody knowing my business. How do you think it feels knowing people are talking about you? And not even bothering to get the facts straight?"

Considering I'd been a recent target of the orchestra grapevine, I sympathized. "Believe me, I know how it feels, and whatever you tell me will stay right here."

He looked at me silently.

"Unless it's illegal."

Gardiner stared at me for what seemed a long time.

I didn't move.

At last he said decisively, "All right. Maybe that'll be the end of it, at last." He closed his eyes. "I went to my ex-wife's."

I was amazed. Big bad Gardiner afraid to admit he'd visited his ex?

As if he'd read my thoughts, he explained. "I didn't want Leanne to know. She's the best thing that's ever happened to me, and she doesn't like Susie."

Wait a minute. "Who's Susie? I thought Clara was your ex."

"She is. Susie was my first wife."

I hadn't known Gardiner married before Clara. Susie, huh? Live and learn.

Gardiner shifted on the couch. "I'd had a fight with Leanne about Olive. I wanted Leanne to move in, but she refused. She said Olive would be pestering us constantly. Susie knows me better than anybody alive. I wanted to work it out with Leanne. She's good for me. I thought Susie could help me figure out how to smooth it over. She always did love telling me what to do. Sure enough, she had an answer."

To risk a cliché, I was speechless. Gardiner showed all the tender feelings one might hope for in a human being. Would wonders never cease?

"Susie told me to get a restraining order. A simple solution to a problem I hadn't seen a way to solve. I called Olive and let her know what I planned. She cried and screamed and, of course, I hung up on her."

Was that the subject of Olive's final text? "In trouble. WRU? CMB!" Probably. I regretted my arrogant judgments about Gardiner. As Mom always said, "It just goes to prove you can't judge a book by its pictures."

"Gardiner, I'm so sorry. I hope I haven't made trouble between you and Leanne. I just wanted to solve this so I can get on with my life."

But, as Mom also taught me, a leopard never changed his coat.

"Just don't bother me again," Gardiner replied. "And I think Lieutenant Gordon should know you've been here. I have to protect myself."

Before he touched the phone, I was out the door and halfway to the condo.

THIRTY-THREE

FRIDAY, FEBRUARY 21, 2010, 5:30 PM

THE BURNER PHONE NOTIFIED ME I had a text as I walked in the door of the condo. KC.

"*Barry advises TUI. CMB!*"

I plopped in a camping chair and phoned. "KC, thanks for the text, but you know I can't turn myself—"

"Gardiner told the cops you're home. Lieutenant Gordon's lost his patience. In addition to the warrant, he's put out an APB. You're officially a fugitive. They're making an all-out effort to find you. And they know you have blonde hair."

"Damn Gardiner. I had no way to know he'd—"

"Em, Barry wanted me to advise you to turn yourself in."

"I can't."

"I know. Don't shoot the messenger."

"I have to—"

"Listen. Now they know you're in town. You haven't shown here, at your house, and you haven't been in touch with me, as far as they know. You're looking guiltier and guiltier." KC took a breath.

"But—"

"And Barry had some new information."

"New information?" I curled up in a cold, bare corner of the room and tensed. I'd told the truth. Why didn't the police believe me? I had to think my way through.

"Yeah." She paused. "Golden's hair matches the hair found at the murder scene . . ."

"Golden's been there a thousand times . . "

"*And* they found your prints on Olive's bassoon. Not on the section that was used as a weapon, the boot. That was wiped clean. On the bocal."

"On her bocal? My prints?"

One of the five parts of the bassoon, the bocal connects the reed to the body of the instrument. A bassoon is nothing without it, but the bocal is thin and small, and could never be used as a weapon. Bassoonists care for them religiously. That care includes cleaning and polishing after every use. Bassoonists might experiment with each others' bocals in the eternal effort to find a better one, but outsiders don't handle them.

"That's not possible. I would never have touched Olive's bocal for fear of profaning a sacred object. And if I *had* touched it, the prints'd be gone because she would have wiped them off right away."

"Except the last time."

We were both silent. "KC, it can't be. There must be some mistake."

Then I remembered. "Wait. I did touch Olive's bocal. Just once. After the last performance of the last concert series she played. She wanted to buy a new bocal and asked Gardiner to go out into the now-empty house and listen. See if it improved on the old one or not. Gardiner responded 'I have better things to do. Use your own good sense . . . if you have any.' Olive shook her head. If she sounded better, the entire orchestra would be a little better. Forget the relationship. As her section leader, Gardiner should have been interested. And he should have been kind—if *he* knew how. Anyway, I overheard his comment, felt outraged, and stepped in on behalf of the orchestra and general decency. 'I'll listen.' It took about twenty minutes. Olive played various passages on both of her old bocals and I went into the auditorium and compared them to the new one. When I returned to the stage, I gave her my feedback. A stage-hand entered when we were almost done and requested, as politely as possible, that we leave the stage so he and his crew could finish tearing down the setup and go home. 'I'll go when I'm ready,' Olive told the stagehand. The color drained from her face and her eyes watered. I thought at the time that she must have felt attacked by everyone in every direction. Anyway, she dropped a bocal. I picked it up and handed it to her. After examining it for damage, she put it in the case with the rest, and I don't remember her wiping it off or polishing it. That must have been it."

"Well, the cops don't believe it has an innocent explanation," KC said.

"I suppose they're seeing it as another piece of evidence against me."

"It'll be okay." She sounded so convinced. "I'll tell Barry and—"

"No! KC, you can't. If the cops know Barry's in communication with me, even indirectly, he'll be in big trouble."

"But if he doesn't tell them you'll—"

"He can't. It's just one more reason for me to find the real killer—fast—okay? Please?"

She finally agreed, and we hung up.

I tried to calm down, but my head felt like it was tearing in two. I had a good cry, but it only made the headache worse. In the end, sleep took me away from it all.

THIRTY-FOUR

FRIDAY, FEBRUARY 21, 2010, 7:40 PM

I WOKE IN THE DARK. Was it a sound that roused me, or the crick in my neck from sleeping in the camping chair KC had brought? I moved to my satchel, took an aspirin from my purse, and went to the kitchen to get a glass of water. I looked out the window. Snow fell. As I watched, two police cars drove into the parking lot from different directions. They must have learned about the condo.

Immediately, I ditched the glass, crouched below window level, and ran for the bedroom. My suitcase would slow me down, so I left it. Cramming my sunglasses and scarf into the satchel that held my purse and flute, I threw on my coat. The bedroom window connected to the fire escape and back alley. I sprinted to it and fled down the metal stairs, satchel on my shoulder, making so much sound with each footstep, the cops couldn't help but know my position.

As I reached the first floor, I saw a dark silhouette at the other end of the building and across the parking lot.

A male shouted, "Hey! There's somebody there. Stop!"

I knew nothing said "guilty" more than running. I also knew that *not* running ensured my arrest. Now I, a formerly law-abiding citizen, ran. I ran down the remaining steps and tried to stay in tire tracks to avoid leaving footprints in the snow, not stopping to look over my shoulder. Terror moved my feet, and I ran as fast as I ever had. Faster, faster, faster.

Dashing down the dark narrow alley, I slipped and fell in my hurry. Heart pounding, conscious of the police behind me, I scrambled to my feet. I didn't see them. My fall had left a form-less blotch in the snow. Beside it, a dark shed in an unfenced yard sheltered the alley. The ground beside it on one side had stayed mostly dry. I'd been lucky so far, but I couldn't outrun my pursuers for much longer. I picked myself up, along with my satchel, and hid behind the structure.

I heard footsteps rush past a few moments later and held my breath.

They ran across the street.

Scared into immobility, I didn't move.

A few minutes later, I heard the footsteps return, walking now, and an electronic crackle.

A male voice said, "I lost her. I'll be back in a few minutes. Let the lieutenant know."

When I no longer heard anything, I called KC from my hiding place. "It's me, Emily," I whispered.

"I've been worried. The lieutenant's been asking questions. Nothing I couldn't handle."

I filled her in on what had happened and told her that the police were nearby. "I have to get out of here and find answers, but I don't have a car or transportation. I hoped you'd help me escape. I don't want to risk it if you think you'll be followed, though."

"Don't worry about me. I'll shake the cops."

I believed her. I was beginning to believe she could outsmart almost anybody.

"Okay. Where should we meet?" I answered my own question. "How about the convenience store at Third and Magnolia?"

She didn't hesitate for a second. "I'll be there."

Now completely paranoid I begged, "Please. Make sure you're not followed."

"No worries."

"And KC?" I shared my gratitude quickly. "Thanks."

"No problem. See you in ten minutes."

Just two more blocks down the alley to the convenience store. I approached it from behind.

Now I had to decide. Was it riskier to wait for KC in the parking lot or the convenience store? The parking lot was dark, and I felt invisible there, but who knows what might happen in the shadows? On top of that, the snow was wet and cold. The convenience store, on the other hand, was safe and warm and well-lit, but probably had security cameras. I chose to wait in the shadows of the parking lot.

It turned out to be a good decision. I spent anxious minutes constantly looking over my shoulder and trying to shrink into the darkness, but I wasn't seen. When KC finally showed up, I threw my stuff in the car and climbed in. "You weren't followed?" This kind of worry was totally new to me.

"I was, but I lost him at the light on Stanford."

Confident she had put my fears to rest KC asked, "Okay, Boss. Where to?" in imitation of . . . I couldn't put my finger on it, but it involved the mob and a classic movie I'd seen long ago.

I hadn't thought that far ahead. "Good question. If I can't go home, to the condo, my mother's, or to any of my friends, I guess that leaves a motel."

"Which one?" KC had a knack for getting to the heart of a problem.

"I don't know. It can't be anything very expensive." I had, after all, only a musician's budget, with a limited amount of cash on me, and no usable credit card.

"I'm thinking the most important thing is that it's close to where you want to go. The less you're out, the better, you know?"

Sounded reasonable to me. "There's a place that's centrally located. The Gold Hill Motor Inn. There's no pool or anything. How expensive can it be?"

I found out how expensive in short order. It would take all my cash and more. For the price they charged for two nights, I could buy a couple months' worth of utilities at my place.

Fortunately, KC had thought ahead. She'd brought enough cash with her to pay in advance. Her cash supply seemed endless. No wonder the salaries of nine-to-five jobs dismayed her.

MY MOTEL ROOM OPENED DIRECTLY TO the parking lot, and I had a clear view of the surrounding buildings. Clean, but no frills. Just a double bed with a worn gold spread, a TV, an alarm clock, a round Formica wood-grain table, and two plastic-covered overstuffed chairs. To complete the décor, a print of Degas-like gold-clad ballerinas hung over the bed. I wouldn't be here long enough for them to grate on my nerves, I hoped.

KC assumed the police were looking for her car, so she wished me luck, gave me all the cash she had with her, and left. I used the motel phone to order a pizza and ate it alone. I felt paranoid, hunted, and sorry for myself. What I wouldn't have given for the comfort of Golden's wet kisses, and, yes, Barry's bear hugs.

Mom always assured me things would look better in the morning. As I fell asleep, exhausted and happy to be in a bed, I hoped that for once she hadn't gotten it wrong.

THIRTY-FIVE

SATURDAY, FEBRUARY 22, 2010, 8:30 AM

I WOKE IN THE MORNING WITH A HEADACHE, still feeling sorry for myself. Headache or no, my thoughts turned immediately to Olive's death. Since I didn't believe Janet or Billie were murderesses, I thought next of Craig Neil, the talented freelancer who played three instruments. I didn't know him well, but we'd exchanged friendly "hello"s a few times. I called KC again. She looked him up on her phone and gave me the number.

Praying Craig hadn't heard the police were looking for me—my visit to Gardiner had only been yesterday evening, after all—I called on the burner phone. "Craig?"

"Yes?"

"This is Emily Wilson, the flutist."

"Oh, hi, Emily."

"I wondered if I could come talk to you. About the musical." I figured I'd hang up if he showed any sign of knowing I was a fugitive.

"Well, sure. You're welcome to come, but I won't have much time."

Whew. No awkwardness or mention of turning me in. I assumed that meant he hadn't heard about the police pursuit and I'd be safe questioning him.

"I'm going out at ten fifteen and I'll be gone all day. Can you come right away?"

"Sure. I'll be right there."

I didn't waste any time. As soon as we hung up, I put on the undies I had washed the night before and the sweater and heavy wool pants I had worn yesterday. I made them as presentable as possible, put on my coat, then walked the two blocks to Craig's house, enjoying the warm morning sunshine and listening to the drip, drip, drip of last night's snow melting.

I arrived at about 8:45. Craig lived in a neighborhood of small houses, close together, but with deep backyards. His place was a tiny bungalow with an attached greenhouse added to the back of the house. He didn't answer the bell, so I went around to the greenhouse and banged on the door. Craig was watering plants.

Even though it was winter, he wore shorts and a tank top with bare feet. "Ooh! Nice look. It brings out your eyes."

I'd forgotten the new hair color and self-consciously ran my hands down my head. "Thanks."

"I have a few plants to water before I'm done. I didn't think you'd be here so soon." He paused momentarily while he turned down the water. "Why don't you wait in the living room. I'll be right along." He gestured at a door which connected to a small kitchen.

On the other side of the kitchen was the living room, where I parked myself in a purple bean bag. Casual, brightly colored furniture pleased the eye. Yellow walls were covered with pictures—all prints of abstracts or snapshots of, I assumed, friends and family. I approved of the colors. Purple and yellow predominated. Someone with taste but not much money had decorated. It was playful, and I liked it.

Craig didn't keep me waiting long. I'd always thought him good-looking. In shorts he was downright striking. He must have been around thirty-eight, at least six feet tall, with muscular, tan legs and a flat stomach. He held a plate he must have picked up on his way through the kitchen. "I'm sorry to be such a poor host. Would you like a cinnamon roll and coffee?"

I didn't want to spend precious time eating. "Oh, I'm fine. I just finished breakfast, but please, go ahead if you want."

Craig took a roll, put the plate on the coffee table, then sat in a recliner across from my bean bag. "You said over the phone you had some questions about the musical. I was a little puzzled, because *Les Mis* only has one flute part, and you're playing it. I'll do the sax and oboe parts." *Les Mis* was the upcoming musical, so, logically, he thought that was the subject of my visit.

"Actually, I wanted to talk about *Cats.*"

Craig looked puzzled, as well he should. The musical had ended, and I hadn't been in the orchestra.

"The police have paid a lot of attention to me because I don't have an alibi for the time of Olive Patterson's murder." I didn't mention the rest of their case. "I'm a little freaked, so I'm trying to fill in any gaps they might have missed. I understand Olive played *Cats* with you and was less than kind."

"I don't understand the connection but, yeah, that's true enough." Craig leaned back, completely relaxed.

"Her behavior must have made you mad."

"I don't pay much attention to people who have a problem with me. It says more about them than me." He took a bite of his roll.

"Well, that's a very mature way to look at it. Kind of unusual." Sounded like the product of years of therapy to me.

Craig shifted in his chair. "I'm used to it. I came out twenty-one years ago and people have had all kinds of reactions. Their feelings are theirs, not mine."

The news took me by surprise. I hadn't known and felt a little disappointed. And naïve. "So, you think Olive was homophobic and that's why she needled you?" I hadn't seen any sign of gay bashing in Olive, but I hadn't looked, either.

"Don't know. Don't care. Other people think what they like. Mostly people don't think about me at all. All that matters to me is I can look myself in the mirror. I do my best in performances or in day-to-day situations. That's all that's important to me and all I can do. Olive and her kind aren't important. I don't lower myself to their level."

I only hoped he didn't include me in "her kind," whatever that meant. It didn't sound like a compliment. "I understand that after *Cats,* several people requested Joe Burke not hire Olive again. Do you know why he ignored them and hired her anyway?" I hoped for confirmation of the blackmail theory.

"Again, don't know, don't care. Who Joe hires is his business. I'm not going to make his job harder. I'm just glad to work."

"Well, you don't sound worried. You must have an alibi."

"I didn't kill her. That's why I'm not worried." Craig took another bite of cinnamon roll.

"Good reasoning. I didn't murder her either, but the police are building a case against me anyway."

Craig stood and walked to a yellow painted desk made of crates. "Okay, okay. I can understand you're concerned. You must be looking for suspects. I guess I would be, too. I'm sorry to disappoint you, but I didn't kill Olive. I don't remember my schedule that day, but I must have an alibi. Sunday the second, right? What time?"

His unexpected understanding and cooperation surprised and relaxed me. Keeping in mind the time of her last text to me and when David O'Malley had found the body, I said, "Between three thirty and six."

Craig opened a drawer and lifted a cell phone. He scrolled to the calendar. "Oh, I remember. A friend of Michael's had an art exhibition that ended that day. I went with Michael to help pack up. The exhibition ended at five. We left home around four, and then helped until around six thirty. Afterward, Michael's friend took both of us to dinner."

The doorbell rang. While Craig went to answer it, I glanced at my watch. Ten o'clock.

"Michael." A man about the same height as Craig, with blonde hair and shockingly blue eyes had come to the door. The two hugged. "I'll be ready in just a few." Craig turned to me. "I have to . . ."

"I was just leaving. Thanks for talking to me."

Well, another productive but disappointing interview. Unless he murdered Olive at 3:30 and then ran home and met Michael at 4:00, I could check Craig off my list of suspects. The list had shrunk further, and I didn't like the possibilities that were left.

THIRTY-SIX

SATURDAY, FEBRUARY 22, 2010, 10:30 AM

WITH A SENSE OF URGENCY, feeling Lt. Gordon poised and ready to pounce, I reviewed my options. I began to understand that I was number one on Lt. Gordon's list of possible killers for good reasons. Only a few suspects were left—Billie, Alan, Janet, and KC's lead, Symphony Board member Curtis Strange. I welcomed other possibilities, but so far there were none. I had to prove that someone other than me had killed Olive or resign myself to a prison sentence. There had to be clues. I would find them. I let geography determine my next interview.

I called on the burner phone, once again blocking the number, ready to hang up if Janet showed any inclination to phone the cops. She unsuspectingly assured me she and the kids would love to see me and invited me over for a bagel.

Janet lived in a brick rancher that some misguided former owner had painted pink. Immense juniper hedges had grown up around the foundation over the years, and no one had yet been willing to expend the effort it would take to trim the bushes and repaint the place. Pink it remained. By the time I arrived Sherrie and Jimmy, Janet's two kids, were out in the warm sun supposedly "shoveling the walks" after last night's storm. They had been distracted by creating a snowman worthy of a Guinness Book category. Before they'd let me in, I had to help them heft the head into place.

Janet greeted me with a beaming smile and a hug, and I was amazed not to be felled by a lightning bolt for the thoughts that had brought me.

"Emily. You look gorgeous as a blonde, girlfriend."

I kept forgetting my new look. "Thanks. I wanted a change."

"You sure are a sight for sore eyes. I'm incredibly pissed at Alan, but I have to keep being Pollyanna for the kids. They're too young to understand any of this, and they keep asking where daddy is. It's about to drive me nuts." While she talked, she led me back to the kitchen, a cheery mint-green room currently cluttered with the remains of what must have been waffles, from the looks of the batter-coated waffle iron and bottle of syrup atop the counter in a brown puddle. "Thank the Lord, Mom's coming this afternoon. Otherwise they'd probably end up being abused."

"I'm sorry." I seated myself at the kitchen table. "I would've helped if I'd been in town." The vacation story seemed meaningless now, but I might as well be consistent.

Janet drew a chair up to the table and flopped into it. "No problem. The kids are my responsibility. But it's taking longer than I thought to adjust to single motherhood."

"You haven't heard from Alan?"

Janet snorted. "Alan!" Her voice was full of contempt, in case I hadn't figured out her feelings from the snort. "He's apologized all over the place, but that doesn't change things for me. It's not worth it anymore. I've had it."

"I'm sorry. You sound hurt and angry."

"Yeah, I guess I am. I didn't do anything. Why should he doubt me? Where's his trust?"

I speculated that a few lonely holidays might make Janet more open to forgiving Alan. Or this might be the best thing for her. The marriage, after all, hadn't been great before. For now, though, time to change the subject. "What's happened with Olive's murder while I've been gone? Have they arrested anybody?" I was the soul of ignorance. They should give Oscars for this kind of performance.

"No. But I thought you'd know all about it. The police've asked about you."

"Me?"

"Yeah. Your finances, and your temper and how long have I known you, and, most of all, did I know where you were?"

"What did you tell them?"

She cocked her head and rolled her eyes at me. "The truth, of course." She thought it a stupid question, apparently. "I told them that, like any musician, you're always short of cash, that you're a patient soul or you'd never have been friends with Olive, and that you'll tell me where you were when you reappear." She paused. "So, where were you?"

Keeping my story consistent, I told her I'd been at a friend's cabin, skiing, without naming the friend, and described the Kennedy's cabin.

"You better phone the cops right away. I promised Lieutenant Gordon I'd let him know if I heard from you, so I'd better call him, too."

Now what? "It's okay, Janet. Don't bother. I'll call as soon as I get home." I left out the fact that it would be a few days before I arrived there, at least. "Didn't they ask about anybody else?" Any use hoping Lt. Gordon had investigated other possibilities?

"Well, yeah. Gordon had the nerve to ask where I'd been. Me!"

"Don't sound so peeved. You haven't hidden your feelings about Olive."

She shook her head. "Alan moved out that day. I won't soon forget it, believe me." She crossed her arms, leaned on the table, and snorted again. "At the time Olive was killed, we were having one last set-to, apparently. The kids were there, looking on, and we were so noisy even the neighbors showed up. What a jerk! You'd think he could at least move out peaceably." She looked disgusted. "But it had a bright side. Everyone told the cops about it, so at least we're not suspects."

Great. Only two possibilities were left, and both were long shots. I had to believe Billie—sweet Billie, elderly, grandmotherly, caring Billie—was a murderess, or that Symphony Board member Curtis Strange, KC's lead, had killed Olive.

Janet chattered on, I think, because her mouth moved, but I felt too sick and dazed to know what she said.

THIRTY-SEVEN

SATURDAY, FEBRUARY 22, 2010, 1:00 PM

Back in the motel, I debated what to do. Its location was close to Craig and Janet but far from Billie, who lived in the wilds of suburbia. The easiest thing would be to call KC and have her take me to Billie's, but I knew the police were looking for me, and I didn't want her to have to dodge them, or risk involving her if I were caught.

I grew more and more nervous. It had been less than twenty-four hours since Gardiner reported my whereabouts, but Billie might have heard the cops were looking for me. I decided to call her on the burner phone. My conversation with her should tell me if she'd heard the police were searching for me. If she had, she wouldn't know where I was calling from, and I'd just hang up.

"Hi. This is Emily."

"It's so good to hear from you."

I didn't hear any hesitation, just joy. Bless her. "I'll be near you and I thought I'd drop in for a few minutes, if it's okay."

"Oh, how perfect. Joe's not here, and I'd love to see you."

"Great. I'm not sure exactly when I'll come, but it'll be within an hour or two. See you soon."

I waited by my window until I saw a bus coming, ran out, and . . . it headed south, not west. I went back to my room and waited for another bus. This time I had better luck. After riding west for about an hour, I exited at a stop fairly close to Billie's, about six blocks away.

Bright, warm sun melted the snow, and my walk should have been pleasant. Instead, it was an exercise in paranoia. I started at unexpected noises, kept my face turned from traffic, and crossed to the other side of the street to avoid fellow pedestrians. Fortunately for me, people were few and far between since the houses were widely spaced, and sidewalks often disappeared or were nonexistent. This was a driving neighborhood, not a walking neighborhood. Also, fortunately, I didn't see any police cars. With relief I arrived at Billie's.

She greeted me at the door with bare feet, wearing a sweat suit, an apron, and a smile. She gave me a hug. "I'm so glad to have company. Joe has a tennis match at his club, and I'm all alone. Let's have some lunch, and you can tell me what brings you out here."

I'd thought about this. "I'm trying that mechanic Joe recommended. My old Subaru is making funny noises. The repair shop is just about six blocks from here, so I thought I'd drop in instead of waiting in the shop." What a convincing liar I had become.

"What a wonderful idea. But you should have let me know you needed a ride. I'd be glad to pick you up."

"I didn't want to bother you. Besides, the weather's beautiful, and I can use the exercise."

As we were talking, Billie showed me back to the kitchen. "I love your hair. What made you go blonde?"

"Time for something new, I guess. It's not permanent. I can change my mind if I want to." Which I might, when Lt. Gordon found Olive's murderer.

In the kitchen, all the parts for bacon, lettuce, and tomato sandwiches were waiting. While Billie assembled the sandwiches, she brought me up to speed on Joe, her children, and the new grandbaby, who developed more each day. "And what about you? What's new since we last talked?"

"I've been kind of out of touch. I borrowed a student's cabin in the mountains for a few days and took a short skiing holiday. What's new on Olive's murder?"

"Such a terrible thing. The police have asked questions about everybody—you, me, Joe, Gardiner . . ."

"You, Billie? Why would they ask questions about you?" Such innocence.

Her face changed. "Remember those 'friends' I told you about? The ones who told me about Joe's night at Olive's? Well, apparently, they also told the police. The police actually thought I might have killed Olive."

"That's past tense. How'd you convince them you were innocent?"

Billie laughed. "Oh, you know me. I'm an unstoppable shopper. When Joe's gone, I go nuts buying stuff. Did you know the big stores keep computerized records on purchases? And, of course, they have security cameras. The police checked. I didn't have to do anything else. Now, if the police'd just pay the bills."

Billie laughed again, but I didn't join in. I couldn't.

When at last I made my excuses, she insisted on taking me to the car repair shop. The one Joe had recommended was nearby and I directed her to it. Once there, I didn't give Billie a chance to get out of her car. I went inside, as if the mechanics were done with my car, and watched until she was out of sight. Then I returned to the motel, via bus.

The situation didn't bear consideration. All my suspects had alibis. KC's lead, Curtis Strange, the Symphony Board member, had to pan out. I could see why Lieutenant Gordon believed I must be the killer. I didn't know what to do. Sick at heart, I had no more ideas, and I cried myself to sleep.

THIRTY-EIGHT

SUNDAY, FEBRUARY 23, 2010, 8:30 AM

I'D SPENT THE REST OF SATURDAY watching TV and gorging on leftover pizza and Chinese food delivered to the door by a gawky, stuttering teenage boy. Then, fully clothed, I fell asleep in a carbohydrate-induced stupor.

Now, I glanced at my watch. Eight-thirty Sunday morning. I should have been getting ready to go to church. Instead, I was hiding out in a seedy motel, in clothes I'd worn for two days, with nothing but a satchel containing my flute, music stand, and purse. Nobody but KC knew where I was. The police would find me eventually. I pulled the covers over my head and tried to pretend I dreamed it all. What else could I do?

It didn't work.

I'd rushed out of the condo so fast; I hadn't even had a chance to bring a book. I'd end up crazed if I had to watch Sunday TV. *Firing Line. Meet the Press.* Wasn't I depressed enough already? I wanted a good mystery. Something to take my mind off my troubles. The idea was irresistible. Why not? I had no other ideas about Olive's killer. I might as well enjoy the freedom I had left. A bookstore would have the perfect book. I'd check it out. Carefully. Thankfully, I'd fallen asleep in my clothes, because when I peeked out the front window to consider the possibility of leaving, a police car was pulling up to the front office.

I threw on my coat and shoes, grabbed my satchel, and walked out the door, away from the police car. Remembering KC's lesson in attitude, I told myself the cop looked for someone in hiding, a mousy musician. I needed to be saucy. Gardiner had reported my blonde hair, but I walked into the neighboring Pic-N-Run casually and confidently. Like I owned the parking lot.

It worked. Safe in the convenience store, I watched through the window as the policeman left the motel office and opened the door of number 121, my recently abandoned sanctuary, then went back to the motel's front office. I ignored the clerk's suspicious looks, grabbed a candy bar, paid quickly, and left the store.

My good fortune held. As I opened the door of the shop, a bus passed, and I only had to run half a block to catch it.

Panting and winded, I found myself fishing for the fare and heading for the end of the line, wherever that took me.

THIRTY-NINE

SUNDAY, FEBRUARY 23, 2010, 9:30 AM

Unsure what to do and desperate for news, I ignored the threat of surveillance and put the battery and SIM card back in my personal cell phone. Hopefully, the police couldn't get a concrete fix on my position because the bus was moving.

No message said, "Low battery," but I worried anyway. Praying the phone would hold out for a little while, I checked the local headlines. Just what I already knew. The police were looking for me and had put out an APB. With the phone on, I checked messages, too. Lt. Gordon had called several times, increasingly threatening. No surprise there. Chuck, the violinist scheduled to play the Friends of the Symphony luncheon with me, had also left a message.

"Hi, Emily. Just wanted to confirm the trio rehearsal Monday morning. I have it down for ten at my place. I . . . I've been confused lately, so I wanted to double check. If that's not right, phone me. The number's five five five seven eight one five."

Poor guy. He sounded lost. The separation from Celia must really be unsettling him.

I turned my cell phone off and removed the battery and SIM card. I had no new information, but something kicked around in my brain.

Rehearsal. Olive had a rehearsal—a quartet rehearsal—scheduled at four the day of her death. Had she played it? I knew Olive, and I knew the rehearsal would have been on her computer/phone calendar, which the police had confiscated. Surely, they had investigated. But if they had, I didn't know the results. I'd have to talk to her fellow quartet members.

In a moment of clarity, it all made sense. I remembered when I'd gone through Olive's music with Patricia, I'd found the Devienne quartet in the current practice pile—violin, viola, cello, and bassoon. String players plus bassoon. Olive had been planning a recital, and the quartet she planned consisted of herself and string players. And, according to her diary entry, she'd asked Chuck and Phil to play her recital. Ergo, the rehearsal must have been with Chuck and Phil and another person. They must know something.

That settled it. Both Chuck and Phil would be at the Beethoven rehearsal Monday morning. So would I. I'd go tomorrow, as planned.

But the rehearsal appeared on my calendar. What if the police were watching and waiting for me? After due consideration, I decided I didn't care. As it was, I was homeless and hopeless. If I didn't do something the police would find me eventually. If they picked me up at Chuck's, I'd go to jail—something that looked inevitable anyway. But if the police didn't find me, I'd be able to follow a new lead. Willing to take a chance, I had everything to gain and nothing to lose.

My bleak mood shifted a hundred and eighty degrees. Of course. Why hadn't I thought of it earlier? I'd been so wrapped up in my dislike of Gardiner and the fact Olive looked for him before she died, I'd forgotten about her rehearsal. There had to be answers there. Now I had a new goal, a new purpose, and a new reason to stay out of Lt. Gordon's grasp.

The bus took me to the farthest reaches of suburbia, and I spent the day swaddled in anonymous safety.

A lovely used bookstore in a strip mall—Hooked on Books— attracted me, and I spent a couple of hours browsing through ceiling-high shelves packed with every imaginable type of book. KC had been an invaluable helper, and I wanted to buy something for her as a thank-you present. But what? She read lusty romances, but I wasn't sure I wanted to encourage that. Finally, in the women's literature section, I found a selection with a gourmet cook protagonist telling a heartwarming story of women's friendships and second chances, and several recipes scattered throughout. While I searched, I found seven more books, mostly cozy mysteries for me. I couldn't carry them all, so I decided on three. I'd spent so long reading, lost in stacks of books and forgetting my situation, that I unthinkingly paid with my credit card.

Too late, I realized my locale might be traced via those purchases. Between that and my personal cell phone use, the police, if they were paying attention, had enough information to lock into my location closely. But I couldn't do anything about it now. I bought a sandwich at the mall's sub shop, then headed for the sanctuary of a nearby park. The day was warm and pleasant. I found a picnic table and read 'til dusk, when the sun went down behind the mountains and the temperature plunged. I knew that to continue to stay outside risked frostbite.

At 5:15 on Sunday afternoon where could I go? A warm place where I could relax. Stores were warm but wouldn't be a refuge. There had to be someplace in walking distance. A movie. A movie would have the advantage of being dark and private. A covered shopping mall with a twelve-theatre complex wasn't too far from here. I guessed it might be about a mile and a half away. If I walked the back streets, I'd avoid the cops, and, by the time I reached the mall, it'd be completely dark. The cold gave me an excuse to pull on the ski hat in my parka's pocket, which completely hid my face. Hoping I didn't look prepared to rob a Pic-N-Run I set off, hauling my satchel and books with me.

Unfortunately, walking the back streets in suburbia confused me. The subdivision was new and unknown to me. I kept running into dead ends or going in circles. The temperature had to be down in the teens, at least.

Cold and exhausted, I gave up on the back streets and instead strode purposefully down Central Boulevard. A police car passed in the center lane moving with the traffic. The officer didn't even slow down, let alone stop me. I could do this. Nobody'd given me a second look all day.

It was 7:15 when I arrived at the mall. The main mall doors were locked, but the theatre entrance remained open and an action-adventure film started at 7:30. Perfect. I bought a ticket and relaxed into the anonymity of darkness for two and a half glorious hours.

The theatre was the ideal hideout, having, as it did, food, darkness, restrooms, and entertainment. At the end of the show, I looked for another movie. Only one choice. Hit the streets or see a gloppy, gooey, romance. I chose the romance. Several girlfriends had invited me to see it, but I had successfully dodged their invitations thus far. Now, however, two hours of mush, and the cost of admission, seemed a small price to pay for warmth, darkness, and safety. I bought a ticket.

I watched the picture with unexpected pleasure. Somehow, it didn't strain my credibility. The hero reminded me of Barry—loving, courageous, handsome, and witty. Oh, lord. Nobody was this perfect. Cynicism came to my rescue. But again, I'd be willing to kill for one of Barry's hugs. In my current situation that might have been a poor word choice, but I craved human contact and felt sorry for myself. Would I ever see him again? Of course I would. He was my lawyer. Would I ever see him again without bars between us? That was another question entirely.

The movie over, I pushed self-pity aside and considered my options. KC had paid for another night at the motel, but I dare not go back there. The police would be waiting. I didn't have enough cash for a room at a different motel and using my credit card would only announce my whereabouts to Lt. Gordon. On a Sunday night, the best I could hope for would be an all-night restaurant. Then I remembered I'd seen one about three blocks from the mall, down Central.

A short time later, I warmed my toes amongst delicious smells. I'd figured the heck with the diet and ordered a grilled cheese sandwich—comfort food from my childhood—so I'd soon be well-fed. I allowed myself to forget my troubles and settled down to finish my book.

The restaurant wasn't as quiet at that hour as I had hoped. Why were all these people up, anyway? Didn't they know decent citizens should be home in bed? But all-night eateries were the only places in town that were open. Because of the blue laws, even bars and strip clubs were closed on a Sunday night. I resigned myself to the noise, tuned out the hubbub using powers of concentration developed in the racket of the practice rooms at college, and immersed myself in my book.

An hour or so later, I stretched, looked up, and found myself gazing directly into the eyes of a uniformed policeman being seated at the table next to me.

FORTY

MONDAY, FEBRUARY 24, 2010, 12:30 AM

IF I'D BEEN THINKING CLEARLY, I would have realized that if the cop didn't recognize me right away, he wasn't going to recognize me at all. But I wasn't thinking clearly.

I panicked.

My back turned to him, I picked up my coat. Then, feeling they were the only comfort I had left, I grabbed the books and shoved them into my satchel. I lifted the burner phone, which I'd been using to check the time, from the table. With my hands full of coat and satchel I didn't have a firm grip on the phone. It fell to the floor. Way not to attract attention. When I leaned over to pick it up, I saw that its face had cracked, and the display died. Damn. No time to worry about it now. Keeping my back to the policeman, I left the phone and hurried to the restroom.

There, I used the facilities and donned my coat, gloves, and hat. Now, as well prepared as possible, I peeked out the door and made sure the cop wasn't waiting for me. I paid the bill and fled. Instinctively, I sought darkness, heading into the residential neighborhood I'd been lost in earlier.

A stupid decision.

Only I moved at that hour. My progress was marked by motion sensor lights and howling dogs wakened from slumber. I ran from the noise, hoping for stillness, seeking the dark.

A small neighborhood park and playground adjoining an elementary school provided both. Between the swings and slide, I
found a round plastic cylinder, five feet in diameter at least, no
doubt a glorious tunnel for innumerable make-believe games. It
provided a wonderful hiding place—dry, dark, and, if not warm,
at least protected from the wind. But I didn't want to share my
shelter. If some small animal had the same idea, I'd find another
place. I checked it out, stooping and looking through the tube . . .
all clear. Grateful for the warm outfit I had donned for my visit to
Gardiner so long ago—was it only two days?—I gave thanks for my
gloves, jacket, and ski hat, and crawled into the cylinder. Using my
satchel and books as a pillow, I rolled into a fetal position. Olive
might not have deserved to die, but I surely didn't deserve this,
either. I wanted Golden. Or Barry. I succumbed to self-pity and
cried myself to sleep.

I woke, by my guess, around 7:00 the next morning. After my
initial teary nap, what little sleep I had snatched had been interrupted in an endless search for a comfortable position. Now my
nose, fingers, and toes were frozen; I felt depressed; my back was in
spasm; my head ached; the shoulder I'd been sleeping on was stiff;
my eyes were swollen and burning from crying; sand had ground
itself into my hands and clothes; I had scraped my backside exiting
from my playground shelter; I smelled bad; and I had to go to the
bathroom. Otherwise I felt fine.

More than anything, I wanted a hot, lavender-scented bubble
bath.

The restroom of a fast-food restaurant would have to do for
cleanup. If I went back to Central Boulevard, there'd be something.
But which way to go? In the dark confusion of last night, I wasn't
sure in which direction I had run.

In the end, I picked up my satchel and went in the same direction as the cars that began to exit the subdivision. Ten minutes and
three left turns later, I found myself back on Central, a fast-food
restaurant visible about two and a half blocks to the left.

With relief, I made the restroom my first stop. The lady who exited the first of two stalls gave me a strange look, and when I checked the mirror, I understood why. My face was scratched and bloody with a streak of dirt across the left cheek, my hair a tangled mess, and my clothes dirty. I felt a rip in the seat of my pants, too. At least I had my freedom, though, and I gave thanks for my playground haven.

I repaired the damages as best I could: washed my face and hands, scrubbed at the dirt on my blouse, and unsnarled my hair with the comb in my purse. It wasn't a perfect job, but I felt considerably better. Then I checked the state of my finances. I was rich. Enough money for an Eggwich, with thirty-five cents left.

FORTY-ONE

MONDAY, FEBRUARY 24, 2010, 7:45 AM

I BOUGHT THE EGGWICH and consumed it with enthusiasm, then made my plans for the day.

If I stayed around the corner from the counter and kept my nose in the morning paper, discarded by some kind soul, I'd hang out at the restaurant until time to leave for rehearsal. Then . . . wait, the music.

I didn't have any music for rehearsal. I had promised to supply the parts for Beethoven's Serenade for Flute, Violin, & Viola. Understandably, KC hadn't brought it when she fetched music, not knowing I would want it. That meant it was at home. I couldn't risk going back for it.

What if I bought the music? The mall had a music store. I could wait 'til nine, when it opened, then use the credit card to buy another copy. But it was unlikely they'd have the Beethoven in stock. And it would require another use of my card if they did.

The college music library? They had the piece, but what if it had been checked out? Besides, the college was across town. I'd have to take the bus and risk Central Avenue during morning rush hour. No telling how long that would take. Besides, I only had thirty-five cents. Even the bus charged more than that. So, no go.

I'd have to call KC. She wouldn't report me to the police. But my burner phone was broken and gone, and I didn't dare risk using my personal cell again. Besides, it had to have been out of battery by now.

My only other choice was a public phone. KC's burner phone number had been lost when mine broke. I'd have to call her on my home landline.

What if the cops had the line tapped?

Though it strained my powers of belief, the visit to Gardiner that had alerted Lt. Gordon to my presence in town had only been two days ago, and those two days were Saturday and Sunday. Possibly the police were too overworked to get a court order to tap the phone this fast, had had trouble finding a judge over the weekend, or hadn't bothered yet.

Or maybe they'd tapped the phone.

I decided to risk it. Again, I had nothing to lose. At worst the cops would arrest me, a fate that looked certain anyway. On the other hand, if I evaded them long enough to find the real murderer, I wouldn't have to spend any time in jail. When it occurred to me that KC could bring me a change of clothes, too, and even some tea, my mind was made up.

In the thrillers I read, the police couldn't trace a quick call. Praying the authors researched their books carefully, I found a public phone next door then dialed.

"KC?"

"Em. Where are you? I've been—"

"Grab me a change of clothes I can wear to a rehearsal, a thermos of tea, and the Beethoven Serenade from the music cabinet in the studio, then come to Benny's on Sixty-Fifth and Central." Benny's shared a parking lot with my restaurant. "Make sure you're not followed, and don't tell anybody where you're going. That includes Barry."

I heard her say something, but I hung up the phone. I dare not talk longer. If the police had traced the call, my instructions would at least keep Barry uninvolved as far as they were concerned. Hopefully, the call had been fast enough that KC wouldn't be involved, either.

I figured she'd take at least twenty-five minutes to make the tea and drive to Benny's in rush hour traffic—twenty if she micro-waved the tea—but I had trouble waiting even five minutes. What if a policeman decided to buy himself breakfast? I hid behind a discarded paper and counted the minutes. The smell of coffee in the air helped clear my head. I checked the restaurant's clock and looked out the window about every five to seven minutes.

KC's maroon BMW arrived twenty-one minutes later.

I strolled casually out to the parking lot and surprised KC by opening the passenger door as she pulled into a parking spot.

"Em. You startled me."

"Sorry. Let's head for McCallum Park, and I'll tell you what's going on." That way if the police had traced my call to KC, we'd be on the other side of town by the time they searched the area completely. "Were you followed again?"

KC didn't ask any questions. She pulled out of the parking space and headed down Central. "Yeah. Last time I saw them they were behind a bus about three miles from here." It wasn't until we were moving with traffic that she asked, "What gives?"

I updated her as quickly as possible. I'd last seen her at the motel two nights ago, so I included the encounter with the policeman and the night I'd spent on the playground.

"Em, Barry's a basket case."

"Too bad. We can't involve him. He'd lose too much if he knew my whereabouts. Don't you think I'd have phoned him if I could?" My chest tightened and my eyes threatened tears. I had to stop feeling sorry for myself or I'd fall completely apart.

The public restroom at the park had been closed and locked for the season, so I changed clothes in KC's car. Clean underwear and a fresh outfit made me feel better, and I looked nearly human again. The tea she brought soothed my spirit. Things were looking up. I checked my watch. Nine o'clock.

Feeling nervous about staying in any one place too long and figuring the police were looking for KC's car, I instructed her to move. As she headed for Chuck's, I told her the plan I'd concocted. She would return to Central Boulevard and circle around until she once again had a police tail, then head out of town, leading them astray. Full of hope now, I asked about her former client and my only remaining suspect, the Symphony Board member. "Have you followed up with Curtis?"

"Don't worry. I'm seeing him tonight."

I felt awful. What if something happened to her? "I don't know, KC. I'm getting a bad feeling. He's my last suspect, and I don't want you alone with him. What if you talked to Lieutenant Gordon and told him your suspicions?"

KC huffed like a teenager, "And said what? That Curtis paid me to date him? I'd have to betray both confidentiality and my own role."

"But . . ."

"Stop worrying. I can handle it." She dropped me near Chuck's and drove off.

I had done my best. She'd keep the appointment despite my warning, and I'd fret 'til she returned safe and sound.

I glanced at my watch. Forty-five minutes early. It would look odd if I showed up at Chuck's at this hour, so I crouched in the alley behind his place, behind a couple of trash cans, trying to disappear.

When I'd waited long enough for the cold to seep through my coat and freeze my fingers, I glanced at my watch again. Ten minutes early. At least that was reasonable. It would take that long to warm up both my flute and my hands. I headed to rehearsal.

FORTY-TWO

MONDAY, FEBRUARY 24, 2010, 10:00 AM

CHUCK'S HOUSE WAS A PRETTY LITTLE three-bedroom stucco on a quiet corner in one of Monroe's oldest neighborhoods. The bare branches of an enormous oak spread themselves completely over the flat roof and sidewalk of the house. Chuck had always kept the place in immaculate order, so I took the unshoveled walks and the two rolled and bagged newspapers on the porch as a measure of his depression at Celia and the kids' absence.

Juggling my satchel and the music for the Beethoven trio KC had brought, I picked up the papers on my way in. When Chuck answered the door, I handed them to him. Unshaven? Chuck? He *was* depressed.

"Hi. Growing a beard?"

"Hi, Emily. A beard?" He rubbed his hand along his chin. "Oh, sorry. I guess I forgot to shave. I'll just be a minute."

Phil wasn't there yet, and Chuck hadn't done anything about setting up for the rehearsal. He'd dropped the two unread newspapers I'd handed him. I counted four more, all of them strewn around the living room where I waited. It looked like a good place for rehearsal. I decided Chuck could use help, so I piled the newspapers in the corner, dragged in three dining room chairs and the big, black Manhasset music stand I found in the corner of the room, then took my wire music stand from the satchel and set it up in front of one of the chairs.

I heard water still flowing in the bathroom when Phil rang the bell, so I let him in. "Chuck's running a little behind. He'll be along in a minute."

Chuck took only a few minutes before he joined us.

He gave a quick glance around the room. "Thanks, Emily." He shook hands with Phil. "It's good to see you." He pulled his violin case from a corner closet. "I'm sorry. I should have made a coffee cake or something. Celia . . ." He stopped, looked confused, and tightened his jaw muscles like he might be trying not to cry, so I stepped into the breach.

"No problem, Chuck. I just had breakfast." I would have given my kingdom, if I had one, for a little coffee cake to go with the Eggwich, but, of course, I didn't say that, and Phil murmured that he, too, had just eaten. I hoped we weren't about to embark on an awkward, uncomfortable rehearsal. Maybe Chuck would cheer up once we started playing.

Each of us settled in, preparing, chatting as we assembled our instruments.

"You look good as a blonde, Emily." Phil stared.

"Thanks. I thought I'd try something different." I opened my satchel, removed my flute from its case, and started assembling the instrument, while Phil set up his stand and both the string players rosined and tightened their bows. I blew air through my flute to warm the cold metal. Luckily, after spending the night outside in the playground, it didn't freeze to my face.

I had risked arrest to find out about Olive's quartet rehearsal, and desperation made me leap right into the topic without thinking about introducing it gracefully. "What's the latest on Olive's murder? I've been out of touch the last few days." I prayed they didn't know I'd been fleeing from police pursuit.

"I haven't seen the papers," Chuck responded.

I already knew that, having piled six of them in the corner earlier.

But Phil gave me a funny look. "Don't you know? The TV said the police wanted you. I assumed you'd talked to them or we wouldn't be rehearsing this morning."

Thinking quickly, I responded, "I've been out of town. I didn't know they wanted to talk to me. I'd better give Lieutenant Gordon a call after rehearsal." *Just answer my questions first.*

Phil's eyes lit up. "Emily, I think you should phone now. You might know something nobody else does."

Phil's enthusiasm more than dismayed me. "What? Me? I don't know anything."

"You might know something without knowing you know it." Phil, the true crime buff, insisted.

"If I do, it'll wait 'til after rehearsal." I paused while I summoned the courage to take the plunge. "There is something I'm curious about, though."

Phil, who had begun tuning his viola with a disappointed expression, looked up from the tuning pegs with a gleam in his eye. "What's that?"

Casually, I asked the question I'd put myself at risk to ask. "Olive told me you guys were working on a quartet for her recital."

Phil raised his eyebrows at me.

"I mention it because the afternoon of her murder, I remember Olive told me she had a quartet rehearsal."

The question left Phil's eyes and he returned to tuning the viola. "That's no big mystery. Chuck and Alice and I were gonna do the Devienne on her recital."

I tried to control my excitement. "Then you guys must have been among the last to see her alive."

Phil didn't even look up. "Nah. She canceled the rehearsal."

"Canceled?"

He looked at me and shrugged his shoulders. "We never saw her."

"Phil, the cancellation might have something to do with why she died. Did you tell Lieutenant Gordon?"

"I'll tell him if he asks." He shrugged. "But it must not be important. He hasn't even talked to me."

Damn Gordon. He must have quit investigating other leads and focused on me. "How can you be sure it's not important? What did Olive say?" *This must be the missing clue.*

Phil had finished tuning the viola and played open strings, testing the tuning. "I dunno. Chuck talked to her. He told me the rehearsal had been canceled."

We both turned and looked at Chuck.

He had been concentrating on tuning his Amati while Phil and I talked. Now he looked at me. "It wasn't important. I only listened with half an ear. She spouted the same old stuff about Gardiner. You know how she was about him. Half-hysterical. She didn't reach me 'til after I'd left for the rehearsal and was halfway to her house. She told me she wanted to cancel and asked if I'd call Phil and Alice so she could keep trying to reach Gardiner. I hung up as quick as she'd let me and phoned Alice first, then Phil. I lucked out and reached them before they left."

That wasn't saying much. Both of them lived close to Olive— five minutes away max. But something bothered me, and I couldn't figure out what. "Well, at least I'll have something to tell Lieutenant Gordon when I call him after rehearsal." This bit of information might keep me out of jail. Chuck had finished tuning his violin. "Speaking of rehearsal, let's start." He had the air of a man who wanted to get this over with.

Disappointed to have to change the subject, I passed out parts and explained that the plan called for us to play as lunch was served, before the speeches.

I began rehearsal without my brain. I tried to figure out what bothered me and relived the afternoon of Olive's murder. Let's see . . . Olive last talked to me at 2:30, and we talked about fifteen minutes. Then she phoned Clara. When did Clara call me? Shortly after 3:00, it must have been.

Oops. "Sorry. I wasn't concentrating. Let's start again." I played by reflex, trying to remember . . . I left to walk Golden . . . when? I didn't remember. Before 4:00, when Olive's rehearsal was scheduled to start, maybe 3:20? Chuck lived about twenty minutes from Olive. If she reached him in his car on the cell, as he said, that meant she had to have phoned him sometime after 3:40. But her last text had been to me at 3:28, according to the information Lt. Gordon had gotten from her cell phone. That was it. The timing didn't make sense. Maybe Olive canceled the rehearsal early, before 3:28. But if she canceled early, she would have reached Chuck at home, unless he left early . . .

Now Chuck showed signs of poor concentration. He'd skipped a key change then miscounted a rest. "Sorry, guys. Can we go back to letter B?"

Mechanically, I gave the cue to start at B, my thoughts uninterrupted. If Olive made her last text to my cell at 3:28 . . .

"It feels like it's slowing down to me," Phil said. "Chuck, make sure you're not late there."

Chuck flushed and clenched his jaw. "Sorry. I just feel it that way. I'm listening to Emily's eighth notes."

Hey. "Let's try it again at B. I'll do my best to be more accurate." Scolding myself for suffering this kind of aggravation without a paycheck to cover pain and suffering, I gave the cue to start and again returned to my calculations.

If Olive's call to Chuck had been before 3:28, when she sent her last text to me, she wouldn't have reached Chuck in his car, because he wouldn't have left until 3:40. Either the clocks weren't synchronized, Chuck left early, or he lied. If Chuck lied, he most likely killed Olive.

"Earth calling Emily." Phil made an effort to get my attention.

"Sorry—"

"Can you try to pay attention here, Emily, and play with a little sensitivity? You ignored my rubato."

Boy, he was the king of tact, wasn't he? "Sorry. I guess I'm not concentrating very well."

"Back off, Phil." Chuck defended me. "She's doing her best."

That insulted me as much as Phil's comment. I played with less than half a brain—way below my normal standard. "No, Chuck, he's right. I'm not concentrating. Let's go back to D and I'll refocus." I couldn't solve the mystery without talking to Chuck, so I resolved to put the problem aside for the moment and concentrate on my playing, before there was a murder in *Chuck's* living room.

The rehearsal ranked as one of the most unpleasant I'd ever survived. Phil continued to jump on every little mistake either Chuck or I made. Chuck busily defended us both, to the extent that we didn't get anything constructive done.

I tried to defuse the situation. "Since we only have one rehearsal, we'd better try to get through it. After all, everybody's sight reading."

Phil tsked. "If getting through is all you care about . . ."

I ground my teeth and managed not to say anything I regretted.

Chuck looked at me. Obviously, we had a common enemy.

I wondered what would have happened in a rehearsal that included both Olive and Phil. They both had the same tactless, perfectionist approach. How had they managed to work together?

Finally, we made it through the piece and rehearsal ended. Phil packed up wordlessly, banging his case shut. Then he stormed out, slamming the door behind him, leaving me alone with Chuck.

FORTY-THREE

MONDAY, FEBRUARY 24, 2010, 12:15 PM

CHUCK SPOKE, HIS VOICE DEEPER AND HUSKIER than I'd heard it before. He said, "He's just like all the others." His face twitched and his eyes watered.

He startled me. What could have brought him close to tears? "Who?"

"Phil. He's just like all the others. Thinks I'm an idiot."

I wanted to soothe him, to calm him, and ask my questions about the cancellation of Olive's last rehearsal. "Chuck, nobody thinks you're an idiot. The Beethoven'll sound okay once everybody has had a chance to practice."

"Nothing will be okay. Not ever again." His voice sounded so, so tired and slow.

He needed Emily's magic cure. "Chuck, let me fix you a cup of tea." I'd find the stuff in his kitchen. I had no place to go anyway, and welcomed an excuse to hang around in a warm house as long as I could. I'd find out what he knew while we talked.

But I never made it to the kitchen. I might as well have been in another county.

"Did you know Celia's left me and taken the kids?"

He'd told me this himself. Why didn't he remember? Had he been drinking? Or taken something strong for his depression? He spoke softly, sounding hopeless. He hadn't moved.

"I heard." I didn't like the direction of this conversation. I sat down and leaned toward Chuck, so his words were clearer. "I'm so sorry. But you know, things have a way of working out."

He didn't even glance at me. "Her parents think I'm an idiot, too."

I shifted my weight uncomfortably, beginning to understand he didn't care what I said or did, or whether I was there at all. I said nothing.

"They've always thought she deserved better."

What parent doesn't?

"I don't make enough money for them."

"What musician does?" This time I said it aloud.

"I could've earned more if it hadn't been for Olive."

"Olive?" Details and theories began to crystallize into foreboding.

"Yeah, Olive." He looked up, eyes focused on me now. His jaw twitched. "She told Peter Hall I messed up her quartet rehearsal. Described every gory detail."

I remembered Peter had mentioned it when he talked about hiring the opera orchestra. "Don't worry about it. Everybody knows you've been under a lot of stress."

He snorted. "Don't worry, huh?" He stood suddenly, grabbing my arm and pulling me up with him. Turning to face me, he seized my free arm. There was no avoiding his glare. "Of course, that's easy for you to say. Don't worry! Olive ruined my chances of landing extra work, extra money. I needed it for my family."

I tried to pull away, but he only tightened his grip.

"Ow! Chuck, let go. You're hurting me."

Instead, he stared at me intensely, not loosening his hold. "Peter didn't care about all we'd been through, or that our kids go to school together."

I wriggled, trying to break his grip, but couldn't. He glared at me. "What kind of friend is that?"

"I understand how upset you must have been—"

"You understand? You understand? I doubt it. I've known Peter for thirteen years." His face reddened. "We do everything together.

Our wives are besties. We're drinking buddies. We cheer for the same teams. And in spite of all that, one comment from Olive means more than thirteen years of friendship."

He shook my arms, sending bolts of quick, hot pain shooting into my neck.

"Chuck—stop!"

He stopped but gripped me fiercely.

When dealing with potentially violent people, I'd heard you're supposed to speak in a calm and soothing voice. Easier said than done. But I tried to sound comforting while struggling in his grasp. "It'll be okay."

His hold didn't loosen.

I winced. "Peter's just scared. He . . ." I shifted my weight, hoping to break free. ". . . he wants to impress opera management."

Chuck didn't relax his iron grip.

Breathlessly, I gasped. "You'll get through this."

But that only infuriated him. "Get through this? Get through it? How can I get through it when you're determined to send me to jail?"

"Chuck, I . . . I wouldn't . . ." I thought fast.

"They'll know!" he shouted. "When you tell the cops Olive cancelled the rehearsal, they'll check the phone records. They'll find out she never called me. You'll be off the hook, but they'll lock me up. They'll know."

Chuck jerked me viciously, and my head pounded like castanets in a Spanish folk dance.

I closed my eyes and took a long breath, willing my voice to be low, steady, and soothing. "You . . . you killed her, didn't you?"

"Yeah, I killed her. The gossiping bitch." He shook his head and took a slow lungful of air. Then he spoke, his voice finally calm. Way too calm. "And now I'll have to kill you, too. If I can keep you quiet, I'll find some way out. I don't know how yet, but the first step is to shut you up. Permanently."

I remembered only one defensive move from the video I'd watched on YouTube. With all the force I could muster, I jabbed my knee into his crotch.

He bent over, hands cupping his genitals, moaning with pain.

Well, look at that. My first knee jab, and it worked.

Panting, I rubbed my newly freed arms, trying to ease the pain of Chuck's finger marks, while I considered what to do next. He was incapacitated for the present, but I had to find some way to deal with the situation more permanently. I headed for his landline.

My mistake lay in turning my back.

I heard groaning. The next thing I knew, Chuck's arm encircled my neck. He dragged me backward, his hold so tight I struggled for breath.

Drat! I didn't knee him hard enough.

Physically, I was outmatched. My five-feet-six inches of pudgy couch-potato-trained flab couldn't prevail against his six-foot-plus of, you'll excuse the expression, fit-as-a-fiddle muscle. Also, he had crazy on his side, and nothing trumped crazy.

My arms flailed out, and I grabbed the nearest solid object. Chuck's violin. The $450,000 Amati entrusted to Chuck's care. He had laid it carefully across the chair nearest to me.

I wheezed, grasping the violin in one hand and waving it. "Let me go. Now!"

He released me as if I had burst into flame.

I turned to face him, holding the neck of the Amati like a base-ball bat. "Take one step and I'll smash it."

"Emily! It's one-of-a-kind. Don't. You can't." His gaze followed the Amati, fear in his voice.

Holding the violin above my head and thrashing the air, I moved toward the wall. "Think I won't? Try me." Like a gong player at the climax of a composition, I wound up to swing.

"Don't! It's irreplaceable. I swore I'd take good care of it. Don't hurt it." Strange that he should care more about the instrument's welfare than his own or Olive's. Preserving the violin was vital to him. More important, even, than killing me. A musician to the core, quite possibly he felt that only the instrument hadn't betrayed him.

He stepped toward me.

"Come any closer, and I'll break it over your head." I held the violin high, ready to bring it down full force. "I'm not kidding,

Chuck. It might not do a lot of damage to you, but the Amati will be in splinters."

He held both hands in the air, fingers spread, demonstrating surrender.

I backed away from him, continuing to hold the violin in the air with one hand while feeling for the phone table behind me with the other. Keeping a cautious eye on Chuck, I lifted the handset and dialed 911. A business-like voice answered, and I blurted, "I'm alone with a killer. I need help. Send police to three ten Chestnut."

Continuing to grip the Amati firmly by its neck and shaking it occasionally in Chuck's direction to keep him at bay, I answered the dispatcher's questions.

Chuck's eyes shifted, alternately gazing desperately at the violin and glaring angrily at me. I guessed he struggled to find a way to attack me without hurting the Amati.

I waved the instrument threateningly and calculated. How long before the police came? I had to keep Chuck talking 'til then. I quietly laid the receiver on the table, keeping an open line to 911, clutching the Amati.

"Even if you killed me, there's Phil and Alice," I said. "You told them Olive called you. They'll repeat that to the police when they're questioned. The cops'll find out anyway."

"I wiped the rehearsal off Olive's calendar. They'll have no reason to question Phil and Alice and they'll never know about the rehearsal, if I can keep you quiet."

I thought fast. "I've already told Lieutenant Gordon that Olive wanted to reach Gardiner before a planned quartet rehearsal." A lie. I hadn't mentioned the rehearsal and only told him she was looking for Gardiner, but Chuck didn't know that. Maybe the fib would save me. "He'll question Phil and Alice eventually."

He stared at me. "You . . . you told them . . ." Chuck's arms dropped limply to his sides and his eyes filled with tears. "You're right." He collapsed into a chair. "I can't do anything right. Not even keep you quiet."

Thankfully, I thought, but figuring Chuck wouldn't appreciate the feeling, I didn't verbalize it.

"I didn't want to kill anyone. But she left me no choice. You're my friend. Even Olive could have been my friend." He looked at me again. "What's wrong with me? What am I going to do, Emily? What am I going to do?"

"If you explain all this to Lieutenant Gordon, I'm sure he'll be able to find you help." I suspected I lied even as I said it, but I hoped my words would comfort Chuck and help me.

Chuck held his head in his hands, ignoring me. "What is Celia going to think? She's always loved me, but I've let her down again."

"Again?"

I listened as he rambled on about the issues in their marriage. He and Celia started fighting over little things at first. Lack of money increased tensions. "As soon as we'd get ahead a little and I'd buy nice clothes or furniture, there'd be something unexpected like car repairs or medical bills. I just couldn't get on top of stuff. And my in-laws kept telling Celia she deserved better. I felt like a screw-up. I guess I *was* a screw-up."

Why hadn't they helped him instead of criticizing? My heart ached. "You work hard, Chuck, and you do a good job. You're not a screw-up, and Celia knows that."

"She loves me, and I love her. We would have reunited when I could afford a bigger place."

Chuck delivered a monologue now, long and sad. He didn't pause for me to say anything as he told me about it.

"I would've done anything to persuade her to come back. That's why I asked Peter for work with the opera orchestra. That money would have made all the difference. I could have paid off the second mortgage on the house. But no-o-o-o. Olive had already told Peter I screwed up the quartet rehearsal. He said he couldn't hire me. Olive ruined everything. The opera orchestra was my last chance to earn a decent living. Now they're all gone. Celia. Peter. My kids. The most important people in my life."

Chuck's eyes went wide, and he glared crazily at me. "And it was all Olive's fault."

Despite my sympathy, I didn't like that look. Keeping the Amati between us for protection, conscious of the open line to 911, I encouraged him. "Talk to me, Chuck. Tell me what happened. Help me understand. We'll make sense of all this."

Finding someone willing to listen, he took a breath and bitterly spat out details. "After I talked to Peter on the phone, I went to Olive's apartment for the quartet rehearsal. I was fuming, but I thought we could talk about it, so I arrived about twenty minutes early."

His eyes moved up and to his right. "She was playing this loud music. *Carmina Burana*. Phil and Alice hadn't arrived yet. Olive started putting her bassoon together. She fussed about Gardiner, and made plans for rehearsal, the rehearsal I had volunteered to play free, as a favor to her. When she said, 'I hope you worked on the last movement of the Devienne,' in that condescending way of hers, I just exploded."

As his anger mounted, his voice rose. "Who gave her the right to judge me? To spread her poison? Destroy a reputation I'd worked years to build?" He formed a fist. "Drive away my friends? Ruin my best chance to take care of my family in years? Who gave her the right?"

His rage frightened me, and I shrank away from him, gripping the Amati tighter and holding it in front of me.

Staring into the air, he made a fist. "I was livid. Furious. She bristled with self-righteousness, so smug. Her bassoon case sat on the end table between us with the boot joint still in it. I just wanted to wipe the arrogance off her face. The boot joint was near to hand. I grabbed it and smacked her." He attacked the air with both hands, as if smashing Olive's head. "The boot joint is solid and it's heavy with metal keys, and I wanted to undo the blow as soon as I heard the 'thunk,' but, too late. She fell to the floor . . . so still."

He closed his eyes and continued, haltingly. "She wasn't moving, and the blood kept oozing. I . . . I . . ." Chuck's eyes popped open. "You know me, Emily. You can see she made me do it."

I made no response but tightened my grip on the Amati. Made him do it? What? She handed him the bassoon boot and ordered him to kill her?

"You have to realize I didn't mean to kill her. But once it happened, I knew I had to erase any trace of my presence. I phoned

Phil and Alice on my cell. Fortunately, I reached them both before they left. I invented a story about how Olive had cancelled the rehearsal and I'd volunteered to help her out by calling the other members of the quartet. I told them we'd reschedule later.

"I put on my gloves and used a tissue to wipe her bassoon boot so my prints couldn't be identified and . . ." He didn't speak for a moment. "Her phone sat right there, on her stand, so I deleted the rehearsal off her calendar and wiped my prints." After a long pause he went on, sounding ever so tired. "Nobody saw me leave. I . . . I . . ."

He quit talking and started crying.

Moments later, several police officers, guns drawn, arrived.

"Careful." I warned them, waving the Amati at Chuck again as I let them in. I needn't have bothered. He cried inconsolably, only semi-lucid.

At first the officers were inclined to arrest me, but I explained, and they took charge of Chuck, to my relief.

I remembered I'd never replaced the phone's receiver. I picked it up and asked the 911 operator, "Are you still there?"

"Yes, ma'am," a calm female voice responded.

"You heard? Did you understand it all?"

"Yes, ma'am."

Relief made me weak in the knees. "Thank you for staying on the line." It was over. Finally, over. Finished. With unarguable proof.

I hung up the call, took a deep breath to recover my composure, then dialed KC's cell. She had followed my instructions and driven to the outskirts of town. She was headed into the mountains when I reached her. I told her the rehearsal had ended. Confident that I'd find a ride home with someone and hoping the police would be done with me soon, I told her I'd meet her at the house.

"House? You mean your house? Is it safe?"

"It's a long story. I'll tell you when we meet, but for now, it's enough for you to know that Chuck Holcombe's been arrested for Olive's murder."

She whooped as I hung up the phone.

Next, I called Barry.

"Em. Where are you?"

I gave him the address. "I'll explain later but come as soon as you can."

While the police dealt with Chuck, I carefully wiped off the Amati, removed the shoulder rest, loosened the bow, and put it back in its case. It had rescued me. Caring for it was small repayment for its service.

When Barry arrived, I didn't mind that his hug threatened to crush me. "Em. You're all right." After a few moments he held me away from him. "Now what's going on here?"

"Chuck murdered Olive." The words were hard to say. "Lieutenant Gordon has to know."

Barry understood instantly and called the lieutenant, only pausing to ask me for Chuck's full name. Meanwhile, the police officers handcuffed Chuck and read him his rights. As Barry hung up, the officers explained they needed to lock the house and urged us to leave as soon as possible. Fine with me. I wanted home and Golden. Now.

Barry obligingly took me to my house. "What happened?"

"Barry, I'm sorry, but I'm exhausted, and KC will want to know the details, too. Can we wait to talk so I only have to tell you once?"

"Sure, Em."

When we arrived at the house, KC met us. "I'm so glad you're safe." She gave me a big hug. "And you solved the crime in the nick of time. When you told me Chuck had been arrested for the murder, I called Curtis Strange right away and cancelled our appointment. I left a message on his voice mail with no explanation. Thank goodness I didn't have to go."

I returned her hug. "Thanks, KC, for seeing him and trying to find information. I know you were doing it to help me out. I worried about you. Thankfully, you're safe, too."

Golden showed her ire at me for being gone so long and pouted. To my disappointment, she ignored me. She couldn't resist hot dogs, though, and I managed to earn my way back into her good graces by shamelessly treating her until she forgave me.

Then, by way of celebration, the three of us took Golden for a walk on the greenbelt, while I told KC and Barry the whole story. I started with my disappearance, since Barry didn't know that part of the saga, and ended with my confrontation with Chuck, to bring them both up to speed.

While I told my tale, I let Golden off the leash to run.

"So, you've really proved you're innocent?" KC gushed.

I smiled with contentment. "At last."

But Barry added, "After I clean up a few loose ends."

Details. You paid a lawyer to take care of them.

When I called Golden to go home, she came running, covered with brown goo. Mud this time. Only mud. Things were looking up. She wouldn't need a bath. I'd give her a piece of hot dog and brush her thoroughly outside, where the mud wouldn't soil my house. A normal problem. I could handle normal.

I went to bed early that night. Between the let-down after my confrontation with Chuck, relief that he had been arrested, my night on the streets, and my victory celebration with Golden, KC, and Barry, I was done in. I wasn't too worn out to have hot spiced tea while lounging in a lavender-scented bubble bath first, though. After my well-deserved indulgences, gratefully, I crawled into bed and fell asleep almost instantly, cuddling with Golden. Life was good once again.

FORTY-FOUR

EPILOGUE–JULY 12, 2011

T HE AMATI WAS RETURNED TO ITS OWNER who, horrified by the ordeal the violin had been through, returned it to the museum to molder in safety. I guessed that he wouldn't lend it out again soon. Too bad. A fine instrument should be played before it deteriorated.

Olive's sister, Patricia, and I went to lunch a few times before she went back to Dallas. She promised to email me, and we did keep in touch for a while but now saw each other only on Facebook. Her mom and dad had become a strong presence in family photos, so I hoped there'd been a reconciliation with them. Patricia married a few months ago. I wished her well and trusted that Olive saw her and could help her, too, from beyond the grave.

The grapevine buzzed about Gardiner and Leanne, this time because she left him to date the new cellist. According to the gossip, Gardiner was heartbroken. Although it might be poetic justice, I wasn't celebrating Gardiner's grief. Olive's brief life and death taught me that life is short and unpredictable; too short to wish unhappiness on anyone. So, I'd wish for Miss Right to be in Gardiner's future. And I hoped he'd learned a little kindness and compassion from his love life. You could always dream.

I had mixed feelings about my hair. I liked it. I got lots of comments like, "you look ten years younger," and "it's hip." Even

Barry said I looked "spunkier." But I knew it wasn't the flattering comments from friends or my hair color that had increased my confidence. Besides, coloring it took a lot of time and constant vigilance to prevent roots from showing. So, I let the dye wash out. KC was right. The "temporary" color lasted about six weeks. I'd glimpsed life as a blonde now, though, and I could always dye my hair again if I wanted.

Barry and I finally managed to coordinate our schedules for a real date, dinner and dancing at the Starlight Room. To tell the truth, it was amazing—amazing enough that I admitted the possibility that a romantic relationship might improve my life. Since then, we'd been on a couple trips to the mountains for some skiing. We met as our schedules allowed for lunch or Sunday dinner, but there were long periods when we didn't see each other since he worked during my off hours, and I worked during *his* off hours. The relationship moved forward slowly, and given my track record with relationships, that suited me fine.

ONE DAY, OVER A YEAR AFTER the murder, I met Barry at the Articulate Artichoke for lunch. Chuck's trial had ended the day before, and we hadn't seen each other for a while. After we greeted each other and sat down, he slid a newspaper across the table to me.

From the Monroe Herald, July 12:

MUSICIAN CONVICTED OF MURDER

Yesterday Charles Holcombe, violinist in the Monroe Symphony, also known as the "Bassoon Basher," was convicted in county court of voluntary manslaughter in last year's February 2 death of Olive R. Patterson, second bassoon in the Symphony.

The prosecution's evidence included a 911 recording of a confession by Holcombe, as well as a bloodstained tissue found in a pocket of Holcombe's coat. The blood on the tissue matched the victim's DNA.

A procession of character witnesses swore to the defendant's good nature and habitual kindliness. Holcombe's estranged wife also appeared and testified to the strain the recent breakup of their marriage had placed on her husband. No other defense was presented.

The jury deliberated only forty-five minutes before returning its verdict.

Asked why the jury acquitted Holcombe of first- and second-degree murder charges, convicting instead on the voluntary manslaughter charge, a juror who asked to remain anonymous said, "We thought it obvious Mr. Holcombe hadn't planned the murder. Who would use a bassoon boot to kill anyone by choice?"

Voluntary manslaughter carries a sentence of four to twenty-four years. Holcombe faces sentencing next week.

I'D BEEN IN THE COURTROOM. I'd testified, and I'd seen the "procession of character witnesses." Chuck embraced his wife after the verdict, and she cried and shook her head as she watched him led away. The grapevine said she'd filed for divorce, to no one's surprise.

Barry had been busy in court with another case, but he'd read the news article. "Glad Chuck wasn't my client. With a taped confession, what can you do?"

"Truthfully, I don't understand why it even went to trial."

"Likely the defense wanted to get the character witnesses on record. Chuck could pull a shorter sentence that way."

"It kind of disappointed me that no one mentioned my help in redirecting the investigation and catching the killer."

"Em, what do you want? Credit or freedom? Take my advice. Give Lieutenant Gordon the credit, and gratefully. You don't want to make an enemy of him. *I* don't want to make an enemy of him. Let him look good."

"Just between us, he did say that, in view of my 'contributions,' he wouldn't bring charges."

Barry helped himself to a croissant. "Yeah. We're lucky you weren't arrested. And even though I think the lieutenant strongly suspects I knew about your temporary disappearance and also where to find you, he hasn't been able to prove anything, thanks to your cautionary measures. He has asked a lot of suspicious questions, though."

I bit down on an ice cube from my water, rolling it on my tongue as I thought. "The murder hinged on such small things. What if Olive had overlooked Chuck's mistakes in rehearsal? Or if Celia had more compassion and patience? What if Chuck had talked to someone about his problems?" And then, for me, the real point. "What if I'd been more understanding of Olive and her problems, even if she only imagined them? If I'd handled my annoyance better? What if I'd concentrated on the positives in Olive and in her life? Refused to gossip about colleagues, so that she knew spreading rumors wasn't right or appreciated? That might have made a difference."

"Maybe. Or maybe not, Em. It's over, though. You can't change it now. You need to move on."

"But . . ."

Barry finally had to resort to his own "what if" to make me see reason. "And what if she'd played the flute instead of bassoon? She never would have been murdered."

Okay. He'd made his point. I let go of the idea that I had any direct role in Olive's murder. The "real trouble" she texted about must have been Gardiner's threatened restraining order. At any rate, the "trouble" she mentioned had nothing at all to do with her murder. She'd already dissed Chuck's playing to Peter. Chuck's rage had been in response to his own demons, his dealings with Olive, and her conversation with Peter. Nothing else had mattered. The killing had happened quickly and without planning or thought.

"How's KC?" Barry asked, changing the subject.

"She never moved out of the guestroom."

He chuckled.

"It's a win/win situation. She cleans and cooks for me, and I give her a place to stay, with flute lessons in the bargain. She's a joy to have around. Golden accepted her as a member of the 'pack' long ago and happily lets her lead dog walks. KC's always glad to dog sit, too."

"Last time we talked about her she was looking for a job. How's the search going?"

At that moment, KC emerged from the kitchen, making the

answer obvious.

She wiped her hands on the apron of her Articulate Artichoke uniform as she made her way to us from the kitchen. "I heard you were here. I can only take a minute, but I thought I'd say hello." As she spoke, she hugged me.

"KC, I had just asked for an update about you." Always the gentleman, Barry stood. "I wondered how your job search is going."

"The search is over, as you can see. As soon as I gave up looking for office work, opportunities opened up. I asked about jobs in beauty shops, and Em," she nodded at me, "encouraged me to apply, but I found the state required a beautician's license for most things. Then I applied here, and voila! I'm a sous chef at the Articulate Artichoke. I've never been so happy." Her smile lit up the room. "You're eating veggies I chopped." She waved at Barry's chair. "Please, sit down and eat. Don't let the food get cold."

Barry glanced at his plate and reseated himself.

KC continued. "The salary isn't what I'm used to, but the appreciation makes up for the paycheck. I've already been here longer than anybody before me and they say I'm the best they've ever had." She blushed. "It's so satisfying to be appreciated for my skills."

"I'm glad you're happy KC. You deserve it." Barry smiled.

KC smiled back. "They need me in the kitchen, but I'm so glad I got to see you."

She hugged Barry and me and headed back to her job.

I sheepishly admitted, "Living with her sets my mind at rest. I can inspect her dates. It's like I'm her mom, in a good way, I hope. She's gone out with lots of guys, and she's suspicious of them all. She says she's grateful for my help. 'How do I know he cares? He's not paying to be with me,' is how she puts it."

"To each his own, I guess." Barry sipped his water.

"It's just as well. So far, no man has been good enough for her, in my opinion. I may be a bit biased."

Barry and I hadn't had a chance to talk for a long time.

"What about the inheritance? I know you felt pretty

uncomfortable about it."

He was right. In fact, I felt downright guilty. I'd tried spending it. "Well . . . after we retrieved my old Subaru, I traded it for a new one. And I paid for Mom's cruise."

"Yeah?"

"She met a man in Alaska who jets cross-country several times a month to visit."

"I bet he's hooked. Your mom's unique."

I nodded and was silent a moment. Barry wouldn't judge me, but I felt embarrassed. I had to force myself to continue. "My friendship with Olive had pretty well run its course, and she had been about to take me out of her will anyway. I decided to use the rest of the inheritance for a fund to honor her."

Barry whistled admiringly. "Great idea."

"It's named the Olive R. Patterson Kindness Campaign. Its purpose is to recognize and encourage kindness and compassion throughout Monroe and acknowledge those who go out of their way for others. The campaign started with 'Kindness Counts' bumper stickers."

"I've seen several of those. Didn't know they had anything to do with you, though."

The waitress interrupted and took our dessert orders—crème Brule for him, chocolate cake for me—before we continued our conversation.

"That's not all. Good Samaritan awards in the schools started last school year."

"That's a good idea. Kids have to develop their humanity, in addition to their math skills."

"And volunteer therapists are staffing family therapy programs."

"Lots of need for that. High-risk kids, especially, can use the help. It sounds like a great program. People should know about it."

"They will. The *Herald* has agreed to run a series of front-page articles on the program. That'll happen as soon as interesting stories have time to develop."

"I'm impressed, Em, and I'm proud of you."

Heat rose in my cheeks. I didn't deserve praise. I hadn't been a very good friend. It was Olive's money I'd used to honor her and to ensure her legacy would be used for good. I had no other way of apologizing. I hoped she'd approve.

B.J. BOWEN IS A MUSICIAN AND FREE-LANCE WRITER whose love of music was awakened by her mother, who played the flute. After discovering her lips were the wrong shape and failing miserably as a flute player, at the age of eleven Ms. Bowen began studying oboe, and has since performed and recorded on both oboe and English horn with professional symphonies and chamber groups throughout Mexico and Colorado. Other experience includes working with various children's organizations, teaching music to children and adults, editing newsletters, and writing grants for non-profits. Her inspirational articles have appeared in *Unity Magazine* and *Daily Word*, and she was a finalist who won Honorable Mention in the 2018 Focus: Eddy Awards for her article, "Letting Go with Grace," published in *Unity Magazine*. She lives in Colorado Springs, Colorado, with two canine friends, and has a stock of musical puns, as well as a song for any occasion.